THE BURNING GLASS

THE
BURNING GLASS

stories by HELEN NORRIS

Louisiana State University Press
Baton Rouge and London

1992

Copyright © 1987, 1989, 1990, 1992 by Helen Norris
All rights reserved
Manufactured in the United States of America
First printing
01 00 99 98 97 96 95 94 93 92   5 4 3 2 1

Designer: Glynnis Phoebe
Typeface: Sabon
Typesetter: Graphic Composition
Printer and binder: Thomson-Shore, Inc.

Library of Congress Cataloging-in-Publication Data

Norris, Helen, 1916–
  The burning glass : stories / by Helen Norris.
    p.   cm.
  ISBN 0-8071-1790-0 (cloth)
  I. Title.
  PS3527.O497B8   1992   92-10557
  813'.52—dc20   CIP

Grateful acknowledgment is made to the editors of the following publications, in which the stories listed originally appeared: *Sewanee Review* (Summer, 1990; Winter, 1992), "Inside the Silence" and "The Wake of a Cry"; *Southern Review* (Winter, 1990; Summer, 1987), "Mirror Image" and "A Bee in Amber"; *Crosscurrents* (September, 1989), "The Inglenook"; and *Virginia Quarterly Review* (Spring, 1990), "Raisin Faces." "The Cracker Man" was first published in the Summer, 1992, issue of the *Gettysburg Review.*

Publication of this book has been supported by a grant from the National Endowment for the Arts in Washington, D.C., a federal agency.

The paper in this book meets the guidelines for permanence and durability of the Committee on Production Guidelines for Book Longevity of the Council on Library Resources. ∞

For Ginger, Wilma, and Leize

Contents

Inside the Silence
1

Mirror Image
33

A Bee in Amber
57

The Inglenook
76

The Cracker Man
105

Raisin Faces
129

The Wake of a Cry
146

Bread upon the Waters
155

Valley of Summer
172

THE
BURNING
GLASS

Inside the Silence

They were returning from Zakopane, the mountainous part of the green land. Professor Kosinski, who spoke her tongue with moderate ease, had turned to her in the back seat, where she was riding with his wife. "Is there something else we can show you?" he asked. "Something perhaps upon your list, the list of things you have come to see."

She had laughed at that. The windows were down. The summer smelled of fern and rain. "I came to see whatever is here, and you have shown me more than I knew." They rode in silence. Her eyes were steeped in the green of ferns deep and lush beneath the trees. Near the road the birches shone in the fading light, and farther back within the wood their ghostly arms embraced the oaks. "Unless," she said, "it is Majdanek."

There was further silence. She listened to it. Perhaps the weekend had drained them all. The strain of turning this land of theirs into words she could understand. She wondered if they resented it. She wished they would trust her on her own. "Ah," he said, "you have heard of it."

"I heard of it from my father's student. He seemed to think I ought to go."

She noted again the long silence. "So . . . we can arrange," he said, "if your father wishes."

She heard his words with some surprise that he thought she would need her father's permission, when she was all of forty-one. Was the place of women so ill advanced? "I shall arrange it myself," she said in as humble a voice as she could command. "I'll ask a student to take me there. Perhaps the one who thinks I should go. . . . What do you think of it?" she said.

"What do I think?" said Professor Kosinski. He spoke in Polish to Professor Wilczek, who rode beside him. "What do I think?" He repeated it. "There is nothing to think. It is there," he said. Over his shoulder after a bit he observed to her, "The place requires official guide. It is a monument of the State."

"Then surely I should see it," she said.

There was much to see when one came to Lublin. One toured the university, of course, where her father had come to lecture on Melville for a month. There was a kind of release in the air, a prolonged breath she could almost hear. By now they were thirty years into peace, the longest period of peace, she was told, that Poland had literally ever had. There were trips to take with official guides. Students with a command of English, glad of the extra she paid, would go, always provided they took the guide or met the guide, who would see to it that she saw no more than the State allowed. "What do they have to hide?" she asked.

Her father shrugged. He didn't care to see the land. She found he wanted to rest from his labor, to read his notes, and even to read his lecture aloud, the one to be given the following day. It made him self-conscious to have her around, listening perhaps, smiling a bit. He liked to mark the places to pause to let the translator catch up with him.

"You won't feel neglected if I go?"

"Go. Go and see it all and tell me about it later on." But she knew there was never a later on. He had reached, as he said, an equilibrium. As much went out in the way of his talk as he had got coming into him. He did not want to become unbalanced. He had known a fellow took in too much at the end of his life, when suddenly one is labeled a bore, and no one wanted to hear him tell it. "Terrible glut. He died of it."

She laughed at him, but she did not like to talk of death, his own death in particular. She had come to get away from deaths, not consciously, of course, not that. But she knew in some recess of her mind that once you have chalked up a few of them in your own land, that land is forever haunted with them. You enter a house.... You travel a road.... You are always fighting a war with them. Or signing a truce that doesn't last.

And here she was given a land that was free of memories, a land of charm, of geese at home in the village streets, of moss covering thatched roofs, of freight wagons and windmills, of gently sloping fields of rye, fields of poppies always red, a man sweeping the street with twigs.... She turned away from the coffins for sale beside the road, the children's on brackets against the wall....

With her father's blessing, then, Lora had gone to Zakopane with Professor Kosinski and his wife. The college officials arranged it for her. They took a pride in their mountain resort. And they seemed to feel responsible for her and vaguely to feel that if left to herself she would get into all manner of trouble, or else return to her own land with a dim view of their courtesy.

The professor, who taught linguistic studies, was a wiry man with flexible hands forever in motion. He found an intoxication in driving. He drove with great elevation of spirit, without much attention to the road. At times he took both hands from the wheel to make a point when his English failed. But he was fairly at home with it. The conversation took basic turns. No philosophic observations. No flights of fancy. He pointed out to her crops and flowers, domestic beasts. His wife had only smiles to give. Her husband revealed that her name was Tekla. Upon occasion he addressed her in rapid Polish, then turned with smiles to explain to Lora exactly what it was he had said. Lora suspected he had changed the speech. The woman's face had not reflected the sunny words she herself was given. He had stashed his wife in back with the luggage, and there she sat, a placid, overweight, speechless woman with large hands and a peasant's face, whose eyes dwelt on the small houses among the hills as if she felt she belonged in them.

To Lora's surprise, Professor Wilczek, the tall and sturdy prorector she had met before, was there before them at the inn. He in fact had reserved a table for dinner. He stood by the door to the dining room, and while he conversed with Professor Kosinski, he watched her cross the lobby floor. She was conscious that he awaited her and that he intended to kiss her hand as soon as she joined him at the table.

Professor Kosinski tucked his wife into a chair. She had donned a shimmering jacket for them and sat in silent awe of it. Professor Wilczek kissed Lora's hand and seated her at the table beside him. "You knew we were coming?" she said to him.

The dinner music surged between them. Wherever she went she always dined to the thunderous peal of local talent. Accustomed to it, he bent to her with a little smile. "I make the plan."

"You are very kind."

"Kind?" he said. He turned to Kosinski. "What is 'kind'?" Professor Kosinski looked up from his napkin. "She calls me 'kind.'"

"Ah, that is good. 'Kind' it means you have a big heart. You are good to her."

Professor Wilczek kissed her hand. "No," he said, "it is for me. I think of it for many days."

Having her hand kissed at every turn had startled her a bit at first. But soon she had grown used to it and found it vaguely pleasurable. It was done with ease and a swift grace. Before one knew it one's hand was lifted, the head was bent, one's skin brushed with the wing of a moth. It had come to seem a natural thing. Not erotic, yet cherishing. Not intrusive, simply . . . ordained. She would miss it when she returned to the States. Yet she told herself it was all of a piece with arranging things for a visitor's pleasure and of course for the pleasure of her father, who must be assumed to wish his daughter an enjoyable stay. And behind all this, a measure of national pride was involved. We can show you, they might be saying to her, as they bent so gallantly over her hand, what the old high ways of courtesy are.

When she and her father had first arrived, a little affair had been held for them in a room adjoining the rector's office. Tea and, inevitably, poppyseed cake. They were offered coffee, but she had been told that coffee in Poland was very dear. So she declined and accepted tea. She was smiled upon. Her hand was kissed a dozen times. The rector was there, a member of a Holy Order, a man approaching her father's age, whose name she was told and then forgot. It was very hard to retain the names. The rector was roughly the chancellor and ran the school, her father said.

She had met the prorector there as well, very much younger, about her own age and not of an Order. He lectured in Polish on English literature. He knew a modicum of her language, and they had been able to make it through with smiles and nods and occasional words. He watched her lips with a gracious intentness while she spoke as distinctly as she could. Apparently he was fluent in German, as all of them were in this part of Poland, and she knew enough to fill some gaps. No more than a word here and there, of course. Her father explained that much of the week he was off to Warsaw. He was liaison between the university and the State. For the moment the State allowed this one institution of higher learning to remain as it was, Catholic. It meant a great deal to the people of Poland. She learned from her father how skilled he was in parrying demands, giving a little, taking as much as he possibly could. "It's a rocky sea. I'm told he keeps the school afloat."

Professor Wilczek had arranged a climb for the following day. More correctly, a gentle ascent. Not more than a mile and a half uphill in the crisp air, with the peaks of snow that were always near, a glimpse of sun on glacial pools. Almost at hand they seemed to her. But Professor Kosinski said they were many miles away. He suggested the air was a telescope. It brought things close that were far away. "I don't explain, I observe," he said. "But it gives us charm, does it not?" he said. His wife trudged relentlessly on, her eyes on the ground instead of the peaks. "It makes us mystery," he noted again, delighted with his transcendent strain. He seemed elated and vigorous.

Two laughing nuns with red cheeks came running toward them down the slope and passed them by with flying veils. The air was spiced with a scent of herb. Bits of cloud like indolent moths were drifting near. The mountain road was patched with sun. There were wares displayed along the way, colorful woolens of every sort, and keen-eyed children who held them up to tempt Lora as she slowed her step, then ran behind her smilingly. She turned to give them each a coin and declined the burden of their wares. Rather, she spared Professor Wilczek, for he would insist on bearing them. He walked beside her, to glance at her frequently with a smile. She found his attention flattering, and yet again she questioned it. Did it belong with kissing her hand? Was it a gracious substitute for the English words he did not know? Once he said, "You will not believe. Last night I study with your words. The words of your country," he explained. "I study them as a schoolboy. I make the list. I try them to the trees and stones."

She laughed at that. "Try them to me."

He shook his head. "I make you surprise. I will say them to you in small parcels."

She found it vaguely touching, of course, that a grown, sophisticated man, undoubtedly brilliant in his tongue, should be reduced to the struggling, awkward speech of a child, and all for her. She was growing deeply conscious of him. She kept her eyes on the scenery, but she knew when his eyes had turned to her. His gaze was palpable, like a touch. It served for speech. She felt in it no discourtesy, only a gentle concern for her, for what she was.

At first she had thought him unattractive, with his coarse, light hair that was cropped too close, his nose a trifle broad for her taste, his head a little the shape of a wedge, wide forehead and pointed chin. A certain flatness below the eyes, just between the high cheekbone and the bridge of the nose, she had come to regard as the Slavic face. Tall for a woman, she liked it that he was taller than she. She liked his eyes with their level, warm, perceptive gaze. When he spoke to her, or tried to speak, at last his eyes were all she saw. Her father had said, "They speak of him with great respect, and his manners are polished, I'll give him that. But judging by the look of him, I'd say that somewhere down the line a peasant wandered through the door and found himself in a lady's chamber."

"How exactly would you define a peasant?"

"A peasant," he said, "is the other fellow, not yourself."

She was used to his answers. They could sound direct but were never something you took to the bank. She wondered if he lectured so and how a translator would deal with it.

Finally at the end of the climb they ate their lunch at a rustic inn—the sour soup she had grown to love, the wild mushrooms caressed with butter. How simple and pure is this land, she thought. It was after that, as they leaned their arms on a wooden rail and drank the view, that he said to her, "You have a husband, is it so?"

It had been before them all along. To reach it they had climbed the mountain, perhaps even journeyed to Zakopane to come upon it precisely here. She held her gaze on a far peak. "When I was young, and then he died."

He did not express the usual sorrow. He said instead, "You are now young."

She smiled and slightly shook her head. "This child who plays in the grass below, I am older than he. . . . These mountains are old. I am not so old."

He stroked the rail. "Sometimes I have the age of the mountain."

"Sometimes I have it too," she said. But at the moment it wasn't so. She felt uncommonly young that day. She knew a rich desire to laugh. Her fellow climbers along the rail, absorbed in the view and one another, were warmly human, it seemed to her, as all had seemed to her long ago. The air itself had a tenderness.

Again she felt the whole of him gone into his eyes that were on her now. He touched her hand so lightly with his that it might have been the brush of his lips. "My name is Jan." He said it out, as a small child will tell his name to another child, and yet as if it summed him up, the simple name, and he offered it, and yet again, he invoked a power mountain-old, the claim on one whose name is known. He was giving her such a claim.

Through a tangle of drifting clouds above, the sun came and went on the slopes. She told herself it was possibly his official duty to lend romance to unofficial college occasions involving the kin of official visitors. "What a lot of trouble I make you," she said. "Professor Kosinski, all of you."

"Trouble?" he said with a puzzled look. He took her hand. He kissed it softly to make amends for his ignorance. And it seemed to her that words were nothing. She recalled that her father was making them, even now as she stood by the rail. The youthful faces were turned to him and, when he ceased, to the translator, and all the while their nimble fingers taking notes. "At first it's annoying," he had said. "But then you get accustomed to it, and finally you come to relish it. For the time it takes, they're not looking at you, and then you're free to blow your nose, have a cough, observe their faces. They're very intense, with the chosen look, conscious of being the one in twelve hundred applicants." And then he complained, "When I make a little light-hearted remark, a witticism intended simply to leaven the loaf, it never seems to get factored in. They never smile. Possibly it isn't amusing to them."

"They're very serious," she had said. "But the translator may not pick up on it. And humor is hard to translate, you know."

"Or he isn't amused and wants to spare me embarrassment. He knows them better than I, of course. Still . . . ," he said, and repeated a particularly witty remark. His voice was wistful. "I'm sorry it was lost," he said.

"Nothing is lost," she reminded him. "Save it and use it on someone else."

"You're right," he agreed. "I'll write it down." But she knew he had already written it down, had probably used it a dozen times. . . .

Jan Wilczek was speaking her name. " 'Lora,' " he said. "In ancient Deutsch it means warrior. Very fine."

She smiled at him. "I have been known to turn and run. . . . I was given my mother's name. It means in Latin 'she who weeps.' "

" 'She who weeps.' "He gazed at the child in the grass below and then at her. He had understood. "I say to you it will not be."

And suddenly she was in his care.

Professor and Mrs. Kosinski approached. "Tekla," he said, "has heard them speak of a little shop with native craft." He bowed to Lora. "Would you care to join her?"

Lora joined the good woman where she stood.

Inside the shop were the customary sweaters and skirts, the wooden plates elaborately carved. She'd collected several from a day in Krakow. But here there were also paintings on glass. The shopkeeper said they were done nearby. Typical of the region, he said. She chose a small one, simply framed, of a shepherd surrounded by his sheep. The shopkeeper wrapped it over and over in coarse paper and tied the fat parcel with a string. "Have care," he said. "Do not drop." He accompanied his words with a telling gesture.

Mrs. Kosinski looked on with a certain anxiety. She had bought an earthenware honey pot crawling over with yellow bees. When she and Lora were on their way, she touched the fat parcel in Lora's hand. "Break," she said with a wise look. It was the sole English word she had uttered. How dreadful, Lora was thinking gaily, if that is the only one she knows.

After dinner they sat on the terrace and watched the moon glide

Inside the Silence

between the peaks, spilling light across the snow, splashing it into glacial pools, farther and farther down the slope till the mountains ran with a ghostly lava and snow light colored the whole sky and hovered, lilac, above the trees.

Professor Kosinski conversed with his wife in subdued Polish. Hush, oh, hush, they seemed to say in the soft sibilance of their tongue. Lora sat between the men. Professor Wilczek was silent beside her. Jan it is, she was thinking of him. They had laid down the burden of speech. And so released, they were freed of the restless search for words, as the search went on in her father's world, which through the years had become her own. If you can name it we'll let you have it, at least till we find a better name and then we have it instead of you. Even she and her father played the game. But the name was never what it was. It only let them circle it. It only kept them from coming close. . . .

Hush, oh, hush, their companions said while she and this man who sat with her sank ever deeper into the hush. Stripped of words, they grew keen of sense. She shared a living silence with him, as if they had brought into being a child too young for speech, who was caught up into the wonder of light and snow and sky. She shared his joy in this child of theirs. Wherever his duty lay with her, she knew it did not extend so far. Slowly he was whispering it: "'Über allen Gipfeln ist Ruh' . . .'"

And after a moment she replied, calling it up from long ago with joy that it was given to her: "Over all the hills is rest."

"Gnädige Frau," he whispered again.

The following day he rode back with them. She had spoken of Majdanek and heard the silence surrounding it. When in the dusk Jan accompanied her to her hotel door, he said, "Do not go, I say to you."

At first she did not understand. Then it came to her. She asked, "Why not?"

She felt him back with the search for words, groping for them amid the chirr of cicadas nested among the leaves. He looked at her long, before he spoke. "Change," he said. "I think you . . . change."

She heard him with amused surprise.

"I desire . . . that you do not change."

She weighed her boldness before she said, "Perhaps you could go with me yourself."

He shook his head. "I go to Warsaw."

"I could wait."

"No," he said, "it cannot be." He kissed her hand.

She felt that a shadow had fallen upon them.

Because of it she did not go. She did not go for a whole week. She had rented a car when they'd first arrived. She continued to drive her father to and from the school. "Don't hover," he always reminded her. She would stand and watch him mount the stairs, conspicuously avoiding the rail, his back straight, a small and really dapper man with carefully brushed and wispy hair, what there was of it snowy white. She wished he would hold on to the rail, or watch the steps at the very least. Perhaps he did when she wasn't there. He was getting old, though he failed to see it, or if he saw he failed to admit it, and she had invited herself to Lublin. He liked her presence. Perhaps obscurely he needed her. Anyway, he had let her come.

She turned when he was out of sight, and on this day Jan was in the hall. She assumed he had been to Warsaw and back. His level gray eyes had been watching her, as if they had never left her face since rest was over all the hills. . . . Rest is in his eyes, she thought. Rest is with us when we meet. She offered gently when he approached to kiss her hand, "I have not been to Majdanek."

His smile was grave. "Your face it says to me," he replied.

She wished he had words to explain to her. I am forty-one years old, she thought. I have seen a great deal in my life. My husband's death. My mother's too. An older brother killed in the war. The loss of a child born dead to me. . . . And she did not like, at the age she was, to be told by a man what she could not see. She confessed there had lingered in her mind a talk with a student, one with a good command of English. She had asked him about the custom here of kissing the hand. The student laughed. "The older men do it. The young ones do not."

"Why?" she asked. "Tell me why."

He had said without any hesitation, "It is putting the woman in her place. It is making her less."

"Less?" she asked. "It seems to me it makes her more."

"No," he had said, "it makes her less. It is saying she is not equal to him. It puts her behind. She cannot freely act or speak. The students believe that a woman is equal. A kiss on the hand is saying to her, 'You are very nice, but do not interfere with us in the way we are choosing to make your life. If you do, we shall no more kiss your hand.'"

She had laughed at him. "Still, I think I like it," she said.

And now she was thinking that if there was to be more between herself and Jan, as she acknowledged she hoped there would, he must allow her the freedom to act as seemed best to her. And perhaps she wanted to prove to him that she could see whatever it was and remain the same. Picking her father up next day, she spotted the student who had told her to go. T-shirt, disreputable pants, like any American student, she thought. Except for the hair, which was cropped short. She asked him to show her Majdanek. He shied at first like a startled deer. He shifted his books and nodded slowly. "Yes," he said, "I think it is so that you should see."

"Why?" she asked.

He twisted his mouth in the midst of a shrug. "You see and then you know," he said.

He had come to her on the stroke of nine. She asked him to drive the thirty miles, since he knew the way. She had to inquire his name again.

"Jerzy," he said. "You call me Jerry."

"That will be easier," she smiled.

They headed out past greening fields, which he said were beets, and factories of brick, which would make of the beets the coarse sugar she was served at table. "I told them we'd need a guide," he said. "I could show it to you, but they think it is too special for me. I think they fear I will take away a souvenir."

"Would you?" she asked.

"Not in a hundred years," he said.

There were oxen plowing the gently sloping fields of wheat. On the narrow road the men walked to the left of the wagons, between the horses and the cars. There were forests floored with the lush fern and clearings with stacks of pine and birch. Beside a stream women washed their clothes.

She questioned Jerry about his work. He studied to be an engineer. Her father had explained to her: "You get a profession and then you belong. You're in 'the intelligentsia' here. It wipes the peasant clean out of you." "Do you have to be voted in?" she asked. "I think," he said, "you're only required to spell the word and not leave out any consonants."

Had he studied under Professor Wilczek? "Yes," he said. "The English literature." She waited for him to tell her more. "He knows much. We learn much." He glanced at her and then away. "We speak of him, the students do. We speak of when he is getting a wife. If he speaks to a woman in the hall, the word is making, he gets a wife." She saw his smile. "He goes to Warsaw many times. It is for the school, but we are saying he goes for a woman. This time it is he brings a wife."

She changed the subject. "And what do you wish to do with your life?"

"I wish to go to America," he said.

She saw at first the dark guard towers, a series of them along the road. From a distance they were giant birds. Then they became tree houses perched on scaffolding, each with a single slim antenna—a single spire that pierced the sky—a single window that faced the field. Jerry turned into the open field, and then without warning, they were there, with rows of narrow, low concrete structures, dark as the towers with recent rain, gray or brown she would not recall. To their left stood a towering mound of earth. A metal ladder led to a narrow metal walk that halfway up seemed to circle it. She did not see a formal entrance. A larger building stood before them, and then the huts, low, monotonous, tunnel-like. She felt a stir of disappointment. "This is all?" she said.

He looked surprised. "It was enough. . . . Over there, the camp commander's house." He pointed to an attractive dwelling some distance to the left of the camp. It was much like any suburban home, softened with shrubs and a few small trees. Beyond the camp for miles around there was nothing but field, with only a dusting of green crop. The land was flat. Across it flew a single bird. She watched its shadow slice the land like a plow that left no cut behind.

A man emerged from behind a building. "The guide," said Jerry, getting out of the car.

She followed him. "Does he speak English?"

"They have chosen for you such a one."

He came to them at a kind of canter, his cap pulled down upon his face. When he was near he pushed it back with a brown finger. His skin was leathery and tan. A short man with a broad forehead, head like an arrow sloping sharply to the chin. Wrinkles raked across the cheeks below the eyes and swept with a scythlike curve to the beard, a rough circle of sandy hair that framed his mouth and pointed chin. The eyes were narrowed, cautious of her. He did not offer her his name. He kept his hat upon his head. His hand extended the tickets to them. She paid for Jerry and herself.

"So . . . ," said the guide. "You will please to follow." His voice was high and monotonous. They followed him to the largest building. He turned to them. "Here begin the German camp. In autumn of 1941 the Nazis establish this concentration camp." He caught her stare at the mound of earth to the left of them. "No," he reproved her, "that is for end. Here is now. . . ."

He seemed to wait, as if accustomed to more than just the two of them. He stood tall and raised his arm, as if he would call in the straying ones, pause for the flock to become unscattered, and then gather them under his wing. He turned with a little duck of his head. "This building here is being the hall where they are gassed in greatest number. The victims told they are taking shower bath to be clean for journey to labor camp. They told to take off all the garment, all of them. And man and woman and child was then told to enter here, so many as this place could hold."

He led them into an open room, the walls and ceiling of concrete. There was an airless kind of chill and a smell of being underground. No windows here. The concrete floor was scrubbed and clean.

The face of the guide had become a mask. He went on in a toneless voice, "While they are standing together so, no clothes on body, only skin, and thinking the water will fall to them . . ." He broke off. "You see the holes above us here. And at the sides are also holes. There are pipes behind, and through the pipes there is coming gas. Cyclon B the gas is call. This gas it makes some blister at once over all the skin. They are screaming with it and die in time of twenty minute. Here," he said, "at the top is hole where official watch and see when all is dead below. Here on the wall you see the bodies dead with it."

"Look," he said, insisting she look. She moved to peer at the photographs of naked bodies with faces contorted and blistered skin. "You see it is instant in raising the skin. A very good way to kill so many people at once." He moved to the corner of the room. "You see in this place some sample of what is Cyclon B." He stroked the cylinders shaped like bombs. There some dozen of them were stacked. "This gas it is not discover till later. At first the ovens, then Cyclon B. Much better, this."

She listened at several removes from him. His recital seemed to her bizarre. They charge for this. They must make it good. They could easily fake the photographs.

He led them into a smaller room that was like the first but with a ceiling very low. "Another room if there is the need for smaller number to be dead. Take smaller gas. You see above where the victims claw the top in pain. You see the marks the fingers make." He showed her his fingers curled and clawing. He pointed to other photographs of victims still alive but dying. They were on the wall. She did not approach. "Look," he said. "I see," she said. She listened to his toneless voice. She saw his face. She felt her own taking on the lean, stunned look of his. She had not been able to glance at Jerry. Now she turned to him and saw that he had not followed them, that she was alone with her guide's voice and his face like hers. She felt a sudden childish panic. He cannot leave me alone, she thought.

"How many?" she asked. "How many died?"

He turned to her his expressionless face. "Many come. Not all dead. Near to half one million dead."

She stared at him. He is lying to me. Someone had told him to say so much. "Are you sure?" she said. He did not seem to understand. "Are you certain it was so many died?"

"Yes. Certain. It is statistic of death camp. Camp is made to make them dead. All this picture capture from German. Here is second largest camp in all of Europe. Oświęcim first. Auschwitz is German name for it. Four million dead. In Poland they place two largest camp. Others too, but not so big. They wish that German people do not know how very much they are doing this. Majdanek is place very central in map of Europe. I show you map. You will see it well. They are bringing people up from south, down from north, every side. Very nice location for many. No making of useless travel, see? Make very good statistic here. Commander not getting good statistic of many dead is getting sent to the Russian front, and there he die from the Russian gun or from the cold. Is all the same, to be dead, yes? So he is making him good statistic." He waved his arm. "Out there in field is mass executions being made. On 3 September, 1943, there is 18,400 Jewish prisoner shot dead. All that many shot one day and burned there. Make good statistic."

She could not remain in the low room. She walked out. The sun was shining. On the worn gray road it pooled in spots of recent rain. He followed her. He swept his arms to include the huts. "Majdanek very good for looking. All building found at liberation." His face was tense with the effort to make her understand. "Oświęcim . . . Auschwitz . . . they burn all building there but two when word is coming that Allies come. Two building all is left there. Make very fine museum there. You see it there?"

She shook her head.

"You come to best. Here is all. Very good. . . . Here," he said, embracing the open space once more, "is where they are entering, yes? The prisoners are coming here. Many camp commanders come. If bad statistic they do not stay." He began to name them all to her. She closed her mind to the sound of them. But she heard him say, "That one they are calling Bloody Mary."

"A woman?" she asked.

He nodded sagely. "Yes, woman. When prisoner woman is entering camp with baby, she is standing here. She is catching baby from arms of mother and breaks brains against the wall." He followed his words with a violent gesture. "Always she is doing this. Is why they are calling her Bloody Mary."

She did not believe him for a moment. What is he trying to do to me? She turned away to look for Jerry. But the guide had shifted to hold her eyes. "Interesting news. They have at this time discover in New York City her sister. Your country is now deporting her." He nodded his head with a satisfaction that he was inviting her to share. She was rapidly resenting him. He wanted some power over her. His eyes were narrowed in the sun. His face was still expressionless, but the toneless voice held a coaxing depth. Listen to me and believe, it said, and I will show you the underside. I'll show you the rubble under the road, more of it than you dreamt was there.

She heard herself speak from her lethargy. "I do not believe what you're telling me."

He stopped, amazed. She amazed herself. She had broken at last his recitation. "Not believe?"

"I do not believe."

He shook his head from side to side. "My English not so good?" he said.

"It could not have happened, what you say."

"*Pani* . . . ," he said reproachfully. He took off his cap and put it back. "I make it clear. You see I will."

He was leading her across the road into the first of the tunnel-like huts. Inside was dark. Out of the sun, she waited there, unable to see, until at the very end of the hut she caught the faintest roseate glow. He pulled a cord and the room was alight. On either side the long, low room was papered with giant photographs, a running strip from front to back. Life-sized faces, life-sized bodies that seemed to be moving with her own. They were walking, running, God knew where. Tormented faces were close to hers. "These picture taken from capture Germans and made so big. Germans make them no so big. Polish government make them big."

"I do not wish to see them," she said, but she could not take her eyes from them. Children were there. Children's faces.

"Come," he said, leading the way to the back of the hut. "Here," he said and pointed to the oven on the right. The door of it was slightly ajar. He opened it. Inside at the back she saw a light. She had seen its glow from the front of the hut. The lighted place, like a small shrine, held a vase of shoddy red paper flowers. Perhaps they were roses faded with time and all but dust. "The oven," he said. "They use before there is Cyclon B. More time it take with the oven, yes? To kill so many. Very small. Is making bad statistic for them."

A chill was creeping over her. It seemed to come from within the oven. "I have seen," she said. "You can shut the door." But he stood entranced by the sight of the roses. She waited beside him, staring into the oven's tunnel inside the tunnel of the hut inside the tunnel of earth and sky. . . . She grew aware of the smell of vomit. From thirty years ago? she asked. Or was it from someone like herself who had come to spy? She was suddenly becoming ill. She held her breath. She quickly turned and left the hut, walking rapidly past the faces, the mouths opened to form a cry, the eyes despairing, beseeching her.

He joined her instantly in the road. "How can you bear to do this?" she asked. "To show these things? To speak of them?" He did not understand her at all. She saw that she had offended him. And puzzled him. She was glad of it. His face had become the enemy's. A bird was crying it overhead.

"My English is not so good?" he suggested. "If *Pani* does not understand, I try more." She saw at once that he was afraid she'd complain of him. He would lose the work. . . .

"No," she said. "I understand."

"I come instead of my brother today. His English is better. Very good. If you tell it I come for him, they will take his work from him. His wife is sick. She is very sick."

"No," she said. "I will tell them nothing."

"Then you must see all," he said. "The guard watch. He ask it why it is not all. He find my brother is gone from here."

She heard his words without resignation. Why was she forced to stay the course . . . as if it were thirty years ago and the gates were locked and she was trapped inside the pain? He seemed to insist if she did not stay she would add to the sum of all that pain that was still alive in his brother's life. . . . She wanted Jerry beside her now. She wanted someone live and young. But he had simply deserted her. They entered then, one after another, huts that were like the one she had left. Along the walls the faces were different and yet alike, expressing their fear and hopelessness. So many faces but all one face. So many bodies with a single end. . . .

"Look," said the guide, rubbing his finger across a face in a sea of them. "He was my friend from being a child. He died here. I find him on the wall one day. He work in the field for them here, see? Strong man. But he get no food. Get weak for work. They kill him for that."

She stared at the face. "Was he Jewish, then?"

"No, not Jewish. Many is killed not Jewish," he said. "First come Russian prisoners, then Poles and peoples of many countries, twenty-six. Please to follow." He led her to a glass-covered bin against the wall. "They take from them when entering here." She saw a jumbled heap of books—Bibles, Korans, New Testaments. "Here," he said at another case, "are toys of children." She saw the dolls and turned away. This has nothing to do with my child. . . .

Across the road they entered a structure slightly larger, set at right angles to the rest. It proved to contain a row of ovens. In the space behind, a tub was set. There the commander had taken his baths in the warm air of the ovens' heat. She looked at the tub with sickened eyes and then at the guide. For now at last she was at his mercy and at the mercy of this place. She knew a kind of communion with him, as if the two of them shared a haunting. She saw he was at its mercy too and did no more than was given him.

Obediently she followed him into still another hut. It seemed to be a place of records. She was shown the faces, again on the walls, no longer in groups. Some were in cases below the walls. Each face was passive and curiously drained. And each was matched with an arm that showed a series of numbers inked in the flesh. To the side of each was the name, the date of birth, the date of entry into the camp. He explained to her. The face of one recalled her mother. She said to him calmly, "I wish to leave." She stated it without any hope. She felt her face as blank of expression as those of the rest, as blank as his. She went and leaned against the door. "How many more?"

"*Pani*, one," he coaxed her gently. He held up a thumb denoting one, in the strange way of his countrymen. She noted this and accepted it, at the mercy of all that was alien to her.

Between the huts a tractor had begun to move, cutting the tall grass with a blade. The driver turned, maneuvering, his face bronzed, at peace in the sun. The gray huts, familiar to him, had lost their power to threaten his peace. He did not even glance at her. She felt she was as dead for him as the bodies that once had fallen here. The sun was soft on the falling grass, which quivered gently as it fell. She caught the scent of new-mown hay.

How long has it been? she asked herself. She could have checked her watch to see, but she knew that its time meant nothing at all. She seemed to have been standing here since they whispered her husband was dead in the crash and she fell down, and her child came dead, and she stood again and waited for this. Once it begins, you stand and wait.... But these deaths had come before. Whichever way, once it begins, it reaches back. It starts again. Hundreds of thousands dead from one....

"*Pani*," the guide said, coaxing her, as a child is coaxed.

She saw that he was back in the road. She closed her eyes and inhaled the scent. "*Pani*," he said. She followed him into the final hut. "This," he said, "where they operate. Make many experiment on prisoner." He indicated a concrete table and then a hole in the bottom of it. "This hole," he said, "to carry the blood. Has been a pipe from hole to there, out there to back to big container which hold the blood. Use for fertilize," he said. "Good business. Fertilize.... Many things is done to them here. Operate to make a game. Make experiment for science or just to see what can be done. Try many things has not been done. Cut some organs out of body to see how long they live without. They tie together the legs of woman is bearing child. To see how long she live with that. Try to bear and cannot do, for legs is tied. See how long to make her die...."

He seemed to be mesmerized with it. The toneless voice could not desist, as if the horror beckoned him.

She broke away from him once and for all. She left the hut. She was walking blindly down the road. She found that she was walking in rain.

He ran after her. "No, *Pani*. Wrong to go. You walk where bones is throwed away. No, *Pani*, back is out."

She stopped at once. She saw before her the earth scraped, enormously pocked. The sight was like a physical blow. Her eyes dropped to the road at her feet. And Jerry was there and taking her arm. She turned to him in a wild fury. "Why did you leave?"

He did not answer. His startled eyes were upon her face. Her tone, her words had frightened him. She pulled her arm away from his grasp and was walking rapidly toward the car. Her anger with him was choking her. She did not think she could ride with him the thirty miles it would take for them. He strode before her to open the door. But seeing him waiting to help her in, she turned aside and walked straight up to the mound of earth and held the ladder for support. She was staring into the packed earth.

And suddenly the guide was there. "Monument," he said to her. "Earth dug in back with bones. Piled here for monument. See how big. Two story high. Full of bones. If *Pani* climb and walk there, she have a very fine look at camp. She see the all of it one look. And up there, see at top, is made some very fine words to say."

She found she was facing chips of bone. A smell of bone was in the rain. And with it the scent of new-mown hay that rose from the cut grass at her feet.

"I read to you fine words is made...."

But she broke then and began to weep. The swiftness of it left him dumb. He backed away. At a loss, he watched. She clung to the ladder and fought for control. When Jerry came, alarmed, contrite, she turned and followed him to the car.

She rode in silence, her head back, her eyes closed. At the hotel he gave her the keys to the car. She left him without a word. Once in her room, she took off her clothes as if it were night instead of noon and went to bed. She tried to imagine that it was dark, that she would sleep, and in the morning she would wake with a mind as free as the one she had waked with hours before. She thought of her father, his innocence. How pure he is, she thought to herself. For all his years he is like a child. It gave her comfort to think of him. For he belonged to another world and in that world she had been a child. Summers ago she swam in a sea that burned with gold. There was warm sand.... With eyes shut tight she recalled the sand, the sea, the gold.... Deliberately she called to her mind the trip to the mountains days before, the moon that broke through the peaks for her and lit the snow and sky for her. And all of it seemed prearranged. The moon itself... all of her pleasure predictable. As prearranged as a trip to the beach for a young child.... She remembered how on one of the trips they had come upon a young man who had drowned in the sea and been washed ashore. That had not been prearranged. She found that now she recalled his face, though she had not thought of it for years. A struggle had been in his youthful features. A kind of horror, she saw now, although at the time she had not known. The fish had eaten one foot away. Her father had picked her up in his arms and rapidly walked away with her. "What is the matter with him?" she had whispered. "Nothing," her father replied. "He's asleep."

How much has been hidden from me? she asked. And suddenly it was not her father, it was she who had been the child. Till in that place she was born again and now the good things smelled of it.

She could not lie still for trembling. It came to her that going there was the only thing she had done for herself and not as daughter and then as wife. Did it make them right, the men at the college, who did not trust her on her own? To go there of her own free will and pay the coins to see and hear. . . . Something seemed to have beckoned her. I went in ignorance, she cried. But tucked in her must have been a knowledge and so a lust for a little more. And so the apple was plucked and tasted. She and the guide had given it life. They had made it happen over again.

She got up and put on her clothes again, but not the ones she had taken off. It would soon be time to go for her father. She washed her face. With all the art that she possessed, she tried to make it look serene. She brushed her long dark hair till it shone and bound it up in the loose knot she always wore. Nothing has changed with me, she said. I am a daughter, once a wife . . . a woman who went to Majdanek and looked at it and then came back. She studied her figure in the glass. She wore her clothes with the same assurance, the slim skirt, the blouse that was open at the throat. She added a chain. She added a belt and tightened it. Nothing has changed with me, she said.

She drove to the university. It was not quite time for her father to come. The halls were empty. She wandered into the library. With her lips set, among the stacks, she scanned the titles of the books. For a time she had worked in a library, until her mother had taken ill. She noted a book that was out of place. The numbers alone were familiar to her. She drew it out and placed it properly on the shelf.

Suddenly, emerging from the stacks, she found that she was facing Jan.

He was holding an open book. He laid it down and kissed her hand. He saw her face. "You have gone," he said.

She did not answer him at once. She scanned the portraits on the walls. "I have seen," she said at last. She wandered away. He followed her. She picked up a book that was on a table and opened it and shut it again. "I was looking for something to read," she said in a voice that was hushed to match the room. "Something light . . . to fall asleep. . . . But here I suppose . . ." She broke off. Students were scattered about the room, hunched over the tables or slouched at ease. One of them slept, his face on a book. She looked at him with a kind of longing.

She turned to Jan. "Professor Kosinski has said to me that here in Poland your poets are honored even beyond your heroes of war." Her own voice was strange to her.

He seemed to be lost in the echo of it. "Is true," he said to her at last.

"Who is your greatest poet?" she asked.

He gazed at her uncertainly. "Adam Mickiewicz, it is said."

"Then read him to me. I want to hear the sound of him in your own voice."

He grew at once confused and sad. "I have not your words."

"You have your own and they are his. I want to hear beauty in words of this land. I want them to drown an ugliness here." Her voice was tight with its urgency.

Her words seemed to break over him. He did not react to them at once. Perhaps he was trying to sort them out. He looked around uneasily. "Not here," he said. He led her at once down a corridor and into an office, his own, she supposed. But she did not want to study it. He closed the door. He stood before her at a loss. His eyes implored her mercy on his perplexity.

"Please," she said.

Whereupon he turned to a shelf of books and chose a volume. He placed her before him at a table. When he opened the book, his hands were trembling. He turned the pages and after a moment began to read.

She heard his voice, his grave way with the sibilant words, calm at first and almost shy, and then the passion in the words, as he gave his best, so bidden by her. Until it became an act of love. With the words. With her. She listened and heard the sound of both. But it failed to drown the suffering. The fervent words were woven with it. They were one with it. And she saw that forever this would be so. Beauty and passion all of a piece with pain of the world.

Glancing up, he found that tears were in her eyes. At once he laid the book aside. She stood before him. He went to her and kissed her hand. But seeing her tears begin to fall, he took her quietly in his arms. "What is to do?" he whispered to her.

She gave herself up to his embrace. This is all there is, she told herself. The rest is nothing. . . . He kissed her hair, her brow, her lips. This is all there is. . . . And she was back in the moonlit night, when over all the hills was rest. . . . Those words were flowering into this. . . . But she shuddered as if she felt the snow and broke away. "I thank you," she whispered, "for being kind. . . . I must go."

"Your father," he said. "I call. I have him taken to home. Is simple to do."

"Nothing is simple," she said to him. And then she was escaping from him and walking rapidly down the hall. Nothing will ever be simple again. At a sudden turn she found herself confronting Professor Kosinski's wife. The latter stared at her weeping eyes. Lora gazed at the simple peasant face, the small and almost cloudless eyes, the plump flesh about the mouth. For the first time she took in the other woman's face in all its fine simplicity. A trace of cunning about the lips but no more culled from a peasant's descent than was needed now to keep afloat in her husband's world with its tricky talk.

The bell rang, but Lora stood as the students emptied into the hall. Freed from class, full of themselves and the joy of being unconfined, they flowed around the women there as if the two were rocks in the stream.

Lora took the other by the hand and led her into an emptied classroom. She scarcely knew what she was about. The coil of her hair had fallen loose. She closed the door and stood beside it with eyes shut. At last she walked among the chairs and dropped to one still faintly warm. On the blackboard words were written in chalk. Alien words she would never know. A pencil was lying on the floor.

Mrs. Kosinski stood looking at her, then very slowly sank to the chair that was nearest hers. Her arms were laden with parcels tightly wrapped in white paper. One by one she laid them down until they surrounded her feet like feeding doves in the chapel square. She sat there watchful and prepared.

"Tekla . . ." Lora spoke her name.

The other nodded, her eyes concerned. Blotting her tears, calming her voice, Lora began, "I went to Majdanek today. . . . I had not been prepared for it. But how is one to be prepared? Has it always been like this, do you know? Is it like this even now today . . . under the surface everywhere?" She asked the questions distractedly, knowing the woman could understand almost nothing, or nothing at all, of what she said, freed by it to hold nothing back.

Mrs. Kosinski pressed her hand. Lora found the gesture hard to bear, so simple it was, so genuine. It was a touch to soothe a child. It simply said, I am here for you. Lora brought the woman's hand to her face. It was large and strong and smelled of soap. "I cannot go on as I have before. . . . I feel somehow . . . I share the guilt. Because I belong to the same race those monsters . . ." She broke off. "Do you know how many . . . how many died? And more were tortured who did not die."

The hair had fallen about her face. With her free hand Tekla smoothed it back. "It is what I saw, as well as what I know is there that I did not see or would not see. All over the world it may be there. The smell is there. Thirty years. It is still there. Not all the sweetness in the grass . . ."

Tekla's eyes took in her face, scanning the features one by one. Lora felt she was seeing her own face for the first time in the woman's eyes. It was a face along the wall. "I feel," she said, "I am one of them. One of those who were tortured there. But also I am one of those . . . I am that woman who stood in the road and took the baby . . ." She broke off and began to weep.

Mrs. Kosinski stroked her hand. "I am the babies whose heads she dashed against the wall. . . . My own baby was one of them."

She whispered as if they were starting anew, "Majdanek..."

The woman nodded. "Break," she said.

Lora caught her breath. Yes. Break. Bodies broken. Innocence and mercy broken. The grace of life . . . my own broken.

She rose late the following day. It was Sunday; her father had no class. She dressed with care and met him for lunch in the dining room. He greeted her with the usual smile. A smile that took for granted her love, her place in his world, her womanly presence that sheltered him. Since her mother's death she was all of that. Don't hover, he said, but he looked for it. Despite his wave of dismissal, he claimed it. . . . He did not seem to find her changed. He did not even question the fact that she had failed him the day before. If it had created a crisis for him—not finding her there when his class was done—he seemed to have forgotten it. "Professor Wilczek called for you. I told him you were sleeping late."

He glanced at her with a quizzical smile and then away. "He said he'd come back in the afternoon. At least he seemed to be saying that. Apparently you get through to him. I find it very difficult. I find myself willing him to sneeze so I can come out with 'Gesundheit,' which is all the German I can recall." Her father was scanning a paper from home. But he lowered it to study her. "Curious fellow. Very intense. I can't imagine how he deals with us, our literature. How does he manage *The Faerie Queene*? Or Chaucer, my God, what does he say?" He raised the paper, then lowered it. "And I rather resent his teaching it with no more command of our tongue than he has. He speaks like an illiterate . . ."—he searched for the word—"garbage man."

She smiled at that. She didn't remind him how little Polish he could command. Their lunch arrived. He ate well. "Eat," he said. "It's very good."

"Yes," she said, but she didn't eat.

He sipped his soup, laying aside the slices of sausage submerged in it. He avoided things that he had to chew. "Not many days left," he reminded her. "Another week. Four lectures in all. Tomorrow I'll begin the winding up."

She envied him his life delivered in small parcels. A course of lectures with four to go. Was that the way one dealt with life? Don't think beyond a chosen point. Choose a point . . . And he was saying, "I think I've had enough of this. What about yourself? I've begun to say my prayers in segments and pause for translation after each."

When Jan arrived she was waiting for him in the small lobby, all leather and oak. She would not see his searching eyes. She led him down a narrow hall and out to a small deserted porch. The servants, it seemed, had forgotten it. A drift of pollen covered the floor. There were pots of flowers in need of water. It overlooked a neglected garden where paths were overgrown with vine. A rose ran wild among the trees. He kissed her hand and did not release it. Instead, he folded it in his own.

She said at once, "I must ask your forgiveness for yesterday. And I wish to thank you for being kind." She heard herself. She had raised her voice. In her effort to make him understand, the words from her mouth were stilted, aloof. It is like a play, she thought with despair.

"Kind?" he said. He recalled the word. It had come between them more than once. "Kind?" he repeated indignantly. He released her hand and strode away. His retreat was traced in the pollen dust. He turned to her. He struck his breast. "I feel here what it is you feel. I sorrow for it. For you," he said. "I wish you not to go," he said.

"Go?" she repeated. Did he mean go again to Majdanek? But surely he could not think she would.

"Go to America with your father. I wish you to remain here."

"Here?" she asked.

"Here . . . with me. To marry," he said.

The abruptness of it quite stunned her. She found she wanted to sit down. Leaning back in her chair, she closed her eyes. Pigeons were bickering under the eaves. She looked at him sadly and tenderly. "You know my name and I know yours, and that is all we know," she said.

He shook his head. "I know what is it sorrows you, for what is joy. It needs more?"

He had not said anything of love. Perhaps he did not know the word.

At once he dropped to a chair beside her and fished from his pocket a small book, incredibly a dictionary. He shook his head and smiled at her.

Quietly she began to laugh. He laughed with her, and in his laughter she heard his love. "Help me," he said, but she laughed the more. She could take the schoolboy in her arms, book and all. He slipped the book back into his pocket. "Words," he said, "of no service."

Her eyes brushed the neglected garden and came to rest on begonias thirsting in their pots. "How could we marry without words?"

"Marry is not a case of words."

At that she rose and knelt to him, knelt in the pollen gilding the floor. She kissed his hand. "I have wanted to see what it would be like, to kiss your hand as you kiss mine."

He drew her to him and kissed her lips. This is all there is, she tried to think. The rest is nothing. . . . They kissed again. She stood and said, "I cannot live here, don't you see? So close to it. Always there."

He watched her lips intently now, trying to understand her words. The garden under the gathering clouds awaited rain. Infant grapes invading the porch were stirred with wind. She caught a tendril that swayed to her and wound it slowly about her wrist. I am bound, she thought, in my own words, and he is bound in words of his. She tried to forget his struggle with hers. She would simply say it out to him, hoping herself to understand.

"I am not safe here anymore. Over the hills . . . there is no rest." Her voice broke on the memory. "I have lost my faith in something close . . . so close I can't tell what it is. But all of you go on with your lives. You hide it. You hide from it."

Her passion only bewildered him.

"You said to me that I would change. Why haven't you changed? Or if you have . . . what were you like before you did? Perhaps if we had seen it together for the first time . . . and changed together. But you . . . but you have had thirty years to deal with it and wipe it out. You are old in it. I am born to it." She turned away. "I think it may be that your land is old and has suffered longer, more than mine. It has learned more. I think you are too wise for me. You would try to make me as wise as you. . . ." She broke off. She had wandered into her father's world, where words kept one from coming close. . . . "It would come between us and spoil us."

"Spoil?" he said.

"Destroy," she said. "Not even your love can do it for me, wipe out the thirty years it takes . . . if it takes so long. That place for me is surrounded with silence. I walk to it and there are no words. To walk away I must find the words. But now . . . I am inside the silence." She gave it up.

He stood up. Of course he had not understood. His eyes spoke his sorrow to her. "Majdanek it comes between."

She nodded and kissed his hand again. Even if she found the words . . . Better she never found the words. She would be like the man her father knew who died of knowing with none to hear.

After this she was more at peace. She knew that she was right, for once. For if she stayed, the decay would spread, to the green land, her marriage, her love. . . . The shock to her had been profound. She was only beginning to know how much. Nothing here could be pure for her. The huddle of huts in the lonely field had touched her own young husband's death, her child born dead, her mother's death. It touched her father's death to come. But these were pure. Those other deaths, those bones like shards of pottery, plowed under, jumbled up with earth, they seemed to her a blasphemy against the deaths she could call her own. If she stayed, the decay would spread to them.

Her father had come to his final class, determined to quit in a blaze of glory with a rousing lecture on Melville's theory of good and evil. He had donned his best gray suit for it. She had tied for him his striped bow tie. "Can evil exist alone?" she asked. "Never," he said. "It will breed the good." She saw the faces along the wall. She found his abstractions hard to bear.

She began to pack her things away, his clothes first and then her own. And the things she had bought along the way, more of them than she had thought. Many of them were generous gifts. The Polish people gifted with grace and always, it seemed to her, with pleasure. In packing the painting on glass from the mountains, she let the package slip from her hand. She held her breath and tore away the layers of paper. The shepherd lay shattered among his flock. "Break," she whispered, recalling Tekla. She could not pack the rest that day.

She had heard nothing more from Jan. He dwelt in her father's parceled world. He could as neatly dispose of evil. But often in her dreams at night they shared a language made for them and spoke their hearts and understood. In other dreams, her husband, dead at twenty-three, had come alive, his face grown older, old as hers. She kissed his hand and the hand was Jan's. And then she was walking through the hut, seeking their faces along the wall. She woke and wept for the loss of both.

She could not leave without a word. When she drove her father to his class, she looked for Jan. His office said he had gone to Warsaw but perhaps by now had returned. They told her how to reach his house. With knowing smiles, they drew a map. She felt the thought being tossed about like a red balloon: He takes a wife. . . .

With the aid of their map she found the house, a brick one tucked among the trees. It was small, undistinguished, banked with fern. There was a yard with a splash of flowers and off to the side a tiny garden with vegetables. There an old man on his hands and knees was pulling weeds. She left her car and approached him slowly, but of course he would not understand a single word she said to him. Perhaps the name if she said it right. "Jan Wilczek?" He did not look up. It seemed to her that he might be deaf. She printed the name on a piece of paper.

He sat back—perhaps it was too much effort to stand—and drew out a pair of steel-rimmed glasses and took the paper in quivering hands. She saw that his fingers were mutilated. Two were missing, the rest . . . She could not look at them. "*Tak*," he said, and gave her back the scrap of paper. And on the arm that he raised to her were the numbers indelibly in the flesh.

She looked away with the shock of it. She felt a single drop of rain and then a steady pelting of drops. He sat at her feet enduring it. She stood, confused, now staring into his broken hands, unable to turn away from them. . . .

In a daze she followed a path to the house and rang a bell. After a bit the door was opened by degrees by an old woman bent almost double. Lora saw the hump across the back, the weal mark across the face. She took it in, the whole of it, and she heard the *"tak"* of the man in the garden as clearly as if it were spoken again. In silence she held out the name. The woman took it away with her. At last she returned and gave it back. And again on the raddled flesh of the arm the numbers there were plain to see. She shook her head and swept the arm to indicate he was not at home. Then, retreating with tiny steps, she opened the door for Lora to enter.

But Lora could not bring herself to further lay bare the secret here. Was it by design it was kept from her that Majdanek was in his home, alive for him each day of his life? Yet why, in God's name, had he let her think that he could forget the horror of it? But of course he had not understood what it was she required of him.

The woman waited patiently. And Lora waited. She found she could not walk away. . . . To walk away I must find the words, but now I am inside the silence. . . . Beyond the porch was a steady rain. A fine slant she could scarcely see except against the trunks of trees. And so on the camp it had rained at the end. In Poland everything ends in rain. She forced herself for a final time to behold the woman. By a trick of light, or a trick of the mind, the woman seemed to be standing in rain, in patience enduring with all the faces along the wall the shower that fell in the concrete room, the heat that warmed the jailer's bath, and last of all, the long table that saved the blood and left the bones to curse the earth. . . .

She bowed to the woman and entered the rain. Off to the side, still pulling the weeds, the old man sat, now slightly grayed with the silver of it, as if he held it of small account, or rising scarcely worth the pain. Slowly she walked away from them. So I have wrongly judged my love, surely the last I shall ever have. . . . But did it mean she could live with him, reminded daily of Majdanek? It would take her years to grow strong enough. Again she felt herself one with the faces along the wall, one with the woman, who now by degrees had closed the door. And I am frailer than she by far. . . .

He drove up beside her quite suddenly before she could get inside her car. He got out very quickly from his. She saw the welcome in his face, the start of gladness.

She shook her head. "I have come to tell you good-bye," she

said, knowing he scarcely understood, but it gave her relief to say the words. "I have judged you wrongly, my dear one. All I have done is weep for them. But you take what is left of them and try a little to make amends. You are finer and stronger than I knew, but I think it is not enough for us. Or perhaps . . . it is too much for us."

The old man was still in his place, but grayed as if with memory. "You were so valiant with my words. If only I had struggled with yours," and then recalling what he had said, "tried them to the trees and stones, perhaps I could make you understand."

She kissed his hand. It was wet with rain. "You were the one bright thing for me."

He held her, moved and at a loss. When she drew away, he turned her hand with both his own to catch the rain. And then he lowered his face to it till she held his face with the fallen rain. . . .

At the school she stood on the porch beside the door and waited patiently for her father. She was too shaken to go inside. Jerry came out of the hall and saw her. Her hair and face were glistening. She beckoned to him. "I never thanked you for going with me. I never paid you."

He shifted his books and shook his head. Like any student at home, she thought. A button missing, scrungy pants. He was ill at ease around her now. She was sorry for that. "I want to pay you before I go. How much?" she asked.

For just a moment their eyes met. "You have paid," he said. Perhaps her wet face reminded him.

"Yes, I have, and the cost was dear. It has cost me more than you'll ever know."

He shuffled a bit on the stone of the porch. "I am sorry I said it that you should go."

"Why did you leave me alone with it?" He shrugged and looked at the dripping trees. "You thought you could not see it again?"

He made a grimace. "Is possible," he said, ashamed.

"What were the words on the monument?" He looked at the trees across the street. "I need to know before I leave."

"'Take care lest this happen again,' it says."

She thought of it. "We must take care, then, you and I."

He nodded gravely. "We cannot take care unless we know."
"Yes," she said, "I see it now."

That day she packed the rest of their things. She came to the shepherd and his flock and gently wrapped the shards to take. She wept for him and for his flock. It seemed to her that the men who had made the huddle of huts in the lonely field had broken him with all the rest. She saw that the breaking still went on for all who went to the place of death and, when they returned, for all they touched. Today . . . today it was she they broke. She wept for herself.

She heard her father whistling as he packed away his books and notes.

Then, as if her hand that held a face, and would forever hold it so, had filled with rain and tipped and spilled, she resolved, in the words of the monument, to have a care lest it happen again. She saw the time to begin was now. The life to save should be her own.

The silence surrounding the huts for her had deepened the silence that circled her love. In silence she cried for an end to it. She told her father when he appeared, "I want a book that will teach me Polish."

He smiled at her and shook his head. "Now? At the end of the run?" he said. "And what will you do with it?" he asked.

"I shall try it to the trees and stones."

"I pause for a translation," he said.

But she thought they would have to wait for one.

Mirror Image

While she was standing there talking to him, she could see herself five minutes from then already down in the street below, taking a cab, riding away in the winter dusk and into the years that would make her forget she was telling her father, "You're scum to me," and watching the shock spread over his face.

The shock in his face spread over her own. It gave her pleasure to feel his shock, to know she had found the words for it. Like the right key that would throw the lock. She had taken his check and torn it across and dropped it onto the rug at her feet. She felt it drift through the floors she had climbed. Climbed instead of taking the lift, because she had waited her life for this and still her anger needed time, a fragment more to be equal to it.

After the check had been torn for him, she had seen the white come into his face. It had given her strength to say the rest. "You weren't around when we needed you. My mother died for lack of money to get her the care she should have had. You let her die. You let me grow up hating you because you left and never came back. Never wrote and never came back. And now you think you can turn it around?"

Then it was finished and she could leave.

But the woman came from another room. A wife, had he said? Another wife . . . with restless hands and scarlet mouth. She now advanced, reflecting his pain. No, simply determined to reinforce it. It seemed the reason that she was there. "Your father was happy that you would come. But this isn't coming. It's worse than if you stayed away."

While the woman spoke the girl was seeing her father plain, a pale and slight, round-shouldered man, with thinning hair, heavy lines from nose to mouth, and eyes that would not meet her own.

A gray suit. He was formally dressed. But then she too had dressed for him. Her best coat. She had kept it on. Her hair arranged to show she was not, nor ever had been, something just to be thrown away. He was not at all, not remotely, like the man who had taught her how to salute and polish her shoes, march double time around the yard, who had fought in a war before she was born and caught a bullet in his chest and many years later left a note: "Try to think I never came back. I died over there and that was it." Left it propped on the counter top between the sugar bowl and salt. . . . But how could she think he never came back when he had whistled her marching songs, lifted her over the wire fence, pulled her flying across the ditch, slipped a knife through the summer melon and held together the giant halves while she guessed if it would be ripe inside, red enough and ripe enough to settle down to in the grass, sweet enough to save the seeds for him to plant the following spring? He had left her with a pocket of seeds. And after many years had passed, she threw them out with angry tears.

She was her mother confronting him. The two of them were confronting him. They had shared him like a common cup, the absent presence they drank each day. Her mother, in dying, bequeathed the dregs: mistrust . . . mistrust of any man, and love cast down the lonely well. Inside the well was the cry of a child. Her own cry? Or the cry of the child she would never have?

A tremor was in the hand that groped for his handkerchief. He wiped his lips.

The scarlet mouth had charged again. "Why did you come if this is what you have to say?"

"Because I have waited my life to say it."

"You can see your father isn't well. . . ."

"I have no father."

She turned and left the room to them. Inside the room and all the while she had climbed the stairs, four flights of them, ignoring the lift, to give her time to face him with a heart as cold as the street below, she had not foreseen that once she was done, that once outside the room, she would break. About her heart the chain was drawn, more tightly drawn than it ever had been. With the pain of it she caught her breath. She shuddered and leaned against the wall.

An aging porter with curious eyes passed her by with a luggage cart. His hair was her father's thinning gray. His sallow cheek was deeply lined, as carefully shaved as her father's cheek had been for her. . . . Her own cheek pressed to the wall, she wept. She had always dreamt he would come again and tell her why he had stayed away. She was swept into weakness, only beginning to understand how much she had counted on hearing him say that he had wanted to come but couldn't. Some terrible reason why he couldn't.

Instead, he was waiting with his check. Things didn't work out was what he said. But now if she needed anything . . . "Need?" she had said, and cried to herself, I need nothing from you but never to see your face again.

Drunk with weeping, she plunged along the empty hall, its carpet patterned with crimson roses. She seemed to be wading through pools of roses caught in the lights along the wall and blurred with tears till she saw them shattered. She did not want the stairs she passed. She wanted the lift that would take her away with all possible speed. His room had cornered the world for her, and there she had fought the abandoned child. But now in the hall, unable to shake herself free of the child, she was conscious of being far from the room she called her home, in a large hotel where she didn't belong. And here she was walking the hall forever, dreading encounters, seeking the lift. Once she heard voices, turned into a passage, and lost her way but stumbled on. She turned again. At last at the end of a passage she found it. She pressed a button. Her coat had all but fallen off. She pulled it close about her throat. She wiped her eyes.

Almost at once the door flew open. She stepped inside. The cage was small and dimly lit. A heavy man, who stood by the panel, was staring at her tear-stained face. Abruptly he reached to press a button. She dropped her eyes and felt the descent. She tried to make her mind a blank. When she reached the street her life would begin.

They swayed to a stop. She waited for the door to open. And when it did not, she turned to the man. He was biting into the peel of an orange. The smell of it was pungent, strong. His teeth were white and small for his face. They dragged a bit of the peel away, then let it fall to his open palm. His eyes seemed never to have left her own.

"It's not too late," he said to her. He pressed the button. The door flew open.

She clutched her purse and stared at him, but she was too spent to feel surprise. She wanted only to leave it all. She stepped out. After the door had closed behind her, she grew aware that the place was wrong. She did not seem to have reached the lobby, or not the one she had seen before. She was standing alone in a narrow hall with rosy tiles beneath her feet. Some twenty feet or so away it fanned into an open space. She took a step. Her heels clicked on the rosy tiles. And still the feel of the place was wrong.

Before her was a Persian rug and elegant bleached-wood tables and lamps. Magazines on a center table. A long sofa and easy chairs. A large, bright room of studied richness framed with paintings about the walls. An alcove with a marble bust. Through banks of fern a flash of gold and silver fish. Most strikingly, the far wall was hung with a giant tapestry that showed a unicorn in flight.

She came to a halt before the sight. Brilliantly lit were the snow-white wings. The single horn was overlong and tipped with cloud, the base of it bathed in a shaft of light that seemed to spring from the room itself. . . .

She drew her eyes once more to the room. It made her think of an empty stage when the curtain parts. But as she was turning to ring for the lift, as if on cue the players appeared, two shadows against the snow-white wings. They walked to her with measured steps. When they were close she grew aware of their measured smiles. Smiles with a measured friendliness, ready to be withdrawn at once, but not surprised to find her there just as she was in her navy coat, the dark hair trapped inside the collar—beneath their gaze she reached to free it—her eyes still red from all her tears. She pressed the handkerchief to her eyes. They appeared at once to accept the gesture. It seemed in fact to reassure them. Their faces visibly relaxed. Incredibly she felt their welcome. She could not come to terms with it.

Except for their smiles they were not alike. One was the taller by a head. Dark and balding, with pitch-black eyes that were velvet soft with a glint of cold. The skin of his face was slightly pocked. The shorter was olive, rapier lean, with a restless body and restless gaze. For just a moment she caught the gleam inside the jacket that swung unbuttoned. She knew with a shock he was wearing a gun. She sensed that the other wore one too. The smiles were suddenly gone from them. She was facing men with a secret answer.

She began to feel at their mercy then. She allowed herself to be propelled by the taller man, who had grasped her arm, down the hall toward the unicorn. She was conscious of paintings on either side, of statuary here and there, of marble birds among the ferns, and at the edge of a table they passed a box of chocolates, open, fragrant. The smaller man, without losing step, caught one up and tossed it into his open mouth. He dropped behind, scooped up the box, and quickened his pace to offer it. She glanced at it and shook her head. His face was rapt with the pleasure of chewing. It told her nothing.

She suddenly halted. "What is this place?"

The one who was chewing waved it aside. "Meetings," he said. He seemed to think she would understand.

She was trying to mask her deep alarm. "I don't know who you are," she said.

The taller one relaxed his hold. "Family," he said while the other swallowed.

She did not move. It was clear she was someone else for them. She freed her arm. "Wait . . . ," she began, but her voice failed.

He looked her over from head to foot. "That's smart you didn't wear the usual thing. You want a cup of coffee brought? How you like it, sugar, cream?"

The man who was still chewing his sweet opened a door near the unicorn. The other gently thrust her in. She heard the door click shut behind. Music was playing, soft and live. A tenor voice surrounded her, beseeching her in tones of love. And then it was abruptly gone.

She found herself in another room as dimly lit as the one she had left was full of light. She sensed at once that the other room had been but an anteroom to this, that here was the core of whatever world she had stumbled upon. At first she could distinguish little. The room was ominously still except for the gentle tick of a clock. She did not move. She let the shapes emerge for her. A mirror that topped what could be a dresser was a little lake of faintest light. She could just make out a bed with covers in disarray. Waves of them that caught the shimmer were tidal pools of the lake of light. The little tick of the faceless clock seemed to surround and define the bed.

A man's voice suddenly spoke a word. It seemed to her like the name "Maria." The name was breathless but firm, with a question. The voice had in it an edge of age and resignation, yet a flutter of stifled anticipation.

She was unable to move or speak.

After a pause, "Then it's Leo," he said in a fainter voice. "Is it Leo come to finish me off?" He coughed once. "You were always one for the dark, boy. Your father's errands run in the dark. I was there with him when you were born. I didn't like the look of you then. Or later on.... It's just as well your errand boy's face is in the dark."

A light came on beside the bed, so unexpected it blinded her. Then she saw she was facing a man in bed, his head half propped among the pillows, the shimmering covers drawn to his chin. Above the covers a gun was pointed straight at her. She saw its gleam in the yellow light.

He lifted his head to stare at her. "Maria!" he cried. "Oh, God, you came!" His head fell back. He dropped the pistol among the covers.

And still she could not move or speak. She held her breath. He seemed to hold his own as well. Only the tick of the clock was live.... A hand was lifted to her and fell. "Come close," he begged her. "*Bedda mia!*" And in his voice was a note she could only describe as joy. "*Bedda mia.*" He whispered it. "Come close to me. It's been so long."

As if his bidding compelled her to, she advanced a little into the room.

"You came," he said. "It's all I care about. You came." She could see him clearly in the light. He was looking at her with eyes of love, a man who was well into middle age. The dark of his hair was touched with gray. The narrow beard surrounding a delicate pointed chin was wholly gray. The face it framed was small and lean. Pale, intent, a priestly face. "Come close and let me look at you."

She forced herself to approach the bed so that he could see she was not whoever he thought she was, and then perhaps they would let her go.

"Maria, *biddizza*. Your mother's hair. Her great dark eyes. And have they shed some tears for me?" The voice was resonant, fairly deep, with the trace of an accent, it seemed to her. Each syllable like the tip of a wave that paused the merest fraction of time before it plunged into the next.

"I'm not Maria." She made her voice sound sure of it.

"If you changed your name I can understand. You're here is all I care about. The little daughter . . . the daughter I lost. I lost you in a garden once."

The urgency of it grew in her. "I'm not your daughter. Look at me. I'm not Maria. Tell them I'm not so I can go."

"Go?" he said. "You want to go?"

"I'm not your daughter. Look at me."

She felt his eyes take in her face. The clock ticked. His hand groped for the table that held it. His fingers all but tipped the lamp. There was now another source of light. She turned to see on the wall a painting suffused with a richly golden glow. The portrait was of a woman somewhat younger than herself, seated and wearing a simple dress. A braid of dark as midnight hair and haunted, dark, impassioned eyes. Her shadow lay across a harp. "You see," he said, "how like you are. Your mother's hair. Her beautiful eyes."

The woman she saw was beautiful. Utterly strange and beautiful. Indeed the coloring was her own. More than her mother's had ever been. "A madonna," he sighed. "She watches over me when I'm here."

She heard him, at a loss for words. He said to her in a muffled voice. "She took you away when you were a child. I saw you once come out of school. I made them stop the car and wait. They told me which you were, you know, but I had picked you out myself. You were too small for all those books. I wanted to help you carry them. . . . But that was a very long time ago. . . . Have it your way," he said at last. A weakness seemed to come over him. His head relaxed against the pillow. The resonance had left his voice. "I thought . . . but I deserve no less. I think your mother always loved me. In spite of all. She never married. . . . Why did you come?" he said to her.

She was beginning, "I took the lift . . ."

He shook his head to stop her words. Over the cover his hand moved down his side and paused. "Before you go . . . There's no one else."

Impatience was conquering her dismay. "I'm not your daughter. Listen to me."

"Your mother wrote. . . . She let me pay for some of your things. The hood . . . she let me buy the hood. They sent for you because they knew. Because they know you are a nurse." He stopped and with a shaking hand he threw the covers from his side. The sheet, the bed were soaked with blood. She thought she had never seen so much.

She caught at the bed to steady herself.

He looked at her with a trace of a smile, as if the blood did not interest him. "You see," he said, "why you were brought. There was no one else. . . . These son-in-laws, they trust no one. The Holy Mother they wouldn't trust. Maria, they said, is one of us."

I'm not, I'm not, she wanted to cry.

He seemed to hear. "Have it your way. But you have a skill. I need you now. . . ." His voice went dead.

She was staring into the mat of towels about his thigh. She saw him lying fully dressed. The leg of his pants had been cut away and cradled his thigh like a blood-soaked flag. The bed itself was a pool of blood, a purple plum and crimson red. She turned away. The room went dark. She was blind and deaf. She held the bedpost to keep from falling. Then the tick of the clock was in her ears. His voice came back from far away. "Stop the blood. It's all I ask."

Desperation was in her voice. "I don't know how. I'm not a nurse. I work in an office. I keep books."

For the first time he seemed to hear. Perhaps the weakness had stilled his protest. The clock was ticking into his silence. She grew aware of something else. Not a sound but a distant pulse. In the mountains in winter when she was a child she had felt such a distant pulse. A gathering fury of plunging snow far away among the peaks. Her father, smiling into her eyes, had whispered to her,

"The mountain shrugs when it's had enough." In the room upstairs she had wanted to say, You shrugged us off when you had enough. . . . But here the fury was in the train. She had been taken underground where trains whip through the hollowed earth. She felt its shudder. Then in the room was a humming of strings, a faint and silvery jangle of sounds. She followed his eyes to the glow on the wall. It was as if the harp within the frame were touched. . . . She could not believe what she had heard.

He reached to shut the picture away, to thrust it back in the shadow again. He drew the covers to his throat and shut his blood away from her. "Who are you, then?" he said at last.

The hum of the strings was in her throat. "Diana Pierce."

"Why are you here?"

"I tried to tell you. I was lost."

"And Dako brought you? The elevator?"

"Someone did. I lost my way."

The faintest smile was on his lips. "He thought your tears were shed for me. . . ." After a while he spoke again. "You see they were looking for someone else. For one who might be weeping for me."

The sound of the harp had died away. "When she comes she will know what to do for you."

Across the room the door was opened. A shaft of light was on the bed. In the doorway was a silhouette. "You found the stuff you need in here?"

She made a move to speak to him. But the man on the bed, now starkly visible in the light, had signed her to silence with his lips. The other came forward into the room. He seemed to be the taller one. He smelled of tobacco.

"Leave us alone," said the man in bed in a clear and cold, peremptory voice.

The other paused, then turned and left.

"You mustn't tell them you're not Maria."

"But why?" she cried. "If they knew, they would find someone else to help."

"They wouldn't," he said, "but they would kill you."

His words were no more credible than the sound of the harp had been to her. "But why?" she asked. Her voice was stunned.

"Because you've seen me. It is enough. They have big dreams, these son-in-laws with greedy eyes. Big deals to make. They want more time."

At that he seemed to drift away. His eyes closed. His face went gray and fell abruptly to the side. Watching him, she scarcely breathed. She knew the seeping of his blood.

"Sir?" she whispered, leaning to him. . . . You can see your father isn't well, the scarlet mouth had said to her.

The lamp had yoked them with yellow light. She laid her coat upon the bed and took the lamp—its marble base was a dolphin shape—and raised it till the cord was taut. The mirror held her bewildered eyes. It held the box on the dresser top.

In a daze she lugged the box to the bed. There were bandages in generous rolls. Square packages of gauze. Balls of cotton wool and tape. Scissors, jars, a small basin. She was at a loss before them.

Biting her lip to keep from shrinking, gently she drew the covers to reveal again his blood. She forced herself to see that the pool of it had spread. She moved the table with the lamp as close as the cord allowed. There glistened below her now a crimson lake. She closed her eyes to pray. Then tentatively she pulled at the towels about his thigh. She held her breath against their warm and secret smell. She slid them into the basin. The wound she saw was gorged. With a square of gauze and water from a drinking glass beside the lamp, she began to wash away the blood. Suddenly it surged beneath her hand. She dropped the gauze in panic. With shaking hands she fell to tearing open pack after pack of it to heap upon the wound. The man was still as death, his face now white above the rim of beard. She found a roll of bandage and circled his thigh, over and over winding it, afraid to stop. His flesh against her fingertips was burning hot. She heard her sobs.

He must have heard them too. She found his eyes upon her. "*Bedda mia,*" he whispered to her. "I never dreamt it would be this way. I dreamt of finding you and begging a long forgiveness." His eyes were burning into hers. "I ask it now. Forgive me, *biddizza.*"

She could not bring herself to speak until she covered his wound. "Are you in pain?"

He shook his head. "Your hand has healing in it. . . . She let me buy your hood. Your mother let me buy your hood. I wish you'd worn it here today." He closed his eyes as if to sleep. "I ask it now. Forgive me."

She shut herself against the echo. She turned her face away.

"So hard to forgive?"

She steeled herself to answer. "For what?" she asked.

"For what?" he echoed her. His voice was faint but touched with wonder. "You don't remember? Then I thank the Holy Mother..."

She could not understand his words or why she wanted to weep.

"You remember a little, is it so?"

"No," she said with effort. "I don't remember. I'm not your daughter."

"You are," he said with passion, "and nothing can ever change it! Not even the scene in the garden can change it. She couldn't forgive me that, your mother. She took you away. She took you from me the following day."

His cheek was flushed as if with health. Gently again she raised the covers. Blood had pierced the layers of gauze. She stifled her cry. "You're bleeding. Tell me what to do."

He did not seem to hear her plea. He threw the covers from his chest. She saw him fully, finely dressed. She brought herself to loosen his tie, a figured silk, undo a button beneath the beard. The throat was corded, deeply hollowed. There were delicate lines about his eyes. The nose was aquiline and strong. A handsome, aging face, with muscles tight about the mouth, yet something generous in the lips. But force of habit turned her face from that of any man and now from his. She began to tug at the jacket, but lest she make his bleeding worse she gave it up. She placed his hands beneath the covers. One bore a curious, glistening ring of green and gold.

She said to him, "What happened to you?"

But he was caught up in the past. His eyes were burdened with memory. "The garden. It was early June. And morning. Was it morning?"

She shook her head.

He closed his eyes. "The path... with roses by the path. He sent his errand boy over the wall. He thought I was moving in on him...." He stirred beneath the covers. "What does it matter now? Can you remember Rico? He would hold you on the pony, round and round the garden. . . . Rico was there and shot him from the end of the path. The spray of it went into the roses."

He opened his eyes. They were bright with fever. "You remember that?"

He drew her into something she had no strength for knowing. She shut herself away.

But he was saying, "You were only three. You never looked at the man on the path. You never looked at the dying there. You broke away from your mother's hand and ran to the roses the gun had shattered. . . . You tried to put them together again."

The horror of it was in his face.

"You mustn't talk." Her voice broke.

"They were white and spattered with his blood. You wiped your little hands on your dress . . . and on your hair."

She would not listen. She turned away. She said, "This has nothing to do with me."

"And on your mother's face and hair. . . . She took you away from me . . . and from this life . . . before you could know any more of it. I never meant it to happen," he said. "I wanted you to be safe from it. I wanted beautiful things for you."

She turned to him.

"Forgive, *bedda mia*. Say it to me."

She could not speak. He raised his head, which she tried to lower. "You must lie still." She was helpless against his fevered strength. Her tears had welled from her despair.

"Say it to me."

"I do," she said.

His head fell back. He seemed to sleep.

Her eyes were streaming. She could not understand her tears. They seemed to come from more than fear. They seemed to come from someone else. From a life that was not her own to live. Yet from a place where she had been. She turned and circled the shadowed room. She was stumbling down the hall upstairs, lost, unable to find the lift. . . . But now there was blood upon her hands. She could not live with the feel of it. She came upon the bathroom door. As her groping fingers found the switch, she shut her eyes to the burst of light and held them shut while she washed her hands with a soap that smelled of lavender. Her face in the glass, when she opened them, was staring back and marked with blood. She plunged it into the running water and felt the wet upon her throat and down her breast and in her hair.

She could not bear to return to him. Over and over she bathed her face. At last she straightened and dried herself. By the bathroom light the room was visible. She saw it now as richly furnished as the other room had seemed to her. A small piano. A wall of books. A Chinese screen with flowers and birds. Porcelain figures here and there, the largest one of a woman and child. A glint of strings from a golden harp. And yes, the girl who was not her mother just discernible on the wall. The girl who had posed with a golden harp, perhaps the one in the corner there.

Slipping into the shadowed room, she shut the door on all but a blade-sharp slice of light that escaped below. She began once more to pace the room, avoiding the bed and its circle of light. A scent of leather was in the air, and then a trace of sandalwood. The fold of a drapery brushed her hand. She drew it aside to reveal a window, which instantly she struggled to lift. A glow from a streetlamp, perhaps the moon, was frosting bars with an eerie light. Beyond the bars she could see the wall. She let the window fall with a thud. Again she was the little girl locked in her room to study her sins, afraid of tigers under the bed, begging her father to change her sentence to double time around the yard, as he had before. . . .

Instantly the door was opened. A darkened figure was in the light. "What is it?" he said, advancing to her. She saw that he was the shorter one. He stopped and then approached the bed. His eyes slid over its occupant and came to rest on the blade of light at the bathroom door. "What was the noise?" His voice was low. Alarm was in it. Suspicion of her.

"The window," she said. "I tried to raise it." Seeing his face, she added at once, "To freshen the air."

He stared at her. "There's not any need. The system here takes care of that. It's top-notch. He owns it," he said. "The building he owns. Anything he owns, it's top of the line. . . . You see that tapestry in there? You know what it cost him? Fifty grand. This stereo system, you know what it cost? You fix him up, he's a generous man."

His jacket was off. She saw his gun. He said in a conversational tone, "I married Leda. His daughter. Your sister. You're family," he said. "Remember that." She could not take her eyes from the gun. "You want some food?" he said at last. "It comes from the dining room upstairs. Top-notch. Anything you want I tell them to fix. You think he can eat?"

She shook her head.

"I tell them to fix you something good. You like Italian?" He continued to stare at the man on the bed. Then he walked away. But at the door he turned again. "You're here to see he makes it," he said. He closed the door.

She could not suppress her trembling. The man on the bed was looking at her. "You don't belong here," he said to her.

She closed her eyes.

"Did you tell me your name?" He listened to it. "Come closer," he said. "You're not someone I'm supposed to know?"

She shook her head.

He looked away. "Maria never came," he said.

"I don't know."

"If she comes they will kill you. That is a fact. Never tell them you're not Maria."

She heard him with a distant shock, like the thud of the window against the sill. "Is she going to come?"

He closed his eyes. "I dreamt she did. What time is it?"

She looked at the clock. "It's after two."

"Two in the morning? That is a long, long time to come. . . . They carried me in here twisted and looped like a braid of garlic. It was daylight when they sent."

"You need a doctor."

"A doctor they wouldn't trust," he said. "I have a doctor . . . they wouldn't trust."

"Not trust to save your life?" she asked.

"Not trust not to tell that I'm lying here. . . . Does it seem to you that I will die?"

As if in a dream she touched his face, felt the rough where the stubble had grown above the beard . . . felt the fever. She raised the covers. The blood had soaked the bandage through. She could not hide from him her shock. "I'm not a nurse. I keep books. I make my living . . ." She broke off. "I pray your daughter will come to you."

"Don't pray," he said, "if you want to live."

She pushed his words away from her. She began to search the box again for something that would stop the blood.

"The bullet is there. I feel it," he said. "It's hot like a chestnut popped from the fire."

Her hands were shaking. "Who did this to you?"

"A friend," he said. "I turned a corner. . . . The gun was waiting inside the car."

"A friend!" she cried.

"It's always a friend. When he wants what you have he's an enemy." Again she felt the distant pulse. After a bit he spoke again. "In the end they always want what you have."

His eyes were resting on her face. "You have a father?"

She looked away to answer no.

"He died, then? He must have loved you. I have loved my daughter since the day she was born. Now her mother is gone, I am all that's left. I must live to go on . . . with loving her. . . ."

He seemed to drift. His voice grew faint. With a touch she roused him. "What is this place?" She faced him with it. "Why are bars at the window there?" She waited for him. She touched him again.

His eyes were puzzled, as if he had lost who she was once more. But after a while he said with an effort, "This is my cave. . . . I call it my cave. . . . I am safe from the friends who want what I have. I listen to music and live in peace. The train comes and I hear her play. Did you hear it then, the harp sound when the train is here? I am in the ground. It is like my tomb. . . ." He paused for a while. "It *is* my tomb. . . . There is no love in my beautiful house. But here I am buried away from them. My wife with her eyes, her prison eyes, and the daughters who give me nothing at all but son-in-laws with greedy eyes. My wife serves time in the prison I made for her miles away, with arbors and waterfalls . . . gardens with flowers but never a rose. A curse is on them. . . ."

The shorter man burst in with a tray. He laid it, clattering, on the dresser. She smelled the food, something rich with spice, a tomato smell. He approached the bed. "Papa? Papa? You wanta eat?"

The older man faintly shook his head.

"You want something to drink?" He studied the silent face below. "You let me know, Papa. I get what you want."

The older man stirred. "The usual," he said.

"Papa, not that. They would know you are here. Who gives the order for it but you? Like signing your name."

"Then get out," said the other, "and leave me in peace."

"It's for your protection."

"No, it's for yours."

When he was gone, she put the tray away in the bathroom and closed the door. She could not bear the smell of the food. Nor could she account for the anger that swept her. It came like a wind that shook her and died. And all she wanted to do was leave, go to sleep, forget this stranger beyond her help. She could see herself, as she had upstairs, walking the street, finding a taxi, riding away . . . drinking the cold as she rode away. She put on her coat and stopped before him. "I don't know how to help you," she said, "but your daughter will come. Now I will tell them who I am and then I will leave."

He looked at her. "You know nothing," he said. "A beautiful young woman, a madonna like yourself, do you want to die? I have seen them kill, blow a man away like blowing a fly. It is hard with a woman, but make them afraid and they will kill you to stop their fear. Greed and fear. It is all they know."

She broke before him. "You make *me* afraid."

"*Bene!*" he cried with a force that surprised her. "*Bene! Bene!* It is what I wish. Now you will wait."

"Wait for what?" she said in despair.

But his eyes had closed. He had spent himself. She was drained as well. Too exhausted to stand, she drew a chair beside the bed. She sat before him resting her head not far from his. She was all but asleep when she heard his voice.

Mirror Image

"Get Tony." It was all he said.

Dazed with sleep, she walked to the door and opened it. She shrank from the brilliance of the light. Beside her was the unicorn, unbearable with his snow-white wings. The men before her were asleep. One stretched at length on the leather sofa. The other slouched inert in a chair. She went to the taller, the one in the chair. She touched his shoulder and saw him spring with a hand to his holster. But seeing her, he stretched and yawned. "Tony?" she said.

He did not deny it.

"He wants you," she said.

"How is he now?" He yawned again. She did not answer. He followed her in and stood looking down at the man on the bed, whose eyes were closed. "What is it, Papa? Tony is here."

"Get me the priest. I want the priest."

Tony shifted. "Papa, what do you want with a priest? Now is not the time."

The older man stared into his face. His voice was hostile, imperious, "Get me the priest."

"A priest you don't need. Maria here is fixing you up. It's taking time. She says you are fine."

The sick man raised his head from the pillow. "The sin of this is on your head."

"I'll do it, Papa." He turned and left. For a moment his shadow pierced the room. Then he closed the door.

The old man, exhausted, lay as if dead. She touched his brow. The fever was gone, but in its place was a moist chill. She took his hand. It was dry and cold. She raised the covers. She drew the rest of the gauze from the box and wound his leg more tightly with it. He winced once.

"Water, please."

She paused then. His eyes pled. She saw in them an alliance with her against the man who had left the room. She had emptied the glass to wash his wound. In the bathroom she filled it and brought it back. She cradled his head. In her arms it was light as the head of a child. He drank for long with the trust of a child. There was peace in his drinking. He could not have done, as if his thirst had waited for her, gathering force until she came. . . . So close to him, she caught the lotion scent of his skin, the laundered scent of his crisp shirt, and over it all the scent of blood that escaped the covers.... Memory came unbidden to her. Her arm about her father's neck while he lifted each of her feet in turn to empty its shoe of sand and shell, their faces close as he brushed the foot. And then her delight to be given the world to walk in without the pain....

She laid him gently down again. After a moment he spoke as if he were telling a tale. "Tony will not get the priest. How many days will I lie here dead while Tony says to the world I live? Till he thinks the whip is in his hand?"

The train throbbed in the sleeping earth. The harp spoke. He was shivering. She took off her coat and spread it over his trembling form. "There's something I ask you to do," he said. "Something you may not want to do."

"I will try," she said.

He waited till the harp was still. "Tony will not send for the priest. . . . I want you to hear my confession now."

She drew away. "I don't know how."

"Listen," he said. "There is no one else. . . ." His fingers slowly sought the table. A sudden glow was in the room. She turned to see the lighted niche. The form on the cross was lean and gray; the eyes were closed. The blood glistened on hands and feet. Turning back, she saw he had drawn a hand from the cover, the hand that bore the curious ring. With infinite care he crossed his forehead, his lips, his breast.

She waited for him.

"Listen," he said. "And then forget. . . ." He crossed his lips. They moved with words she could not hear. Then she heard him speak. "I was born to this. I was born to it and what could I do? But every crime I acknowledge now. God sees them all. I acknowledge them. Over and over blood was spilled. Not my own, until today. Not by me. There was someone else to spill the blood. With a word from me. Is it better or worse to give the word and keep your hand . . . ? He broke off. "I lost my way. I had a wife and a beautiful child. I loved them more than life itself. . . . I lost them too. I lost my soul. I have lost enough. This hour it is my life I lose, but it's not enough. . . . I buy the beautiful, costly things. Paintings, art . . . so everywhere I look is good. I fill my eyes with what is good. And music. What I hear is good. In my house I allow no words not fit for the Holy Mother to hear. No love is there, but the words are good. . . . Gifts for the poor. . . . It's never enough. It comes from blood."

His eyes were on the lighted niche. "When I was a boy my mother said I would be the priest. We need a priest in the family, she said, to take the curse from so much blood. She prayed for it. In the church I watched her kneel and pray. I knew her words. Before the Virgin heard I knew. I wanted it too. . . . But my father died, my brother with him, and I was next. It was almost dark when they came to me. The room was full of the shadows of men. 'You are next,' they said. I was twenty-one. My mother knelt and wept for me. 'What can you want with a boy?' she cried. 'A baby to be the father!' she said. 'Turn on the lights and leave,' they said. 'No,' she said, 'what you have to say will be said in the dark.' And in my heart I wept with her.

"But when I saw Maria's mother, radiant, lovely as the moon, I was glad then I was not the priest. And when her daughter was born to me, I was glad again I was not the priest. But when she left and took her from me, I wished my mother had had her way. The blood I poured would be God's, not man's. And that is life instead of death. . . ."

She was hardly aware of the words he gave. She heard their sorrow. She took their pain. She watched him cross his lips again.

"I am that man of crime . . . of sin. I wept for it in the dark of night, and in the daylight I sinned again. It is my blame. . . . But I am that boy who was almost the priest. I am that man whose soul belonged to the purest of women and to her daughter, my beautiful child. I came to love them more than God. Because of that, He took them away. Not for the killings. . . . I went to the priest with all of that. But because I loved them more than God and never told it to the priest. . . . How could I tell what I would not change? I knew in my heart . . . I knew it better than any priest . . . without that love I was nothing more . . . than a man of crime, who gave his money for beautiful things . . . to hide the blood."

He seemed to have drifted into sleep. She waited, watching over him. When he woke he was looking at her with joy. "I dreamt you came. Can you forgive me, *bedda mia?*"

Moved by his joy, she wept for him. Or for herself. She could not tell. He touched her hair. "Can you, Maria?"

"Yes," she said.

"For my whole life? And the garden too?"

"Yes," she said. It gave her a strange delight to say it.

"Don't cry," he pled. "No need to cry. . . . We'll go away. We'll tell no one. We'll ride the carousel," he said. He brushed the tangled hair from her throat. "You remember that?"

She covered her face. "Yes," she said. Strangely, there was a memory of it. Was it Maria's or her own? The horses leaping with the song, the world gone still to watch her as she rose on wings of music. Like the unicorn.

"I need the music now." She thought he meant the carousel. But he raised his hand with a backward thrust. Behind the lamp she found the switch. Live and sweet was the tenor's cry. It came from every corner, faintly thrilling in the harp. Warm with passion, it besought her now to live and love. The words were strange, but not the voice. She had heard it in her dreams. Then very close she heard her own, so like it seemed to be her own. It answered, yielding, joining his. She could not bear the sweetness of it. Or the pain. . . .

He signed to her to halt the music. She pressed the switch. He spoke into the silence. There was singing in his voice. "There is a country in my heart. A place between a priest . . . and what I became." He gazed at her with longing. "We would be happy."

She pressed his hand.

"It's getting dark. I can't see you."

She bent her head to him. Her dark hair swept his face and she brushed it away. But he whispered, "Don't take away your mother's hair."

She felt his hand begin to tremble. She was caught in his trembling till it was hers as well. She saw his lips were moving. "In my will you have the money I made when I was young. A boy. A boy's wages. I worked after school. It is clean. . . . I never spent it in the world I was given. I saved it for you. . . . Take it, you will take it from me?" The pleading in his voice was encircled with the question.

"I will," she said.

"A ring of my mother's. A girl's. Before my father. I have written it is yours. You will wear it for me?"

She dropped her head to his pillow. She felt that she was sleeping. She did not want to wake.

He turned his face into her hair. "Can you know how much I love you . . . and your mother in you? Can you feel it?" She had never heard the note in any voice before. "I have waited my life for this moment with you."

Her tears were on the pillow.

"Have you waited, too?"

She felt his simple waiting, his blood racing out of him and filling her silence. "Yes," she whispered.

At that he seemed to fall asleep. She rose and walked to the window and pulled aside the drapery. The bars were stark as bones in the early light. Through a drift of mist she saw the wall. Who am I? she said. Daughter . . . stranger, what he finds in me I am. I have waited my life . . . She was dazed with his words. If she took the elevator she would find the very words still alive in the room where she had made them hers. . . . Like the beat of her blood, she knew the coming of the train. It burrowed in her body, deep, insistent, closer, with the singing of the harp, until it died away. Then above, the swift percussion of a manhole cover as a truck rode it down in the dark and sped away.

She heard his voice from the bed. She went to him quickly, and she saw with mourning that now she was no longer his daughter but herself. He held her eyes with his. She sensed that he was gathering his forces for an effort. "What is it?" she said.

His lips were forming words, then she heard them. "The time?"

She glanced at the clock. "It is early morning."

Again his lips were forming words that had no sound. She shook her head. "Leave here. Now."

"I want to stay with you."

He turned his face from side to side. "No! They will kill you." He was silent for a moment. "If my daughter comes . . . or Chico. They sent him for her. If he comes . . . Water," he said.

She raised his head and brought the glass to touch his lips. He drank from it with effort, as if he drowned with each swallow. Once more she knew his lightness, the child in her arms. She laid him down again. She sensed his desperation. It surrounded them like air. "Food," he said, struggling.

In the bathroom was the tray. There was wine in an opened bottle. She poured him a little, red as blood, and held him while he wet his lips. He drank but a sip, then turned his face away. But it seemed to revive him.

An urgency was in his voice. "Listen to me now and do as I say. Tell them there is a drug you need for me. It takes a prescription, but the hospital has it. They keep it locked up but you can find the key. Tell them you mustn't wait for Chico. They must give you taxi fare."

"I'm afraid of them," she said.

"No . . . no. If Maria comes you will not be safe. If Chico comes . . . They will ask you why he isn't here . . . where he went when he brought you. . . ." He shut his eyes and seemed to think. The effort was on his face. He beckoned her close. "Tell them you sent him for things you need and couldn't wait to get yourself. . . . You sent him back for them. Tell them that."

"What if they don't believe me?" She fought her fear.

His voice was failing. "Make them believe." Then he drew his hands from beneath the covers and pulled from one the curious ring. "Wear this," he said, "and let them see it."

His fingers shook beneath the lamp. She took from him the ring. It was a serpent of green enamel, twisted, biting its own tail, the scales and eyes inlaid with gold. They flashed in the yellow light. "What does it mean?"

She could feel that he summoned all his strength to speak. "It means to them . . . unending power." He seemed to swoon, but she touched him and he spoke again. "When they told me she was dead . . . the wife I lost was lost again . . . I knew the ring was endless evil. I had made a circle of it. And so it would be. . . ."

She held it out to him. He waved it away. "Wear it," he whispered. "My power is in it. They took an oath on it and kissed it. They will believe you have my trust."

She put it on, and he kissed her hand. "You have been a daughter to me this night."

She would not take away her hand. She had lived for thirty years and none had kissed her hand before.

He said in a voice that she must strain to hear. "When you are gone from here you must throw it away. You won't be safe if it's found with you. Promise me."

"I promise," she said.

His hand was groping among the covers. "The gun?" he whispered.

She found it and put it into his hand. "No," he said, "it is for you."

She shook her head. "I can't.... I can't."

He nodded slightly and closed his eyes. He moved his lips and she bent to him. "I need the music," he seemed to say. "Go ... go ..."

She pressed the switch for him and heard the soaring of the tenor. She put on her coat and found her purse. She shut the music inside the room.

In the outer room the two men, slouching, came to their feet. She began to tell them about the drug, how she would get it and return. They listened to her with expressionless eyes. Beside her the unicorn listened too. His single horn was in her breast.

"Well, is he better?" Tony asked.

"He needs this drug."

"What drug is it?" said the shorter one, whose name now she would never hear. If they let her go.

She began to say, "It's a chemical name..."

But Tony broke in with "Jesus Christ, it don't matter the name." He advanced upon her. She grew afraid he would take her purse and open it, see who she was, who she was not. With terrible effort she stood her ground. "You have blood on your skirt," he said at last.

She belted her coat. "I'll wash it later. There isn't time."

He nodded. "Chico should be around. Where did he go?"

She found she had forgotten her speech, where Chico was, why he wasn't here. Instead she answered. "My father said ... he said to give me taxi fare." She steadied the hand she held for it. She felt their eyes upon the ring. Till Tony, reaching inside his coat, was drawing the money and not the gun.

She saw that she took it and walked away, with the voice of the tenor following, though it was locked inside the room. She saw that Tony rang for the lift. She found herself inside the cage....

55

Outside was the cold of early dawn. Into the mist the streetlights bloomed. But as she walked they faded away, one by one, as morning came. The voice of the tenor was with her still, rising, falling, beseeching her. The ring she wore was cold and loose. She let it fall inside her coat. Her fingers traced its circle there. Evil turning, beginning again. The horses going round and round . . . rising, falling like the song. Her fingers traced a circle of pain, the pain of the woman like herself for whom it was now too late to come with the word of pardon, late for that.

She turned a corner, as he had done. And suddenly the singing stopped. She stopped as well and held her breath. She felt the breath gone out of him, the circles stopped . . . the blood stopped. The pigeon roaming the still street was the only thing in the world that moved.

A Bee in Amber

A woman in a white coat rushed headlong into the heavy glass doors leading to the restaurant. She slumped and then lay stunned upon the black slate floor.

Mrs. Carroll had been crossing to the desk, and now she stopped. She was in Gdansk and waiting in the lobby of her small hotel, where she had just been paged and smiled upon and wordlessly escorted toward a phone. People loitering in the lobby turned. Those who had been sitting rose. The government man in the brown suit quit the corner bench he made his home. The whole room tilted and abruptly centered where the woman lay. Waiters rushed to press white towels against the blood upon her face and coat as if they had rehearsed it for a play.

Mrs. Carroll, remembering the phone, glanced up to see her own shock mirrored in the eyes she met across the helpless form. She was aware that for the first time the man she had been seeing for the past week had looked directly at her. Then he was with the waiters, who helped the woman to her feet and placed her in an armchair. She was like a wilted leaf.

Mrs. Carroll moved uncertainly to the phone. It was Eve Novak, her traveling companion, who said she was in a small town with a name that Mrs. Carroll did not even try to catch. The names were hopeless. Eve wasn't coming back today as she had promised. No, her cousins were insistent on another week. For now there was a whole new generation to be seen to; it had been that long. "Are you comfortable?" she called out in a voice that flaunted her compunction. "Buy yourself some amber," as connections faltered and then failed and Mrs. Carroll held the dead receiver in her hand. She watched the woman rise and sway and limp away into the lift. Two waiters followed her with towels.

Another week of rain! Mrs. Carroll walked disconsolately back to sit again in the alcove by one window of the lobby. Leather bench seats faced each other like a train compartment. She found it vaguely comforting to be there, as if she were indeed once more upon the rails with fields of shimmering green beside her and the forests banked with fern beneath the boughs. She felt a little chilly and alone and something past her sixty-seven years. The encounter of the woman with the glass doors had depressed her. Across the room an old man with a shredded towel was polishing the doors. She took her glasses off and put them in her purse.

And then the man whose eyes just now she had encountered was inquiring if he might share the alcove with her. "Mrs. Carroll? Forgive me but your name was called."

She smiled a little, truly pleased to hear a voice from home, and noted that he was indeed the man she had been seeing for the past week in the dining room and lobby. She noted also that his eyes were gray and that his face was younger than his hair, which too was gray. But she observed especially his need. Eve said she always looked for sadness in a face. Of course that wasn't so. But often it was there for anyone to see who cared to look. Now she was aware that he would tell her what it was. Not at once of course. For he must tell her first that he was called Nick Rawlins, that he was from a town in Maine, that he had been here for a week.

He did not sound to her like Maine, where in her younger days she had been living till her husband's death. He sounded . . . it was hard to say. She decided he was shy. He had a little hesitation in his speech, a frequent pause between the words, as if they might have been a burden he was reluctant to impose. His earnest gaze supported them. Even so, she grew aware of a slight preoccupation, as if his mind were wandering among the others in the lobby. When someone entered the revolving door, he did not quite look up but seemed to note it. "I have been waiting here for someone for a week. Oh, yes," he said, "today it is one week."

And then he drew the wallet from his breast and slipped from it a picture that he studied carefully and passed to her. "I thought perhaps you might have seen her."

She took her glasses out and put them on. She was looking at a woman, young, not past her twenties, with blue eyes and with hair that might be called a chestnut. Almost pretty in the way that all the young who are not actually plain will have a kind of sheen upon them. She shook her head. The government man, she grew aware, was watching from his corner. Eve had said he was a government man, and she would know. "What is he for?" "Who knows?" Eve said.

A couple stopped beside them. They were speaking in the softly sibilant Polish—which always made it seem to her as if a fretful child were being hushed. She felt them wanting to be in the alcove where she sat. "Is she someone close to you?" she asked. The couple left.

He looked after them. He said quite low, "It has been thirty years. I knew her in Warsaw. Then the war was over and I lost her." He turned to her a rich full glance. She saw the kindness in his eyes. "A month ago I found her. . . . My wife, you see, has died. It was arranged that we should meet here in this hotel the first day of June. . . . I have waited." While she was studying the face again he added, "It never did her justice. The liveliness. The animation in her eyes."

She gave the picture back to him. "I'm afraid I've seen no one like this." She wondered then if she should say it, but she did: "She may have changed."

"Of course," he said. "And I as well. . . . But I would know her."

"No word?" she asked.

"Nothing. I check with them." He waved his hand and held the picture toward the desk. "They are quite bored with me and sometimes shake their heads across the room to keep me at a distance."

She sensed his waiting need. There was something in it suddenly that matched her own. Or rather summoned up her own from where it lay among the voices and the falling rain. "I'm sure there is a reason." She saw that he was worn out with the ebb and flow of reasons and the steady expectation. It was better to be paged as she had been, escorted to the desk and granted a reprieve, however disappointing.

He laughed uncertainly. "Here I am," he said. He glanced around the lobby. "You will be as bored as they are at the desk."

"Oh, no," she said. "I know myself how hard it is to wait for someone." Whom had she meant by that? Surely not Eve Novak.

"You have been waiting here for someone?"

"Only my friend, who tells me now that I must wait another week."

Someone entered the revolving door that led into the street. She felt at once how in a curious way he was inside revolving with the occupant to be released into the lobby. His eyes were wandering about the room and came to rest upon the government man. He stood up suddenly. "Forgive me. I must let you wait in peace."

Then he was gone among the sibilant voices.

She did not see him again until the dinner hour, when quietly he greeted her as he approached her table. She had the impression that he wanted to be asked to join her. And she wanted it herself but was too shy to ask. Yet all through dinner she was thinking of his waiting and of how it would delight him and indeed herself—for she had taken on his waiting; it had replaced her own—if suddenly through the glass doors the woman would come in. She pictured her grown lovelier through the years. The kind of face that blooms from suffering and loss. . . . And he would stand, oblivious of the diners, and go to meet her with his glad eyes, with his hands outstretched.

After dinner she took the groaning, swaying lift to her room. Each time she entered it alone she made a vow that on the next occasion she would walk. Once she was locked inside, sometimes it waited, hoping she would change her mind and take the stairs. But when she stood her ground they slowly rose two floors, enduring one another, until the final lurching stop, when for a moment they were panicked by the gate that always stuck.

The lobby below her was a grim renewal, a determined refurbishment of drapery and leather, of brass and slate. And the dim sea chamber beyond the glass door like a wall of water, where at certain hours the waiters glided, was a slightly modern, aquatic touch. The upstairs belonged to the world of the lift—ancient, shrouded, with a smell in the hallway of something long past, a musty memory, perhaps the wine of revelries now gone to dust. It sprang to life in the corners; it was faintly heady. Here and there were the stains convivial with roses in the pattern of the rug.

She was walking to her room when through a partially opened door she heard a woman's muffled weeping. She slowed her steps, passed by, but lingered in the hallway by her room three doors away, where still she heard the gentle murmur of distress. Then, because all sorrows touched her and because all losses, for a reason she could never name, at last became her own, she turned, retraced her steps, and found that she was knocking lightly on the open door.

The weeping stopped. At last she peered inside. The curtains were drawn, but in the twilit room the figure of a woman lying on the bed was clearly visible.

"My dear . . . ," said Mrs. Carroll.

The woman sat bolt upright.

"Forgive me, but your door was open and I heard you in the hallway, and I thought . . ."—she waited just a bit—"that I might be of help. My name is Mildred Carroll."

The woman did not move at once. But then she blew her nose and slowly thrust her feet into the slippers by the bed. She switched the bedlight on, and in its radiance Mrs. Carroll was surprised to see the woman of the morning who had rushed into the restaurant doors. A swollen, purple bruise was on her forehead, and now her eyes were swollen from the weeping.

Mrs. Carroll was all distress. "Oh, my dear . . . I know you. What a blow you had this morning! I can see the nasty bruise. But has a doctor seen you?"

The woman shook her head.

"But of course you are in pain."

"It is nothing," said the woman. "It was stupid of me. Very stupid." She spoke with a certain accent. "But now I am all right."

"But you are weeping . . . and your head . . ."

The woman stood. "It is not my head," she said with swift impatience. Then once more she was in tears. "It is my heart."

Mrs. Carroll was uncertain. "Your heart? You are in pain?"

"No, no, it is . . . my sorrow . . . my heart."

Mrs. Carroll understood at last and all too well. "If you could speak of it," she offered as kindly as she could.

"I would not burden you," said the woman in desolation, now beginning to pace. The bed lamp threw a tender pool of light on the rug, and the woman trod upon it each time she turned.

Mrs. Carroll advanced. "You wouldn't burden me at all." She

spoke it from her heart. She sensed that something now was ready for unfolding. And for a moment it seemed to her she might have come to Poland for this very thing. She observed the woman closely, the prominent, slightly raw-boned, almost masculine features, the graying hair and softly wrinkled skin. Mrs. Carroll surmised that she was well into her fifties. Lying stunned upon the lobby floor, she had not looked like any age at all. Finally the woman sat again upon the bed.

Mrs. Carroll found a chair and drew it up beside her and listened to the halting recital of her woes. How long ago in Warsaw once and forever she had been in love. How he had left for thirty years and now had returned, how she was to have met him in this very hotel on the first of June.

"But my dear," cried Mrs. Carroll, overjoyed to be the bearer of good tidings, "he is here! I have spoken with him this very day. He has shown me your picture. He is waiting for you now."

The woman nodded sadly. "I know. I know."

"But if you know . . . ?"

"Look at me," the woman cried out. "Look at my face. He doesn't know it. Would you know it for the same?"

Mrs. Carroll was forced to admit to herself that the woman and the picture were extremely unlike. "But perhaps if he were close enough . . ."

The woman was weeping softly. "This morning when I ran into the door . . . he was one of those who helped me. He looked at me. He took my hand. I was a stranger to him."

"But if you made yourself known."

The woman rose and paced the room. "I could not bear it," she said. "He has seen me for a week and has not guessed who I am. His eyes slide over me. I cannot bear to be so changed. My life has not been easy. . . . But he . . . he is wonderful to look at. Just the same. The hair is gray, but the flesh is firm and young."

"Perhaps if I explained to him," Mrs. Carroll began.

"No!" the woman moaned in grief and horror. "He must never know me. You must promise. You must swear." She drew a locket from her breast. "You must swear on this likeness of my mother who has gone to her death, tortured, shamed by the enemy . . . but dying in dignity."

"I promise," said Mrs. Carroll in the greatest haste.

The woman wept quietly. Mrs. Carroll watched her sadly, all her sympathy gone out to another in such pain. A pain that recalled her own of long ago and the dear young husband whose death had marked the finish of her happy years. And now her only joy must be in others' joy, which she could welcome to her breast as if it were her own. She said very softly, "Please tell me your name."

"What does it matter?" said the woman. "It is Sofia."

"Sofia," said Mrs. Carroll, awkwardly repeating the stress upon the opening syllable. "It does seem to me he must not go on waiting and expecting you to come."

"At last he will leave. And I will leave."

Mrs. Carroll repeated, "Expecting you to come and feeling ill of you at last. Feeling betrayed. Or knowing the sadness of thinking you hurt or dead."

Sofia was silent.

Mrs. Carroll went on. "Let me tell him how it is with you. Then he will know how much you wish to spare yourself and him. Then he can go away. With sadness, yes, but without the bitterness."

"You will not let him persuade you to reveal me?"

"That I will promise. I shall not even speak to you again unless you wish."

"But I will wish to know what he has said."

They left it so.

When Mrs. Carroll told him the following morning in the alcove of the lobby, she did not look into his face, knowing as she did how all the years had crashed around him. Instead, her eyes sought out the government man predictably in his corner. Over the top of his daily paper he was watching her, it seemed. When at last Nick Rawlins spoke, she found him more accepting than she had feared he would be or even in her timeless, romantic heart had wished him to be.

"My dear lady," he sighed, "what a burden each of us has laid upon you. . . ." His speech was larded with the silences. "Do you know, you yourself, how little value I would place upon the outward form . . . the face . . . and how much upon the pilgrim spirit?" It was almost like rehearsing for a play, the slightly formal way in which he spoke to her. Of course he was shy. She must remember that. And the beauty of his final phrase had echoed in her breast.

"I know," she said, tears starting in her eyes, so deeply she mourned for him, mourned for them both, and mourned for herself and the waywardness of things.

"This is too much," he said at last. "How could I have known that she would do this to us both? Can you not persuade her? Can't she be made to see that I have waited thirty years and crossed the sea, and now when I am almost with her, when she may be at this moment in this very room . . . ? Isn't it unfair that she can know me and I not know her?" His words in spite of hesitations spoke rebellion, but their tone was resignation and it broke her heart.

She laid her hand upon his arm. "Believe me, I shall plead your cause."

The door beyond them was revolving. Although he did not stir, she felt how within he circled half a turn. And she knew that even now he was waiting for his lady. He straightened with an effort. "She will change her mind. I must believe it." His eyes were sweeping the room. At last they came to rest upon her own as if he found in them a home. "In the meantime I shall take you somewhere you would like to go. You may refuse me if you wish, but I feel close to her when I am with you. Do you mind, dear lady?"

She did not mind. She felt she loved them both. She loved to be the link between them.

"Where would you like to go?" he asked. "The shipyards? But no, they would be dull for you. There is a famous organ in Oliwa." His tone pronounced it even duller than the shipyards.

"I know so little of the place. It always rains."

He was peering through the window. He announced the sun. And indeed beyond the window was an opalescent glow. She refused to believe it. "Come," he said, "I think we'll buy a gift for you and one for her. You will deliver hers for me. And perhaps . . . who knows? Even so. Even so, I want her to have a gift from me. Some piece of jewelry, I think. What could it be?"

He was quite animated now and looked at her with speculation in his kind gray eyes. "What would suit her, do you think?"

"She seemed so sad. It's hard to tell when one is sad."

He brightened visibly. "A piece of amber. It's said to have the property of healing and to bring good luck. Shall we put it to the test? Here is the place for amber. Baltic amber."

"Yes," she said, remembering Eve's "Buy yourself some amber" before connections failed.

"We mustn't wait," he said. "I want her very much to have it. And then the rain may come again." He was smiling at her with particular sweetness. "Can you go at once?"

"Why not?" she said, and she was smiling back. His warmth had banished all her gloom. She was thinking how like a fairy tale it was. The quest, the princess in disguise, the gem. It had to have a happy ending, and it would. And then she was wondering if a cosmetician and a hairdresser, the perfect dress for Sofia . . . The money she had brought to spend and had not spent. The amber money, Eve had called it. What do I want with amber at my age? Better to let the money buy a little courage for a woman like herself with painful losses. Loss of youth. Loss of love, which need not be if courage could be purchased.

The government man rose with them, folding up his daily paper, and followed them to the sidewalk, where they took a cab.

They left it at the Old Town to walk along the shimmering canal. Pigeons were drinking from the pools of recent rain. The air was fresh and full of grace. She felt a lifting of her spirit, as if she were a part of something dear and wonderful, the way it was in bygone years before her husband's death. In the distance there were church bells. . . . He was telling her of the ancient amber trade routes and of the gem itself. He described to her the fallen trees exuding resin, how they had lain for eighteen thousand years beneath the sea, sometimes with a leaf, an insect, trapped in resin, making the amber far more precious by its presence.

They passed two handsome granaries on the left. One, a soaring thing, was delicately ornamental. It seemed designed for their occasion. Late Renaissance he called it. She paused to study it with mounting pleasure. But he was at her elbow saying that they must have time to see the shops. She was fairly giddy with their mission and the sunlight.

And then before them was a sidewalk painter. An old man like a marsh hen waiting for her to love him because he made the gray walk bloom for her with colored chalk. She stopped to try, at least to try, because she knew herself how it can be when you are old and not quite used to it and wanting to get back inside the glass bowl of the world where things are moist and green.

He had sketched the long and festive table to the very street, heaping it with purple grapes and golden fruit, a blue bowl spilling out wild strawberries, the king and queen beneath their golden crowns, and down in front before them kneeling with hands raised in supplication, her hair a golden shower, could it be Salome?

The man with chalk was smiling with such joy. Look, his smile was saying, she is you when you are young, as you are young this moment. Indeed the girl was very like herself as she had been. The breasts, the little dancer's feet like nesting doves. But all of it a shimmer from the tremor in his hand or from the recent rain.

Smiling still, he bent and made a gold ring for her finger and seeded it with sapphires. For her throat a string of pearls. His crippled fingers took such care with each to give it luster that each was like separate gift. She was suddenly too frail to meet his glance. How much was he expecting? She had no coins of his own, nor any words that he would know. . . .

But he was busy with a circlet for the wrist of gold and amber. . . . Before her wondering eyes he drew a small knife from the nest of chalk beside his shoe to prick his thumb and press a jeweled drop into the circlet. Then while another gathered like a red plum swelling on the bough, he swiftly traced a white rose for her breast and veiled it with a spill of blood that stained her flesh. And over her, wild strawberries were spilling down into her wounded hands.

Her knees were aching from the pavement. She could not rise until the woman at her feet was past adorning. To be so richly gifted by a stranger . . .

"Come," Nick said. "He'll keep you here all day if you will let him." He was impatient, but she instantly forgave him for she knew the cause. He dropped some folded bills among the chalk. He is a generous man, she thought. He is deserving of his lady.

Now they turned. All about them in the air, like tiny flakes of snow, were floating bits of floss from some mysterious source. A tree? Like bits of down from some mysterious passing bird. "This is the street for amber," he was saying. "Here are the little shops on either side." Some were well below the street. He took her arm and they crisscrossed the street to view the windows for display. He would not give her time to study them. Pigeons flew after them to skim the pavement at their feet and walk beside them.

Once she glanced back. Incredibly, the government man was there and window-shopping. "Look," she said, delighted with all things. "The government man. He must have followed us."

He laughed at her. "He follows everyone. Once I saw him following a cat."

"Perhaps the government man is shopping for some amber."

But Nick refused to turn and look. He had a special shop in mind. For when at last they reached it, his manner changed from gay to grave. "We must enter this one. It has some treasures you will want to see."

They went down a step into a shop much larger than the rest, with a smell of sandalwood and something sweet. He pointed out the cases for display upon the walls, but they were almost bare. "We must ask to see their things. They keep them locked away." From the ceiling in the center hung a slender gilded cage. And just above it flew a bird with scarlet feathers tipped with gray. When the girl approached them he inquired of her softly, "May I see the owner?"

She turned without a word. And soon the woman was beside them, diminutive and handsome, dressed in black, her pitch-dark hair drawn backward from her face into a chignon that was cradled in a net of gold. Her lips were pale and finely modeled. Mrs. Carroll could not guess her age.

Without a word the woman seated them before a smallish table. She sat behind it, facing them, so close that Mrs. Carroll felt the brush of the woman's skirt. Her eyes were dark and soft as butter. Then she unlocked the drawer in front of her and drew from it three pieces made of gold and amber. Her tapering fingers with the coral nails caressed them.

"Does she speak English?" Mrs. Carroll asked him. She slipped her glasses on.

He shook his head. "She understands it."

One by one he raised the pieces and examined them. An amulet like a giant drop of honey laced with gold, a ring, a bracelet. "What would you like?" he said to Mrs. Carroll kindly. "You must have something."

The bird was fluttering over her. She shook her head.

"But I insist. I will not take you back without a gift of amber."

"Nothing so fine as these," she said. She could not really tell if they were fine. She read the manner of the two who touched them.

He was lost in contemplation. He picked the bracelet up again. In a golden circlet was an oval carved of amber of a variegated color—milky yellow, palest fawn, and clearest honey. "Do you see?" he pointed out with reverence. "There is a bee embedded in the amber. Quite the most perfect I have seen. Very rare. Thousands of years ago this poor unlucky fellow left the hive on a sunny day like this, was caught in resin, and now he finds himself immortal. . . . I think I must have this for her. Will the symbolism please her?"

She looked uncertain.

He smiled at her and prompted, "I was caught and never have escaped."

Mrs. Carroll nodded swift approval. "I will explain it if she doesn't understand."

He raised the bracelet. "I should like to have it wrapped."

There was something hard and gemlike in the woman's face. Without a word she took it. She swept the ring and amulet into the drawer, turned the key, and with a brush of her skirt she left the room. The bird flew after her. Mrs. Carroll was vaguely ill at ease. The room, the woman and the bird, all but Nick were suddenly alien. She wanted to join him as he studied amber in the cases on the wall, but he was utterly engrossed. Instead, she walked to the doorway. The government man was standing outside with a slightly bearded older man she had not seen before. Bits of the floss were visible on the government man's brown suit. Suddenly she heard them speaking in American English without a trace of accent. "Take over for me," said the government man. "I need to make a call." "If you say so," said the other.

For a moment she accepted what she heard without a question. Then she was aware that she had overheard Americans, not Poles.

When she turned back into the room Nick was holding up a

chain for her inspection. Each link was carved from amber of a different hue. "Quite unusual, don't you think? I have chosen it for you, and you must wear it now."

She protested but he put it on her. Indeed she thought it lovely. Tears came into her eyes. "You're very kind."

"Here we are," he said. "She's wrapped my bracelet." The woman was beside them, and from her tapering fingers he received the package. Before they reached the door, he handed it to Mrs. Carroll. "You may as well, since I depend on you to give it for me."

Once outside the shop she told him gaily, "I've discovered that the government man is not a government man. He's one of us." He looked at her. His eyes were smiling. "I overheard him talking to another American."

"These Poles are really wonderful at picking up our language. They study it for years," he said. "You can't detect an accent."

She protested, "But I'm sure. He sounded more American than you or I."

He laughed it quite away and pointed out the tower of the granary, pink and lovely in the sunlight. Little clouds resembling birds were moving through the sky. Down below, like shadows of the clouds, the pigeons strolled. In the distance was a flash of water.

When they had turned the corner she looked for the sidewalk painter. He was nowhere to be seen. Only a smudge of color where the fruit, the royal couple, and Salome once had been. "What a shame!" she cried. "Why couldn't he have left it?" She found her eyes again with tears, as if a memory of her youth had been erased. She thought she saw the dark stain where his blood had been. And for a moment she recalled the woman on the floor, the waiters with their towels, the blood. . . . At once she clutched the package in her hand as if it were a relic that could heal, restore.

When they had reached the lobby he held her hand for just a moment. "And now," he said, "I have no choice but to rely on you." He looked into her eyes and touched her cheek.

"Thank you for this," she said and put her fingers to the chain. He waved her words away and turned into the street.

Once more she found herself succumbing to the lift, for she was tired from the walk and did not care to climb. The dusty wine aroma of the carpet was sharpened by the smell of coffee from a cluttered tray beside a bedroom door. It reminded her that coffee was very dear in Poland, then that it was lunchtime and she had no time to eat. She passed the door to Sofia's room and went straightway into her own. Harboring the package in her hands, she sat beside the window and watched the sky begin to gray. She recalled with gentle yearning the painter in the street and how the walk had bloomed with her very youth when she had held her dear love in her arms. . . . At last she prayed to God to restore this man and woman, Nick and Sofia, to each other and to make them happy as she once had been. She thanked Him for the privilege and the joy of touching with her life their long-abiding love.

She rose and took the gift to Sofia's room. When the door was opened at her knock she was surprised to see that Sofia was rather smartly dressed in a dark gray suit with pearls about her throat as if for going out, and that her eyes fell instantly to the package that her visitor was holding. The bruise upon her brow had disappeared. Mrs. Carroll would not have known her for the pale, disheveled, battered creature of the day before, and now she gazed at her through a mist of kindness. "How well you look, my dear. How well you look."

She waited and began, "I've told him you are here and why you will not see him. But oh, my dear, if you could hear how much he wants it. . . . He sends this gift, a token of his love." She turned away and then turned back. "If you could hear, I think you would relent, I know it." She found she was too deeply moved for more.

Once more in her room, she grew a little puzzled that Sofia had thanked her briefly but had not asked her in. But she reassured herself: She wants to be alone when she is opening his gift.

She thought Nick might have reappeared for dinner if only for assurance that his gift had been received. She did not see him. She retired early and lay for half the night in silent reverie, mentally supporting with her thoughts and prayers the two whose lives were now her deepest dear concern.

After tea for breakfast in her room she knocked on Sofia's door with plans and soft suggestions to be offered. She waited in the hallway for some moments, then knocked again before the door was opened. Sofia stood before her in the same gray suit with pearls, as if she had not been to bed at all. Mrs. Carroll was amazed to see that an open suitcase on the bed was packed for a departure.

She caught her breath. "You can't be leaving."

Sofia smiled a little tightly. "Yes, I must."

"If you would let me tell you how he needs you . . ." In her distress she moved into the room. There on the bed beside the suitcase was the bracelet. Mrs. Carroll gazed at it to gain support for what she was about to say. And then she stopped. She stared. She could see the bee was missing. . . . There was only a tiny hole where the bee had been.

She turned. She met the eyes of Sofia. They were stone.

Afterward in her room it seemed to her that it was she who had run headlong into doors of glass with eyes for what was on the other side, and now lay stunned. She could not think. She only knew that somewhere she had gone astray, that things were not what they had seemed to her to be. Outside, the birds were bickering on the ledge below her window.

Toward noon she heard a knock upon her door. She thought of feigning sleep, but if it were the maid, it might be well to have the cleaning done with. At last she roused herself to unlock the door. To her surprise the government man was standing in the doorway. Behind him was another in a Polish uniform.

"Madam," said the government man—except that he was not a government man at all, "would you be pleased to show us what you purchased in the amber shop a day ago?"

She looked at him in wonder. "Nothing at all," she said. "I purchased nothing."

"But something was purchased for you, and may we see it if you please."

She brought the chain and held it up before them. The men examined it with scrupulous care. Each link was caressed between their fingers. At last they shook their heads and gave it back. "Would you be pleased to let us look around your room before we leave?"

She was incredulous. "You mean to search it?" But seeing the man in uniform, she guessed she had no choice. They went through her belongings silently and swiftly while she stood in the doorway listening to the birds and staring at the stain that years ago had spread among the roses in the carpet of the hallway. Like the spill of blood that only yesterday had veined a white rose on the pavement. She saw the waiters with their towels and the blood on the white coat. . . . Or so it had seemed.

When they had finished she watched them go away. She watched them pass the room that had been Sofia's. Now the maids were getting it in readiness for another. She went inside and locked her door and walked slowly to the dresser, where she dropped the amber chain. She put her glasses on to stare into the mirror at her wounded eyes, her mouth that quivered for a moment as she gazed. Hardly Salome kneeling on the sidewalk. Something has happened to me and I don't know what it is. Something was happening all along and I didn't see.

She sat in her window chair and tried to recall the whole thing, from the time the woman rushed into the doors. . . . How much of it was what it seemed to be? When she reached the sidewalk painter she wanted to pass over him and leave his painting innocent of guile, something made for her that spoke to her. But then his drop of blood on the amber bracelet . . . was like a sign . . . was like a finger pointing to the bracelet . . . was like a spoken word to someone else. What was behind the bee or in the bee? What was the service required of him that after eighteen thousand years his grave should be disturbed?

She dressed and slipped the chain into her purse and walked the streets, stopping to look in shops and seeing nothing. Groping with her mind behind the bee for something small. She had heard of a tiny chip. On it could be written secret, desperate things—part of an ugly war that was always going on below the surface of things. It had to do with nations being greedy for others' secrets and was betrayal, not love. It was the furthest thing from love. She had an aching memory of the package being put into her hands before she left the shop . . . and of the words: "You may as well, since I depend on you to give it for me." He had touched her cheek. The eyes of "the government man" had always been upon her. Perhaps they followed her still. Once she turned to see.

Clouds were banking overhead. She felt their shadow chill her as she walked. When it began to mist she had a cup of tea and returned to wait in the lobby for a man who once had told her that his name was Nick. The government man no longer sat in the corner with his paper.

She chose a seat where she could clearly see the entrance. A little boy had trapped himself inside the circle of the door, and someone, taking pity, pushed him screaming and revolving till he fell into the lobby. Then he ran past her in a trance of grief.

The afternoon was late when Nick appeared. He walked in from the street, revolving with the door, gray hair a little ruffled from the rising wind. She rose and called to him when he was close. He stopped and smiled as if with pleasure and came toward her. "I must speak to you in private."

"Of course," he said and mentioned tea.

She shook her head and led him to the very bench the government man had quitted. She dropped the amber chain beside him. "I have been visited by the American who used to sit here and by what looked to be an agent of the Polish police. They have searched my room. They have examined this—for what I do not know—and now I do not want it anymore. I do not know the man who gave it to me. Or why it was given. Or why the bracelet I delivered for him now has lost its bee."

His gray eyes smiled indulgently upon her. "What can you possibly mean?"

"I don't know what I mean. I think you do." She faltered for a moment. "I have been trapped." She caught her breath. "I am like the bee."

His fingers stroked the amber chain. "I want you very much to have this."

"For the service I have rendered . . . like the bee?"

"For being the kindest and most gracious woman I have ever known."

She would not have it so. "You spotted me," she said. "Something in my face betrays me, is it that? Or you are good at reading an old woman's heart."

He shook his head.

"You saw that I was hopelessly romantic. You saw I could be used in that direction."

He simply pressed her hand but she withdrew it. "But why all this . . . charade? Why all . . . so much?" Now it was she who spoke with hesitation, groping her way from phrase to phrase in darkness. "I am a simple woman. You could have done with less." She shook her head in wonder. "The two of you . . . I was so easily deceived. I keep thinking that it couldn't all have been for me. It must have been for someone far more sensible and wiser than I."

He raised his hand in protest and let it fall.

"Tell me one thing," she said and turned her face away, for tears were forming in her eyes. "Have I been led . . ." She stopped and looked to him again. "Have I betrayed my country?"

"Dear lady, no, believe me you have not."

She stood up then. "I take your word for it because it seems I can do nothing else."

"Believe me you have not."

She did not want to talk about it anymore. It was something dark and ugly that struck at her life. She turned and walked away, past the heavy glass doors where a woman had lain stunned. Or so it had seemed. Nothing was real but her thirst to leave behind whatever it was. A cold thought struck her as she left the lobby that it might be a recipe for blowing up the world. But of course he wouldn't tell her, and something deep inside her cried out not to know.

Feeling unequal to the swaying lift, she climbed the stairs. Inside her room she calmed her beating heart. And Eve? she thought. She too belongs to all this world. Did she leave me at their mercy, knowing me for the fool I was? She wept a little. But she knew the snare: because of one betrayal to see betrayals springing up like mushrooms. Standing by the window, she wept a little more.

At length she dried her tears and lay down in the twilight. I have been used, she thought with sorrowful logic, staring deep into the gathering dusk. I have never minded being used. It is that I mind what I was used for. . . . Or that I mind not being used for something I would like. A fool she was, but yet an honest fool. I mind not helping to restore a woman to the kingdom of her joy.

Incurably she lingered with it, lingered with a woman and the kingdom of her joy. And shouldn't you be allowed to choose when you were older . . . when you couldn't if you tried get back inside the glass bowl of the world where things were moist and green? No one could tell you what to look at through the glass. . . .

A girl can make a dream into her own sweet world, until the clamor of noon overwhelms her song. But some in later years will find again the power to remake the world, to trump all aces, to restore the dream. Mrs. Carroll beautifully was mistress of that power. Lying in the dark, she quite deliberately unwove the final days the way they were and wove them back into the image of another's joy. Sighs, tremors, whispers, starts of recognition, yieldings of the heart.

And then she thought, I might as well. . . . And so she wove the rich encounter and the long embrace.

The Inglenook

Until she was thirty-five Rachel's life was like any woman's life—a husband, a house to keep, and summers and winters. Winters indeed, for they lived in the North where the cold was long, forever eating into the summer and into her husband, who was older than she and never well in the cold. So they moved to the South in her thirty-sixth year. And after that . . . her life was a tale out of some old book, something she might have read before the fire and pondered. A tale for winter telling, though now the spring came early with a promise of joy.

She had no children. It had lain upon her heart. And her husband with the passing of time touched her less. But when they reached the South they bought themselves a farm with a burned-down house. While they waited in the fall for their home to be built, they lived in the nearby one-room smokehouse, which had escaped the fire. It had but one window and was full of moving life in the corners and the shadows. And it was warm and dense with the smoky scent of hams and sides of bacon that once had hung from the hooks in the sturdy rafters. At night it was like sleeping with peace and plenty and waking in the dim light cured to a ripeness. They clung to one another for the first time in years. Before the house was finished she would have a child.

They waited for the house, and they waited for the child and saw to the building of a room for him with a window seat and a wall of windows to let in the light. They planted pears and plums and a few apple trees to remind them of the North, although they were told that it was too far south for the kind they had planted to set any fruit. And they made the house with a special thing to sum up the winter they had left behind: in the living room wall a great fireplace, long and wide, made of stone. One end was an ingle-

The Inglenook

nook, a corner by the fire with a seat of stone deep inside the hearth. The very oldest houses where they came from had them. She had seen a woman nursing her newest born in the bower of stone and embers, all rose and warmth. She remembered it with longing.

When she knew about the child she felt as if the moon shone clear through her body, such light was hers. Later she felt as if the moon were inside her. She sat in the inglenook before the house was done, and the moonlight from her body shone about the hearth. She sat and waited in the womb of the nook to be born again when her child was born.

But for all the moonlight and the sweet months of waiting, the child was stillborn. A hard thing to bear in any land, but in a strange land it was harder still. The house itself was like a stranger that did not care. And to tell what came after and get the telling of it done, in the spring her husband, Dirk, had a stroke and fell. He fell among the new apple trees he had planted. And when she came upon him, with the blossoms from the maiden trees drifting to his face that was now like someone's she had never known, it seemed to Rachel then that she fell with him. She could move her own limbs, but her spirit lay as still as the stone in the pond, as still as her husband and the child stillborn. Afterward he lay in the four-poster bed they had brought from the North, as if he had become her stillborn child.

Her bewildered mind shackled it all as one. For while her husband lay motionless, never, for sure, would there be a child to wake and sleep in the room where the cradle held its breath, as motionless in its way as Dirk. And what was the cause of the double harm? She pondered this in the days that passed.

Then she came to believe that the cause was herself. The two-fold evil had sprung from her. Something in herself . . . but she did not want to know what it was. Whatever her fault, it had done its work. She grew worn with the effort to keep it at bay. She had set her will not to think it by day or dream it by night.

As for being forgiven, of what use would it be? She did not care about her soul. She cared that her child lay cold in the earth and her husband lay too cold to give her another. And that was the flesh and the bone of the matter.

When things go well, a woman can be like a leafing tree and a thousand forms with the wind in her leaves. But when things are ill, she is only one shape and a root gone down to the center of the earth.

She was still a young woman, handsome enough, with auburn hair that was dark as wine and a throat that was firm as a column of stone. She covered them both with a silken scarf when she went into town and bought supplies. Her hours she spent in tending Dirk, feeding him with infinite patience and care. Sometimes she seemed to be feeding their child. The ritual of it passed into dream. If she stroked his cheek, after a while he would open his mouth. Then she stroked his throat till he swallowed the food. She could not tell if he wanted to live or die. And until she knew, she could not wish him one thing or the other. Tell me, her sorrowful eyes would say, and then we can both want whatever you want. Long ago in the North she had heard it said that if two hearts desire the selfsame thing, it would come to pass.

She searched her memory for words from the North, where life had been simple and cold and clear. Here it wept rain that misted to a cloud in the warming fields. Here it was confused with blossoms that drifted to a face gone strange, blossoms from trees that would never set fruit, or so it was said of their apple trees. As she was a tree that would never set fruit.

The doctor came to look at him once a week. He remarked each time, "I knew a man like this for goin' on a year an' one day he sat straight up in bed. I wish I could recall the first thing he said." He stood beside her staring down at Dirk and trying to remember what the man had said.

In his silence Dirk was well-favored still, with a face now refined and forever in thought, the gray at his temples spreading each day and the dark hair curling about his neck. Each day she shaved him with special care, weeping a little if she cut his flesh, kissing away the trace of his blood. She saw how the skin of his face grew tight and then how the planes of his face relaxed as if from a constant, invisible weight. Before they were married Dirk took her to see his Canadian kin, and she watched him now turning into his father—pale, skintight, and French to the bone. The livelong day his opened eyes had a puzzled look, as if he had forgotten what had come to pass, his fall and the blossoms that covered his face. At night she would close the puzzled eyes with a gentle sweep of her hand like a wing. She could not tell if they ever slept, but in the morning she opened them. She gave to him all the mothering care she had stored in her body and mind for the child. She sang to him songs laid by for the child, songs she remembered out of her childhood. Indeed she seemed to have lost the rest.

Meanwhile she must take her life by the hand. She must see to the farm and the head of beef cattle, all black as Satan, they had bought to graze and to sell in the fall. Cattle would be easiest for Dirk, they thought. They had wanted sheep. But lambing time can be bitter hard, and the war had taken much of his strength.

She placed an ad in the farmers' bulletin, which came twice a month. She asked for a man to help with the cattle and to make her a garden behind the house. A farmer appeared. His name was Peavy. He was taut as a wire and leathered with sun. His eyes were razor-sharp on her land. He lived somewhere. She knew only the direction his finger had pointed. Places and roads were still strange to her. He would come once a month. . . . After each trip she counted out money into his hand while he looked into the line of oaks in the distance as if his mind had gone back into the fields of his own. He did not care for her land or her cattle or the garden seeds she had brought from the North. She felt it was so from the way his eyes skimmed over it all, herself as well, grudging the time it took him to look.

Once he said to her spitting into the grass, looking into the trees, "You best git married to someun' be aroun' to take keer o' this."

She waited, listening to the bees in the clover. "I already am."

He cut across her with his razor eyes. "That a fact?" he said.

She saw then how little she and Dirk were known in the land. Or perhaps he was only fishing for facts.

"He gone off someplace?"

She turned away. It was a way of putting it. Gone off someplace.

But wherever he was he was also here. And she needed someone to help with his care and to leave him with when she went for supplies. She was not at ease with the young black girl she had used at times. She had never got used to blacks in the house to do her work. She put another ad in the farmers' bulletin.

Once she dreamed of walking alone in the woods and finding a man she had never seen and lying with him to get a child.

After that she braided her wine-dark hair and bound it tightly about her head. But then each night she loosed the braid and lay with her head across Dirk's chest, feeling the stir of his breath in her hair, hearing the crippled beat of his heart and trying to time her own with his, to make between them one beating heart that was not their own but another heart. It was like being again with child.

One Sunday morning the girl Cassie appeared in answer to the ad that Rachel had placed. The girl was small and almost pretty, with watery green eyes and sea-foam hair that crept and scattered along her back and rounded features that were like a baby's and a way of speaking that was like a child's. Her lashes were white, as if they were powdered. She was soft and young. But her hands were large and red with deep orange fissures gone into the knuckles. It was hurtful to see them. After a week Rachel gave her a jar of cream to use. She smelled of it and smiled and put it into her pocket. When Rachel asked her later if the cream had helped, she looked half afraid.

"Yes, ma'am. But I let my sister use it. The baby has such a rash . . . I'll bring it back."

"No, keep it for the baby."

It was the first Rachel had heard of the baby. A little boy. The sister's husband had left before the baby was born. They lived with Cassie . . . "till she can git married to someun' be aroun' to take keer of things."

Rachel paused in wonder. The words were an echo of Peavy's to her.

When Cassie spoke of the baby her eyes narrowed with memories and she fell into smiles. And when she fed Dirk she was patient as if she were coaxing a child.

Rachel came upon her once in her own child's room, which she had left in its state of waiting. Rachel stood in the doorway and watched for a moment, how gently the girl rocked the cradle to sleep, how she ran her hand through the sheen of its rim, and finally lifted the little white pillow and laid it softly against her cheek.

The Inglenook

At once Rachel stepped inside the room. The girl looked up and their still eyes met. Rachel stared until Cassie lowered the pillow and placed it carefully back in the cradle.

"I heard you had a baby died."

Rachel nodded.

"Born dead?"

Rachel turned away.

The girl sighed and looked with longing at the little table with its tub and the tray of things for bathing.

"My sister would really love to see these things." She added after a moment, as if she had not told it before. "Her husband took off and lef' 'fore it come." She waited. "She would really love to see these things."

Rachel was mourning under ice. "I couldn't give them away. . . . I couldn't do that."

"You might have another one and get to use 'em. . . ." Between them was the motionless figure of Dirk. The girl asked, again touching the cradle, "Did you have this made?"

"No. No, it was handed down." But she did not want to talk of it.

Cassie looked away into the depths of the cradle, rocking it into a kind of mind-motion. And again her eyes were narrowed with memories.

It seemed to Rachel as plain as day that the child was Cassie's, though nothing was said. Her clothes had a smell of powder and milk. Though mostly it was the soft of her eyes, and the bloom of her skin, and a dreaming stare. As if her own dream, Rachel's dream, had mellowed and dropped into Cassie's arms.

But in the heart of it all was a sadness, which at first Rachel took to be her own. And then on the mornings that Cassie came, another thing entered the house with her. At times she surprised Cassie looking at her with a tenderness it was hard to explain. Each day that Cassie swept the hall her footsteps slowed by the baby's room. She lingered there, as if she would call it out of its sleep.

Rachel hedged herself round with a quick impatience. Then she listened to Cassie coaxing the food into Dirk's still mouth—the wheedling, the edge of a cry in her throat. She held her own breath,

81

and in spite of herself she listened in wonder, afraid to guess what it was she heard.

She never asked Cassie about her child, but he lay between them full of need. Sometimes in the night Rachel woke to his cry in the house miles away Cassie said she had rented. When she went for supplies, leaving Cassie with Dirk, she bought extra milk and gave it to Cassie.

Rachel was hanging the laundry one day. Cassie had gone to fetch corn from the smokehouse. When she called to the hens they would come at her bidding, running as if they were waiting to hear it. Then she fed them, teasing them, tempting and luring and full of sweet talking, as if they were children that gave her delight.

"If you was to find a baby . . . what would you do?"

Rachel swallowed and frowned at the sun.

"Reason I ast: my aunt found a baby oncet under some leaves at the back of her house. It was mostly dead. She had to breathe in its mouth. But she got it to goin'. An' it live an' become her favorite chil'. Res' of the chil'ren took off and lef'. . . ."

Rachel shrugged and went cold. "I don't really like to talk about babies. . . . Surely, Cassie, you can understand that."

"Oh, yes, ma'am. Yes, ma'am. But sometimes I ast myse'f what would I do. Like if'n my sister was to take off an' leave. . . ."

And this was how it was laid between them. Like a length of quilt they were piecing together, and each in her secret heart knew the pattern and where in the middle their fingers would meet until at a glance one could see the whole.

When they worked in the kitchen side by side or met in the yard, a kind of trance enveloped them both. Each avoided the glance of the other. Their gestures grew measured and even slow. And the air between them was filled with dreaming. The two of them wore a listening look. Sometimes they paused in the midst of a task, as if they were hearing a distant cry. . . .

And most of all, the baby was never mentioned now.

The spring days passed. One afternoon Cassie came late with a basket, the kind that is found in the market with produce. Open slats and wire handles. It was covered over with a flour sack. "I got mendin' to do while I set with Mr. Dev'reaux, ma'am."

Rachel hardly gave the basket a glance. She was ready and waiting to leave for town. When she returned Cassie was standing by the kitchen door. "Ma'am," she said, looking past Rachel, "you reckon I could have my money today?"

"Of course," said Rachel and laid down the groceries. She gave the money and then some extra.

Cassie folded it quickly and thrust it into the pocket of her skirt.

Rachel turned away. "I got extra milk."

Cassie waited. "No, thank you, ma'am. I got enough to last." Her eyes were shining. Rachel had a feeling of something they had made being almost finished. Something they had worked in the dark to make.

Still Cassie waited. "Good-bye, ma'am," she said with her eyes on the lemon balm in the window. "I give Mr. Dev'reaux his soup like you said." Her voice had an edge of distraction in it. "I wanted me a cutting of that," she said, and she walked to the window and stroked the leaves.

"Take it now," said Rachel. "Dig down at the side. Get one of the roots."

But the girl turned away and shook her head, her green eyes shining. She walked to the door.

Rachel called after her. "You came with some things. . . ."

Cassie half turned. "I'll get 'em tomorrer, that be all right." She was scarcely audible. And then she was gone.

Rachel stood in the kitchen with her eyes on the balm. She listened for Cassie's step on the walk. Slowly she walked to the living room and bent and slid to the inglenook and sat there listening with all her might. Her throat was full. She stroked it softly, the column of stone, as if it were not her own but Dirk's, and swallowed once, and her eyes went soft on the lines of stone.

At last she rose and slowly walked the length of the hall past the room where Dirk lay to the baby's room. She stared at the cradle and turned away and walked the length of the hall and back. Then she entered and stood looking down at the basket inside the cradle. The wire handles were loosely draped with the flour sack patterned with lavender blooms. Her heart was beating into her throat. She turned away and she sat for a while on the window seat. Then she went again to stand by the cradle, and quickly she drew away the cloth and saw the baby lying asleep, folded together to fit the basket, his knees drawn up as if he were waiting still to be born. He was so quiet that he seemed to her dead. And her own dead child came into her womb. Then his small puckered mouth made a rhythmic motion, and she knew that he slept.

Her eyes went blind. Her unborn child was heavy within her. She drew the cloth to hide him again. She turned away. She scarcely breathed. And she sat again on the window seat. At last she got up and went to Dirk where he lay gone down to silence and bone and dead to her question and all her need. And she said to him, "Dirk, there's a baby been left here. . . . What do you want me to do with it, Dirk?" Then she came closer and touched his face with a trembling hand. "Answer me, Dirk." She whispered it tightly, her need and her tension gone into her voice, all her excitement, her hope and fear, and a kind of deadness that lies in a seed in the wintertime.

Then she sat in the rocker beside his bed and rocked herself into the words she made. "Sometimes I think that I lost the baby because if I had him I couldn't tend you. You're just about all I can handle, Dirk. . . . There's that little Littie, that little black girl. I guess I could get her to come in and help." It amazed her to hear how settled it was that Cassie would never return for the child. "You hear me, Dirk? Cassie won't be back."

She began to weep now without any sound. And after a while her tears seemed to come from the room down the hall where the baby lay. She got up and went to him, but he lay asleep. She drew back the cover a little more and saw that a bottle half filled with water was placed beside him. To his shirt there was pinned a penciled note: "He likes it you hold him. This is how you make his milk. . . ." His legs and stomach were covered with rash. He stirred and strained and his face grew as red as his mother's hands.

She glanced again at the penciled note. At the bottom was added: "I lef 4 bottle in the frigre . . ." The phrase was crossed out and above it was written: "nex to the ice." And under it all: "When he wakes you might shud feed him."

She had never taken care of a child before. She found herself startled and deeply anxious. She warmed a bottle and fed him just as he lay in the basket.

Then she paced the hall, unable to rest, unable to think. The wine-dark hair came loose from the braid. When she fed her husband his early supper she fell to brooding while she held the spoon. She could hear the lowing the cattle made. The sound of it was her own disquiet loosed upon the field and sky.

At twilight the baby began to cry like a little lost kitten, a mewing, deserted, insistent wail. She fed him again and walked with him, his tiny body surprisingly heavy, tensed, unyielding as a stone. The weight of it grew till her shoulders ached. The house began to take on a chill, and the baby's flesh was cold to her touch. She laid him down while he howled with despair and churned his fists in a dark protest. She built a small blaze in the fireplace and sat with him in the inglenook. She turned his face to the leaping flame, and at once he grew quiet and still as an animal watching the campfire, craning his rash-covered neck to the light.

And she stared at his face where it lay in her lap, an ancient face, red in the light as his mother's hands and nothing at all like the child fair of flesh she had carried for months and somehow lost. This child was alien. Even as she held him still in her arms he strained away and she let him go. She could not fold him against herself. Instead, she allowed the flame to warm him.

She began to weep and the baby listened and down the hall Dirk heard her tears. Or so it seemed to her as she wept. I cannot love this child, she wept. I cannot turn from my own little boy. To take this red imperfect child began to seem like a deep betrayal of the child her dreaming body had formed. An easy way to blunt her grief, but a wrongful thing to take a child and give him the care that was meant for another, and all the time to withhold her love.

Or so she reasoned, mourning and weeping, growing soft in her heart and hard by turns. She placed him once on the seat beside her, but he cried like a kitten lost in the night. Guilty, she took him again on her lap. And she sat with him for the rest of the night, afraid, if she slept, the child would slip to the hearth below. The fire fell into ember and ash. Her body grew stiff and cramped with pain. And in the darkness she came to see that the power of her mind and the strength of her body belonged to Dirk. Her mothering spirit belonged to him. He was her child. She could have no other.

When it was daylight she warmed a bottle and fed the child. She lowered him gently into the cradle. And mercifully he fell asleep. With stumbling hands she changed his wet clothes for dry ones Cassie had left in the basket. She touched the rosiest spots of his rash with a little lotion. It was all she had.

Then she wrapped a scarf about her head and ran in the early morning light down the road to the house where the black girl lived. "I need you to come and stay with my husband. . . . For just a little while," she said. And she waited in the thinning mist like a supplicant. "For just a little while," she pled.

Littie stared into the burdock trees.

The black woman loomed in the door behind her. "I heerd you had a white girl he'pin' you out." Her voice had an edge of resentment in it.

"She couldn't come. . . . I'll pay your daughter."

"I skeerd o' sick folks," Littie said.

"Shet yo' mouf," said the woman, "an' git."

Rachel at last was in the car with the baby packed again in the basket and the meager store of his clothes she had found tucked away into its corners. She had taken his bottles from the ice. She placed the basket at her feet. The baby's mouth was a puckered ring, and even in sleep his face had the ancient weariness.

She drove straight to town and stopped at the bank. Inside, while she waited she prayed that the child alone in the car would not wake and cry. She asked for eight hundred dollars in cash. As he counted it out, in the polished glass of the teller's window she caught a glimpse of her haggard face and the dark half-moons beneath her eyes. The teller stared at her curiously.

Cassie had told her how to find the house. As she twisted and turned in the rutted road, she planned her words: Cassie, this money is all I can spare. I want you to use it for your little boy. . . .

But no, she would hand her the child and the money, and between them the rest would be wordless and clear. Nothing between them, nothing that mattered, had ever been spoken, and now it was better to end without words.

The late spring sun was shafting across the face of the child. Her old car sputtered and almost stopped. Cattle egrets flew out of the field and across her path, rising and falling as if they were blown about by the wind, but the air was still and heavy with mist rising out of the grass. The sky was faintly enameled with blue.

She found it at last. The house was little more than a shack leaning into an oak that leaned away. A chimney was shedding its bricks on the roof, which looked to be tin and streaked with rust. In the yard filled with weeds and thistles in bud stood a pickup truck. In the bed of the truck she could see a chair and an unpainted table. She drew up beside them, and at once an old man reeled through the door, on his back a mattress. His hair was white. His face was tanned. His shirt was unbuttoned and his chest was covered with cobweb hairs. He heaved the mattress to the bed of the truck, then gave her a sharply curious glance.

She got out and stood by the side of her car.

"Is the girl moving? Is she moving away?" In her surprise she could not remember Cassie's last name. Perhaps the house wasn't Cassie's at all.

He rubbed his face with a flower-print cloth he pulled from his hip. He was breathing hard.

"Is she in the house? I need a word with her."

He spat on the weeds. "Ain't nobody here."

She stared at him with a growing alarm. "Then why are you taking her things?" she asked.

He mopped his throat and then the cobweb hairs of his chest.

Her voice began to tremble and shrill. "Tell me why you are taking her things." Then, as still he made no reply, "She works for me. Put her things back in the house at once." She seemed to be speaking out of a dream.

The baby woke and began to cry. The stab of her fear was making the cry.

"She give 'em to me. I ain't steal her thangs." His cold, thin face was a judgment upon her.

The weeds at her feet seemed faintly to shudder. She steadied her gaze on a thistle in bud.

"I'm a God-lovin' Christian man," he said. "I carried her to Delta to catch the bus. She dint have no money, er say she don't, to pay me fer it. She say I could take what thangs she had. We had us a covenant. You understan' what I'm saying', lady? We had us a covenant I could take these thangs. Ain't nothin' much here. Like I say, I carried her clear to Delta."

Speechless, she leaned against the car. They stood with all her despair between them.

He looked down into her face with scorn. "You tend yer young-'un an' leave me be."

He turned away and went into the house.

She felt as if he had struck at her. It seemed there was something about herself. Perhaps it was that she came from the North. Or was it because her luck was bad and people could tell and feared to catch an evil chance? A cattle egret, white as milk, was walking toward her with delicate grace, dipping and lifting its pencil beak. She closed her eyes. When she opened them it had disappeared. . . .

She started the car, and the child at her feet stopped crying at once. She found herself driving along the road without a thought as to where she would end. She tried to think what it was she must do. There were agencies who might take the child, but she knew of none or how to find them. And how was she to explain to them how she came to possess this child she had? How explain to them that nothing was said, nothing that mattered was ever said? She could see Cassie sitting straight on the bus that traveled a different road from hers and how the green eyes swam with tears but how they trusted in things unsaid. And she herself could not bring down wrath upon that head . . . when things had been that were never said.

She seemed to move deeper into the land. The trees were taller and hooded with dusk, and river willows lay in wait and threw their shadows across the road. Here comes the Yankee woman, they said. She put out a hand to get her a child and kept the other behind her back. She kept the other to give him back. What kind of woman is that? they said. She tricked herself for good, they said. . . .

The child at her feet was lying awake, turning his face to the wavy pattern of trees and sky, dark and light. His face was old, as if he had lived through another life.

She saw by a sign at the side of the road that she was entering another county. She must be very far from home. She seemed to have lost the power to turn. And she wept for Dirk, who was helpless without her, with only Littie to sit with him, with only Littie doing God knew what. She wept because he was lost without her and she was powerless to turn around. To turn would be to say to herself, I'm taking this baby home for good.

She quickened her speed. The tree frogs shrieked above the sound of her car. And then abruptly the trees were gone. The fields were beside her. The child at her feet frowned into the sun. She slowed to a halt and shifted his basket and felt of the bottle she had placed in the blanket. It was still quite cool.

Then she heard voices. Ahead of her children spilled out of a tunnel below the road. One child after another surfaced, their faces and stomachs smeared with mud. One of them held a stick with a minnow impaled upon it. He was spitting out dirt, and the others were laughing and grabbing and twisting. Eight or ten, perhaps a dozen, they moved so fast it was hard to tell. Their half naked bodies were lean and tanned. They stopped when they saw her. The smallest ones ran to hide in the tunnel. The older ones stood and stared at her.

Then down in a hollow she saw the trailer. A woman was sitting in a chair beside it.

The day came together with a clap of silence: the long, sleepless night, the running through mist and begging for Littie, her own voice shrilling at the old man reeling under the mattress, then endless miles when she could not turn. . . .

There were trees, a forest, behind the trailer and a clutter beside it, and off to one side something quite familiar. It looked like an apple press for cider. She had not seen one since coming South. She saw it with tenderness and then with wonder. It seemed to be weaving her into the hollow and binding her with the woman below, who was too far away to be seen quite clearly . . . who was looking at something she held in her lap. Rachel watched her, entranced.

A faint golden light crept over the land. And it seemed to Rachel that down in the hollow lay the turning home.

At last she got out and stood by the car. Her loss of sleep had begun to unsettle and distance the world. Beyond the trailer a cloud like a pearl-gray giant hand seemed to hold the sun. But light spilled over and struck the trees. And this she could see was the golden light. There was not a sign of a path to the trailer.

After a while she picked her way through patches of sedge and cone-flower weeds that had gone to stalk. The field looked dead and deep into autumn. In a dream she seemed to approach the woman. In a dream the child in the car cried out. She stopped for a moment, then walked straight ahead till his cries grew faint.

The woman by the trailer must have seen her coming, but she did not look up till Rachel was only a few feet away. Then she raised her head. "You got trouble with yore car? Nobody 'roun' here can fix a car." Her voice was colorless, detached. Her hands were busy with a basket of beans. She never stopped stringing and snapping and stringing.

"It isn't the car."

The woman looked her over from head to foot. "You sellin' somethin'? I don't have no money." Her hair was pulled straight back, pitch-dark but white where it was skinned from the temples. Her face was tanned, with cheeks high boned like an Indian face, and deep-cut lines from nose to mouth. Her arms in the sleeveless shift were broad.

"Your children," said Rachel, "seem healthy and strong. . . . They seem to be happy."

The woman looked wary and wiped her hands on the breast of her shift. "You come all the way here to tell me that?"

Rachel could not speak. Flies were buzzing at the door of the trailer. The sunlight was striking the apples press. The woman picked at her basket and went back to the beans. "Yore youngun' in the car don't seem none too happy." She brushed her tanned cheek against her arm.

Rachel found in her weariness she could not stand. She walked to the trailer steps and sat. A wind from the forest blew under the trailer with a smell of rain. An egret was circling the apples press. Halting, he dipped his slender beak. Just for a moment, in her weariness, he seemed the bird she had left at Cassie's.

The woman ignored her and ignored the children advancing, retreating, and whooping it up till the cattle egret took wing and left.

"I done said I don't have no money to buy what yore sellin', whatever it be." She spoke in her flat voice as if to herself.

In her dream Rachel said, "I see you have an apple press next to your house."

The woman did not look up. "That what it is? It was here when we come."

"I used to have one where I lived before. . . . You press out the juice . . ." She could not go on.

"You wanta buy it?" The voice was toneless.

"No . . . no, I don't. I don't have any apples."

"Won't do you no good then."

Rachel could not take her eyes from the sinewy hands that were tumbling and snapping, breaking the silence that grew between herself and the woman. Till the woman observed, "Yore youngun' could be smotherin'. I don't hear 'im no more."

Rachel stood in alarm. Then she ran through the weeds that pulled at her skirt. The children followed her at a distance. It was hot in the car, and the child mewed softly. He had worked his head into the basket splints. She found a small splash of red on his cheek.

She picked him up. The tears stung her eyes, and she wept for them both. She sat on the ground in the shade of the car and fed him the milk. It was like feeding Dirk, the slowness, the patience. And her heart grew panicked at the thought of her absence, how long it had been. . . . Her hair had come loose and the heavy braid fell across the child.

The children were near her and circling the car. At intervals they pelted one another with gravel. The smallest, a girl, wore a shift like her mother's. The rest were in short pants, their chests bare and muddy. They did not appear to be watching her, but she felt them drawn by the fact of her tears. She felt their alertness, their curious faces, their bodies coiled and ready to spring into ditch or tunnel. She felt they were waiting for her to sleep.

The child was quiet. He looked to her neither asleep nor awake. She folded him carefully into the basket and found her purse. And slowly she walked through the field again. The dried coneflowers were brushing the sides of the basket she held. As if she dreamed it she heard their whisper.

The woman ignored her. But when Rachel stood in the weeds beside her she looked up expressionless, simply waiting.

Then Rachel said evenly, almost as if she had rehearsed the words instead of their coming so new to her lips that she heard them now with a cold surprise. "This baby was left inside my porch. I don't know how to take care of him. And my husband is sick . . . unable to move."

"That's nothin' to me," said the woman at once. "I got all I can take keer of now."

"I can see that you have a great many," said Rachel. "I can see that you know how to care for them." Then she put the basket on the ground at her feet and opened her purse and drew out the money . . . in bills of one hundred, eight in all. She put them on top of the beans in the basket. "This will help to buy him whatever he needs. And when I am able I promise to come back and bring you some more."

The woman looked at the bills spread across the beans. She did not speak. "I got eight," she said at last in a tone of resentment, "an' one on the way."

"I will bring you more. I have promised you that."

Still the woman waited, her eyes on the money, her face gone hard. She touched the bills. She seemed to be counting.

"Is the youngun' yores?" She asked it slowly, not looking up.

"I told you I found him inside my porch."

"I heerd what you said."

Rachel felt the lash of the woman's scorn. It stunned her so that she could not speak. She watched while the woman fingered the bills, while she rolled one over a limber bean and slowly unrolled it and rolled it back, and plunged her stained hand deep in the beans and scooped them up to bury the money.

The sunlight was caught up into the cloud. The trees behind the trailer swayed. And then without warning it began to rain. The cold drops struck the baby's face. A startled look came into his eyes. Rachel held her breath. The rain would decide it . . . the rain would decide.

The woman stood up and looked down briefly at the child. She lifted the basket by the wire handles. Then she lifted the basket of beans with the money. And walking between them, she moved to the trailer and went inside. In a moment the door was fastened shut.

Seeing her go, the children came running out of the rain and flattened and crawled beneath the trailer and huddled like chicks beneath a hen.

Rachel felt their eyes as she turned and left. . . . She was miles away and she felt their eyes.

As she drove, the tension went out of her body. She knew a lightness. She dared not think. She gave herself up to the road and the trees and the patches of field that were rimmed with fence. And then the lightness became a void. She could feel the void in the midst of her breast. And now the rain was steady and sure.

She had eaten nothing since the night before. She stopped at a crossroads beside a car that was decked with baskets of yellow plums. But when the man limped across in the rain and lifted a basket, she could not speak. It was the kind that had held the baby. And it came to her like a blow to the face that she did not know the baby's name. Incredibly she had left behind a nameless child with a nameless woman.

She sat with her head on the steering wheel, her wet hair loose and winging her face. She was wild with a longing to go to sleep. She felt the darkness like a bell ringing her down into earth and rain. And she knew that if he had had a name she could never have turned and left him there.

Far down the road she began to eat the cold wild plums that were drenched with wet. Sweet and bitter and sour they were. She ate them with a desperate hunger. It seemed to her that she drank their rain.

When she reached her house she went at once to where Dirk lay. "We're alone, my darling," she bent and whispered. She closed his eyes and dropped to the bed and slept at once with her arm thrown out across his chest. Down the well of sleep the rain like apple blossoms fell.

Toward morning she roused. It seemed to her he had gone to stone, that she lay with death. She could not move for the weight of loneliness she bore. With an effort she drew her head to his chest and heard the crippled beat of his heart . . . and then the sound of waking birds and the low of cattle deep in the grass. But the emptiness would not leave her world. At last she knew that it rose from the room across the hall.

All morning she moved about the house in a trance of something akin to sleep. At times she would pause for a distant cry in the withering fields she had left behind. She would listen as she and Cassie had done. And when she gave Dirk food at noon, the fear of her waking sleep was back. "Don't leave me, Dirk," she whispered to him. "You hear me, Dirk. You're all I have."

She would not pass the inglenook. But the smell of ash was in the house and in the baby's empty room. As she paused to stand inside the door, she knew that her life with Dirk was timed. The measure of it was almost full. And because it was so, perhaps the child had been granted her to give what remained a reason to be.

She sat with Dirk for the afternoon and listened to rain that was falling still. She held her gaze upon his face. But in her mind she was seeing the child and how with the days his limbs would grow and his eyes would follow her through the room, how the two of them on the window seat would watch the summer come and go, and how she would build a blaze on the hearth and sing to him in the inglenook and they would hear her echoing voice round and full in the bower of stone . . . singing life into all their days.

In the morning she walked to Littie's house and stood again like a supplicant. "I skeerd o' sick folks," Littie said and hid in the house, but at last she came.

The rain had stopped but the air was fogged, and the fields were patched with lakes and streams. In stretches the water had taken the road. And Rachel drove with the words to say. I will leave her the money and take the child.

When she found the place the trailer was gone. At first she was stunned with disbelief. She tried to think she had lost her way. But there was the tunnel beneath the road and the bare ground space where the trailer had stood and the children had huddled away from the rain. The apple press had disappeared. . . .

She sat and stared at the vacant field till it blurred with the silent wood beyond. She closed her eyes and bowed her head. The loss of the baby bound her breath. But loss was swept up into guilt. The eyes of the child were upon her now and upon the life she had made for him. By her hand, it came to her, she had brought this empty place to pass. The forsaken child, in forsaking her, became the tool of her punishment. For her she knew it was fair and just. But for the child it was very hard. She turned her car around and left.

In a way it was good to know her blame and have a reason for evil luck. Deep in herself there must have lain this guilty thing she would surely do. And this would explain the rest of it, Dirk and her child, the rest of it.

The road was muffled in silken haze. She passed the turn to Cassie's house. . . . If only all had been spoken and clear, as it was with the old man mopping the cobweb hairs of his chest, calling out there had been a covenant. Then Cassie's face came out of the mist as if his word had summoned her. And in her eyes was a covenant, the one two women had worked to make. It was the covenant they had left unsaid.

When she reached her house it seemed deserted. But Littie came out of the kitchen crying. "He wouldn't eat nothin'. I give 'im the spoon but he wouldn't eat."

"It's all right, Littie. Sometimes he won't."

She opened her purse to get the money. But the girl was already past the door. Rachel stopped in the act with a clutch of fear. She ran to Dirk. At first she thought he was just the same. The bed was the same. He lay the same way, straight and lean. Then she saw he was gone. . . .

Her covenant had been with God. She might have known it would be with God.

Late in the week she buried her dead. Her father came. She had not seen him in several years. He was older now, with whiter hair and slower speech, and a memory that whistled things down the wind. She thought how good to be already old and all of it past and the mind grown dim. He wanted to take her back with him. She shook her head. "My child is here," she reminded him. She saw that it had slipped his mind.

From the porch he gazed at her Angus herd. "Why black?" he said. "They look like death. I'd get me another color," he said.

"Their heads are small. They're easily born."

"You could sell 'em," he said, "and come back home."

She could not really explain why not. Except that her life was in two graves and a plot of earth where a trailer had been. He would think it would make a reason to leave. He stayed for a month and went away.

After that there was nothing for her to do but wait for the years to pass away. They passed in a guileful, cunning way, drawing her into the hours and days, the work with the farm, decisions to make, money to borrow and then repay, and all the things she must learn to do—making time seem slow and hard, but filled to the brim with smell of rain and the shudder of tall corn caught in the wind and racing toward her or running away. Her cattle drifting, haunting the grass, and haunted in turn by cattle birds that were white as milk. Drought and flood and the chatter of sleet in the dried cornstalks. And bleating calves that were lost in the woods. And her heart made flint when they came for cows she had fed with her hand. . . . Yes, making time seem slow and hard. When all the time it was running away like corn in the wind into years she was hardly aware had gone.

And surely she wasn't born to farm, to be at the mercy of sun and rain. Nor to have at her mercy cattle and corn. There was something in her that longed to withdraw, to let things be whatever they would, to inflict no life on any seed, to plow under nothing whose time had come.

As time went by she was more alone, the Yankee woman with Yankee ways. Her hair lost much of its wine to gray. But her throat was still a column of stone. When she stroked it with her weathered hand, it was almost as if the throat or the hand belonged to another, and which was she? She needed a husband to see her whole or a child to make an image of her.

But all of that she had not deserved. After a while she ceased to mourn for Dirk and her child. But the covenant child was another thing. She could never be finished and done with him. When she stopped to rest he was always there. Like a shaft of moonlight in her day, strangely cold, forever there.

Her health was good till her middle fifties. Then most of one winter she lay in bed against the cold. In the spring she would make a blaze on the hearth and sit for hours in the inglenook, where in

The Inglenook

fact she had not sat for years, raising her weathered hand to the flame. It brought to her mind how long ago she had sat in the nook, her child within, and how she had held the other child one livelong night and formed her resolve to give him back. And then they would merge into a single child. And she would give herself to the nook. There was always deep in the burning log a trace of the woods from which it came. More than a trace of the violet haze that hung above the farthest trees, a curious spice of wildest honey locked in wood, a singing that came from the heart of leaves and blew across to her on the wind.

As the spring advanced she knew that the iron was gone from her. She would need some help, perhaps for as long as she kept the farm. Peavy had left her a decade ago, and the work since then she had done herself. Now, with a war, men moved elsewhere for better pay. There was no one dear for this war to break. She told herself how good it was.

She began to plan. She hired a carpenter to give the smokehouse an air of home. She ordered low windows to catch the air and a little porch where a man could sit and hold his pipe or watch the sun go behind the trees and the egrets mount and fly to nest and the black ghost cattle lie down to sleep. . . .

But the rich smoke scent was locked in the beams. It caught her up in the warm dense life when she lay with Dirk and conceived her child in peace and plenty.

When all was done she placed an ad in the farmers' bulletin and waited until the month was gone. The rains had stopped. The fields were green and the cattle grazed. The time was passing to plow the land and plant the corn. She put another ad in the paper.

And then one noon when the clouds were piling high in the east, he came to the door and knocked and waited out in the yard, kicking the gravel with the toe of his shoe. Rachel opened the door and shaded her eyes.

He came to attention.

"What is it?" she asked. He must have walked. She could not see a car or a horse.

He did not answer her at once. "Ma'am, I come for the ad," he said.

He looked far younger than she had in mind. Eighteen or so. Twenty at most. And really slender, not very tall. "I need a man who can farm," she said, "and help with cattle."

He stood looking down at the gravel path.

"Have you done this sort of work before?"

He looked at her briefly and down again. "I might could do it. I reckon I could." His speech had a deeply country slur, too clipped for a drawl.

"Where are you from?" she asked him then.

"Differnt places. I git aroun'."

"I need a man who is willing to work. And one with experience."

He looked up into the clouds in the east. "I reckon I might could do it," he said.

And after all she had no choice. The spring was running away from her. She led him at last around to the back. She showed him the cows and the field to be plowed and the shed where the tractor was kept and the rest. She showed him the house where a man would live. "I plan to buy a stove," she said.

She waited and turned to look at him. He was formally dressed in a dark brown suit complete with vest, a little small. She guessed that it didn't belong to him. The planes of his face were beginning to form from a boyish round. The ridge of his nose was pink with sun, and the pink spread into the tops of his cheeks. There was rust in the places where freckles merged. And rust in the hair that was mostly fair. The eyes were green.

He walked away to look across the fence. "Ma'am, how many acres you got?"

"Fifty," she said. "A little more." She had bought some after Dirk was gone. "A lot of it is in woods, you see. I keep a patch of pines to sell."

"How many cows you reckon you got?"

"It would be fifty in all, I guess."

Egrets were riding the backs of the cattle. She watched the shadow of clouds unfold.

"Ma'am, I see you got a pond. You reckon it's got some fish in it?"

"I think it does.... It used to have."

"It's nice," he said. "A place to fish."

And the shadow unfolded across the pond.

He turned to look at her pears in bloom, spilling over the fence of stone. "You sell these off?"

"When I have a good year." The apples trees were in her mind. Long ago they had passed away.

The rain began to fall on his face. His face in the rain. It chilled her heart.

"Come inside," she entreated him. "I'll make you coffee."

He seemed to consider, his eyes now turned to study the house. Smoke from the chimney was drifting low. "Ma'am, you reckon I could have some milk?"

"Of course you can." She climbed the steps and entered the kitchen. But still he waited, circling the house, scanning the land. He picked up a rock and skimmed the pond. Once she thought he had gone away. But then he appeared on the walk in front.

"Come in," she pled. "You'll take cold in the rain."

"I never git nothin' wrong with me."

But at last he came in, to leave a trail of mud on her rug. A fire was going upon the hearth. She threw on some wood to build it up.

His suit was wrinkled and striped with rain. "Sit here," she said. She showed him the seat of the inglenook. "It will dry you out while I bring the milk." She turned at the door. He was standing before the rising flame. "I could fix some cocoa. It would warm you up."

He turned to her. His green eyes scanned her face and left it. "Ma'am, it's milk I reely like."

"Of course." She thought how young he looked. And how could he ever do the work? But his hand on the stone above his head was large and firm. It moved her and she turned away.

In the kitchen she poured a glass of milk and put some crackers upon a tray. She did it all with accustomed ease. But deep in her hands a tremor grew. In her mind she saw him stooping to enter the inglenook. She saw him touch the blackened stone. And she waited awhile. She went to the window above the sink and looked out over her rain-gray field. The cattle were ghosts that bowed their heads. And she thought of what her father had said. "Why black?" he said. "They look like death." And now he too was gone to the grave. A dozen years or so ago. "I'd get me another color," he said.

And she had said, "Their heads are small. . . ." She whispered it now: "They're easily born."

She turned from the sink. And why should anything ever be born? Ancient losses were rich and fresh.

She picked up the tray and went to him. He was sitting inside the inglenook, holding the poker in his ample hand, touching the burning wood with its tip. He did not rise. He let her serve him deep in the nest of fire and stone.

She did not trust herself to speak. She retired to sit where she could watch. She gave herself up to seeing him. As he leaned to the light, she caught the gleam of a trace of beard. How folded he was in fireshine. She stared at the glass he brought to his lips and it seemed to her that she tasted cold. The flicker was moving over his face, turning it young, then old, then young. The flicker was in her dreaming eyes. . . . And slowly the glimmer of firelight gave her the face of the vanished child. She had sat with him while he strained in her arms away from her and toward the light. She knew it beyond a shadow of doubt. Not the green of his eyes or his massive hand or the hair like straw. Not any of this that was like his mother. But something that sang with the flames at his feet and cradled his face in rose and gold.

From head to foot she was bathed in the singing and rose and gold. She seemed to be kneeling upon the hearth to drink from the shining glass he held. And she saw how at last if you waited long, all things lost were given back. She saw how over the numbing years this child had been growing into her own. This man child had become her child. . . . The broken covenant was whole again. Nothing was broken or lost for good. The guilt and the loss dissolved like mist.

She was stunned with joy. Too stunned to move or speak. At last she found her voice in the flame. It was quiet, not to puzzle him. For of course he could not be aware of all that his coming would mean to them.

With an effort she spoke in a homely voice. "I'm beginning to think that on days like today and in the winter . . . the house in the back wouldn't do at all. There's a room down the hall I could fix for you. No one has lived in it before." And only after she had made the words was she aware of the wonder of them. She spoke of the room that had slept in waiting.

He had finished his milk and the crackers too. He wiped his mouth with the ample hand. Gravely he watched the restless flame sink into the embers and disappear.

"Would you like some more? Have you had your lunch?"

With the tip of the poker he touched the wood and shattered the gold. "I ate a little spell ago. I guess I better be on my way." He rose inside the inglenook and now the chimney obscured his face. In a moment he bent and came out to her. He stood and seemed to study the room with a questioning look she could not explain. But of course somehow he remembers, she thought. Somehow he knows. A miracle will work both ways. Or he senses that it will belong to him.

Indeed it all belonged to him now. And she saw the room as it first was made. The generous beams, the walls with a scent of living pine, the stone the color of milk and sand. An abiding place with a promise of ease.

But then he turned away to the door. She roused herself. She stood and followed. "We haven't discussed the pay," she said.

He opened the door and looked at the rain, and then at her, and again at the rain. "It don't seem exactly right for me."

Her heart went dead.

"But it is," she said. "I would help you with it."

He shook his head. "I had in mind to look it over, but now I seen it . . . I'm obliged for the milk and crackers, ma'am."

Her life was gone into hearing his words. "We haven't discussed what I could pay."

"It ain't the pay. . . ."

"What is it? Tell me."

"It just ain't anything I could name."

But she saw his face and she knew with certainty that he could name it, that even before he had come he named it. "Don't go till the rain has stopped," she begged.

But he pushed the screen and went onto the porch.

"Tell me your name," she pled with him.

He did not turn around to reply. "That's a reel good question, ma'am," he said.

Then she was sure in her heart he knew. She watched him go from her into the rain. She watched the ruts in the road grow soft. . . . She saw the startled look of the child as the cold drops struck him in the face.

In the open doorway she shivered with cold. Leaves were sobbing against the roof. She went and sat in the inglenook. His empty glass and tray were there. She took his empty glass in her hand.

How could he know? Then she pondered something that never before had occurred to her: her own identity could have been guessed, and might with a little trouble be known. The Yankee woman with the Yankee speech. The auburn hair. The kind of car. Perhaps her county from the license plate the older children might recall. And if he had come to know who she was . . . then he could believe, as the woman indeed had seemed to believe, that he was her own ill-gotten child.

At last he had traveled, finding her ad, to see what she was and to see what might have belonged to him. As he looked them over, how sweet it must have tasted to him to reject as he had been rejected. For a moment she too could taste the sweet, until it became her bitterness. Like tasting the wild of the yellow plums.

All night she lay as if a stone were upon her chest. At last she knew she would sell the farm, the coal-black cows, the pears in bloom, the corn that it now was too late to plant, the tall young pines that grew of themselves in the corner lot in the acid earth where the huckleberries massed in the spring. She would sell them all with the loss and guilt, and buy her peace with the money she got. She would make a covenant with God to leave her alone for the rest of her days. I'll do whatever you want, she said.

She rose with daylight and washed her face. At the kitchen table she began to write what the place was like, a notice to sell. There was far too much she found to say. At the end she found she had sold herself, all her labor, her rebel strength. She made a clean copy to take to town.

Then she sat again in the inglenook without a fire upon the hearth but with warmth enough from the fire past. There it was shadowed and memory crammed and timeless the way she liked it to be. And she wept because she was selling the nook.

It was hard to say how long she sat. She dozed a bit, with her head against the milk-warm stone. Into her dreaming there came his knock.

She roused and opened the door for him, all unprepared to see his face or deal with him in the noonday sun.

He stood in the yard with a frowning face. She could tell he had walked for miles in the heat. His shirt was wet. The burn and the rust were deep in his skin. She did not think to ask him in.

"Ma'am, I been thinkin' about this place . . ."

She listened to him, still deep in her dream.

"Ma'am, this war. I got my notice. A year, they say. But it could be more. An' I got to thinkin' it might be nice to have a job to come back to then." She could tell he had rehearsed the words. He said them quickly without a pause. And yet they seemed to come hard for him.

Still she was hearing them in her dream.

"O' course I ain't gonna ast you to save it. If you was needin' somebody now. But in case you was needin' when I got out . . ."

He gazed at the house as if he could see through the doorway behind her and into the flame that had kindled the hearth and then beyond it into the field where the cattle grazed and the pear trees bloomed and fish were moving deep in the pond. "I ain't got a place to reely be. . . ."

Noon had gathered his shadow close and rooted it, so still he was.

Her voice broke out of her winter sleep. "The job will be waiting when you return."

He looked at her, straight into her face. "I got no right to ast you to save it." Almost he seemed to be questioning. Or crying out. She could not tell.

She clung to the door. She wanted to meet his cry with hers: You have every right . . . But how they belonged to one another had never in all the years been said. Into the moment that held those years an egret flew to the grass nearby.

"Well, then, I reckon I'll see you, ma'am."

He said it gravely and turned away. And still she had not asked him in. She called to him, "Take care of yourself."

"Yes, ma'am," he said. "I never git nothin' wrong with me."

"I'm glad," she whispered. She watched him leave. The world was wider than she could bear. She closed her eyes against the egret taking wing and the boy gone into the morning sun. But in the twilight behind her lids a countermovement began to form. The child in the swing you have thrust away, the farther you fling him the more he returns. . . . She saw him enter again the house where now he would take his appointed place.

The Cracker Man

She rarely ever went as far as town. There were places to shop just short of it. Today, just short of the Fourth of July, by the side of the road in the dancing shade of a cottonwood tree, she saw the stand with a banner that read: FIREWORKS FOR SALE. Gloria Turner slowed to a stop and read the smaller print underneath: BIG BANGS FOR LITTLE BUCKS. The words, blown out of a painted volcano, were sailing up and out of line. Tied to the roof at either end was a cluster of sassy red balloons.

The stand itself was a sassy thing. It was sitting all alone in the field as if it owned the world in sight. She used to know who owned the field, but the stand looked nothing to do with him. She guessed the Lord didn't take an interest in stuff like this, but yet the stand was a sign to her, right in her path beside the road when it hadn't been there a week ago. She sat in the truck and looked at it while the cars passed—not many around; it was early still—and the crickets sang aloud in the grass. She liked the little pitched, shingled roof that made out like it was big enough to keep the rain off a county fair. She liked the volcano blowing up words that were orange and red. She even liked the red balloons. Kid stuff. When it happened you didn't have kids yourself, she guessed you stayed one down to the end. She guessed they could nail you down in the box with a big red sucker in your hand. Or maybe, along with a lot of things, she saw it with her grandpa's eyes, the way they'd see if they weren't wore out.

When the leaves stirred and sunlight riddled the cottonwood shade, the luminous paint swung a flash at her. It seemed like maybe the fireworks stand was planted there to flag her down. I guess this is where I was headed, she thought. . . .

* * *

Not everyone feels the way she did, but Gloria felt that her great-grandpa was a precious person handed down to be preserved. And every year that he survived added to what he was worth to the world. Like a gold coin, she guessed he was, that was dug up out of a wreck at sea that happened a thousand years ago.

Not that he was worth money to her. He hadn't a cent when he came to her, only a burial policy so old it fell apart where the creases were and its company probably had as well. But he kept it folded under his mattress as if it was worth a lot to him. And she kept him folded on top of it, folded up like the policy—much of the time he stayed in bed—as if he was worth a lot to her. As a person, he was all she had. Her mama and daddy had gone in a wreck ten miles away nine summers ago. Their will had left her the farm, the truck, and her great-grandpa.

She reckoned that if she ever got married, which now that she was thirty-three and nobody feasible in sight, it didn't seem likely she would do, but if she did she said she would have it understood that grandpa was a part of the deal. For a fact, she was mighty proud of him. She didn't know of a single soul, not anywhere in the countryside, who had a relation of any sort about to turn one hundred years.

For his birthday she might have had people in, but she didn't know any people to have. She lived way back in the countryside. The woods were on each side of her and stretched behind for miles and miles. If she asked anyone from the hardware store or the feed store or the grocery store, she doubted they would know how to behave around a person one hundred years. They might not see how special he was or what fine shape she kept him in. She kept him clean and his hair slicked down. And once a day she got him dressed. If the weather was good she slid him into the red wagon and wheeled him around the yard a spell and then she parked him under the trees. He liked that. He would sit and smile at the cottonwood leaves and wave back when they waved at him. Or if it was winter, in front of the stove he grew alert when she opened the door and poked the coal to a blaze and a pop. He raised his fist and shouted, "Charge!" or "Fire away!" and stuff like that. He had fought in a war one time, she knew, but he couldn't remember which one it was. The way he was keen on light and noise, anything that was bright and loud, it could be just they were something easy to see or hear. But she thought it had lots to do with the war. As old as he was, he might have been in more than one. The words he said were scrambled up, but she got the stuff like "Hit the dirt!" and "Shoot to kill!" She thought it was why he loved fireworks.

Because he was born on the Fourth of July, every year when his birthday came, she fixed him a cake and lemonade. She was precise about the candles, counting them twice to get it right. She lit them all. He didn't have enough breath to blow, so he just sat and watched them burn, watched them till they flickered out. And then she put in his store-bought teeth and served him a slice of cake and wax. After that, when it got dusk, she woke him up from a good doze. She lighted a sparkler for him to hold and shot him off a torpedo or two. If it happened to rain, she lit one and pitched it under the porch. He seemed to like that best of all. "Cover yer rear!" he yelled at her. "Dammit to hell, that un' was close!" The rest of the night her teeth would hurt. . . .

Now it was almost the Fourth again. This time it had to be something more. Godamighty, she said to herself, a man don't live a hundred years and nothin' get done to mark the day more than a damn torpedo or two. . . .

She slicked her hair down close to her head, then kicked up the ends with the palm of her hand. She got out and walked through the coarse stubble. The crickets were singing out in the heat. And the mown grass lay dried and sweet. She walked straight up to the stand and stopped. She didn't see a soul around. The air was still, but the tree was chattering overhead. Cottonwood leaves could find a breeze that nothing else could. They made her feel at home at once. Her grandpa loved to watch them talk. "I wish them things 'ud speak up," he said. But they couldn't shout the way she could.

Beneath the plunging roof was a counter. Nothing there but a can of paint. She leaned way over and looked inside. There on the floor was a man laid out in a red T-shirt. There were boxes around him, head to foot. She thought at first that he might be dead.

"Mister?" she said.

She saw him yawn and stretch an arm till he hit a box. He sat straight up. He smiled at her, and his eyes were a deep-down golden brown, deep down and lazy sweet, like cane syrup in the wintertime. She saw that he hadn't lived long enough to practice up on a look like that. She guessed you were maybe born with it. She guessed he hadn't hit her age. He kicked a box and stood up straight. He was medium tall and lean and mean, except for his eyes, which were lazy sweet. His hair was sand and ribboned with paper, the shreds you find in a packing box. He shook his head like a wet dog and it all came out on the counter top. He brushed it back inside the stand, as if it was something he always did and there it would be to sleep on next. He smiled again.

"You lookin' to blow up the world?" he said.

She couldn't help laughing aloud at that. She had to remind herself not to shout. "You got enough here for that?" she said.

"You'd be surprised what all I got." And the way he spoke he seemed to mean more than fireworks.

She fluffed her hair a bit with her hand.

"What can I do for you?" he said.

"Well," she said, "I guess what I really need . . ." She stopped because she had started to yell. She surprised herself, the way she talked. She was usually shy around a man, unless he sold nuts and bolts or feed, and then it was kind of an all-out war. Men who worked in a store like them didn't think a woman should step inside. "What I really need is some advice."

"I got it," he said. And again he seemed to mean more than that. She could tell his stand had nothin' on him; he was ever' bit as sassy as it.

The red balloons at the ends of the roof began to stir. They squawked a bit, they were jammed so tight. It occurred to her that she wanted to talk about lots of things, she guessed because she hadn't talked to a soul in weeks that she didn't have to shout it out. She wished she had worn her pale blue slacks.

She swung her purse to the counter top and wrapped the strap around her arm. She told him about her great-grandpa and how he was born on the Fourth of July and how she wanted a big display. "What all I can afford," she said, "bein' he's lived a hundred years." She held the hundred years to the end, just to finish it off with style.

He listened to her with his eyes fastened upon her face, as if he was counting the freckles she had. He nodded at times. The tree frogs sang aloud in the leaves or scraped their legs, whatever they did, and the crickets died of a broken heart, the way they carried on in the grass. She was all but dizzy with hearing them cry and the red balloons jumping up and down and his eyes fastened upon her face. "Am I crazy, or what?" she finished to him.

He seemed to consider it seriously. "Not in my judgment you wouldn't be. A hunderd years is a major thing. I wouldn't be in this business o' mine . . . You got to consider, the way I do, is what you doin' makin' folks glad or bustin' 'em up."

"I guess," she said.

"I put it this way: I never did handle nothin' like this they wasn't happier when I left. A whole lot happier, I could say. I kep' one kid from leavin' home when he was packed and rarin' to go."

"Kept him for good?"

"Well, he stayed the night was good enough. I got two kids in the mood to marry. I don't know if you would call that good." His eyes, still fastened upon her face, were golden brown and lazy sweet.

She looked away. "If they was old enough," she said. She fanned herself with her open hand. "It's turnin' hot a'ready," she said.

He suddenly ducked behind the counter, and then he appeared at the side of the stand with a folding chair. He brought it around to where she stood and brushed it off. His fire-red shirt was tucked into jeans. "A lady talks business is got to sit." And he leaned against the counter top as straight and slim as a rocket, it seemed, about to go off in his red shirt, if somebody struck a match to him. Two cars passed and slowed their speed, then moved on. "I don't want to take up your time," she said, but she sat down.

And he assured her, "It's good for business, folks see you settin' here purty like that." The sides of his face were acne-scarred, but all of that was behind him now. It made him old enough to trust. And she was smiling into his eyes and not any reason why she would. It was just that in the summertime the things you did were warm in the sun and easier to do than not.

She pictured herself as she looked to him—a farm girl with too much sun, brown hair that she whacked herself, too much of it to be civilized, her nose freckled. She slid her purse to cover her hands, which were freckled too.

He snaked a notebook out of his shirt and a pencil stub. He tossed the stub and caught it before it hit the ground. She could see that he had some clown in him, but she liked that. She had a speck of it in her too, bein' life was crazy as it could be, so why not be some crazy yourself?

"It's gotta be somethin' special," she said. "Real special, if you know what I mean. You got somethin' good?"

He smiled at her with his golden eyes, till she had to shift her own away. "I got it all. But it might could cost you more than you want." Again he seemed to mean something more.

"I want it to be the best thing ever in all his life."

"Like I say, I got it all. And somethin' I don't stock I can git."

The cottonwood leaves were clapping hands. Behind her a red balloon went pop. The way she jumped, it was like a torpedo under her porch. . . . He looked amused. "That a publicity stunt?" she asked.

"No way," he said with a deep-down look. "Sometimes a customer sets one off. A lady built in a certain way . . . But let me give you my business card." And he snaked one out of the pocket of his shirt.

She took it and slipped it into hers. She could feel his warmth against her breast. This is one crazy deal, she thought. The sun kept rippling through the shade, and she knew her freckles were popping out. She narrowed her eyes and looked away. "I ain't goin' into this blind," she said. "I'm a businesswoman. You tell me what you would recommend." He rolled his eyes a little for her. She had to laugh, but she sobered and said, "I got to know exactly what and how much and when."

She was sorry she had to get sharp with him. Men liked their women soft and dumb. But she was sinking some pigs in this, the fertilizer to grow their corn, the time it took to pray for rain. It cost a heap to make a pig. With a deal like this, it was just like striking a match to a hog and blowing him to kingdom come.

"Well, when is the Fourth of July, ain't it?" He opened the notebook and wrote it down. "My policy is the pay up front." He got a faraway look in his eyes. "I generally start with the basic things.

And I got to explain, the names you has heard maybe all your life, like Blue Bottle and Old Glory, I got my own names for all o' them."

"That's fine with me. I want it purty but plenty loud. You got somethin' loud he could maybe hear?"

"For racket a cherry bomb can't be beat."

"Fine," she said. "I want a lotta them. And somethin' purty up in the sky. His eyes ain't good but they still work. Especially bright and it's dark around."

He made some notes with a serious face. "You may not be familiar with this: Rockets comes in two main types. Oriental style it makes a flower up in the sky. Italian style is precisionlike, with more comin' and then some more. Unless you got a particular cravin', I'd like to give you a mix o' them. A thing o' this kind, it should be planned like plannin' a meal, a little o' this and a little o' that, to give it balance, you might say. What you want is a nourishin' combination, one'll keep you goin' till dinnertime."

"That's fine with me."

"To mention a few I would recommend: Two days' time I can git all them. . . . There's 'Love in Bloom' for color and beauty and really sweet. Recommended for anyone on in years. Carry him back to sweet sixteen and guaranteed. I could give you a honey called 'Grapes of Wrath.' Blow his hostilities off the map. All his grudges, you git my drift? Case he got some o' them stored up. Lotsa folks has but don't recall what set 'em off. I'm talkin' psychological now, but fireworks is a mix o' that and sound and light. . . . For somethin' spectacular, hard to beat, I'd definitely go with 'Watermelon Bustin' on the Way to Heaven.' Give him a thrill, I guarantee. I could furnish you with a fountain o' lights. Though maybe not. It really don't do a lot for me. It really don't have enough lift for me. . . . I generally finish off the show with 'Swing Low, Sweet Chariot' to bring 'em down. Pull the customer back to earth, all in a sweet and easy way."

"That the best you got?"

He looked at her slantwise. "O' course it ain't. You aimin' to do this all by yourself?"

"Well," she said, "I can strike a match."

"Reason I ask, the woods is dry, the trees and grass. My personal service comes with the rest. No extry charge. First come, first serve. Close to the day I git booked up. Already I got some strong requests, which I ain't said if I would or won't."

"Well," she said, "I didn't look for that. Like I say, I can strike a match."

"Ma'am, sometimes, and I don't say ever' time it is, but sometimes it can make the difference."

She looked at him from under her brows.

"You got to take into account," he said, "this is my profession. I give it study. I give it practice and dedication. Dedication is what it takes." He smiled at her.

She could get suspicious of services thrown in for free. The price was generally out of line. But she smiled back.

He held her smile till she couldn't let go. "I feel like with you and with your kin hittin' that even one hunderd mark, I want to be satisfied it's right. I done it once for an old folks' home. Somebody there hit ninety-six, but he passed out cold on Mogen David 'fore I got to fire a shot. I never done it for a hunderd before. Ma'am, it would be a privilege for me."

She held her smile, though generally privileges turned her off. "I reckon you wouldn't knock off for the privilege?"

He sobered at that. "As it is, I pare it down to the bone."

"I'm kiddin'," she said.

"Reason I ask about bein' on hand, I could see it done right without no danger o' settin' the world on fire. And then I could recommend somethin' else, if I was on hand to do it right."

"What else?" she said.

"I got a beauty that takes some handlin'. In my own judgment, it's the best there is. A rocket I'm callin' 'Stars Alive.' For color and beauty and stayin' power. Keeps explodin' till you wouldn't believe. You think the end of the world is here. I might should call it 'End of the World,' but it ain't a name that'll sell as good."

"How much?" she asked.

"Just one?" he asked. "Reason I ask, I got a special on two today."

"It's as good as you say, one is all I need."

He nodded and smiled. "Seventy, even."

She caught her breath.

The Cracker Man

"It's worth it," he said.

She turned around and looked at the sky. "Wow!" she said.

"I guarantee if his memory ain't good, here's somethin' would really stick to it. It has a tendency to wipe out ever'thing bad you done and leave you tastin' the sweet o' life."

She faced him then and laughed a bit. "It done that to you?"

He met her stare. "It done that to satisfied customers. . . . It's a question o' money, I would recommend cuttin' somethin' else and includin' this. I would likely recommend cuttin' out . . ."—he cut his eyes to the red balloons—"say, 'Passion on the Loose,' which at his age it probably wouldn't do all that much."

"Seventy dollars! For one little pop?"

He looked grieved. "What I'm tryin' to say, it's a awesome thing! You are witnessin', ma'am, the end of the world and the start of another. I never git used to seein' that one. It's like them stars keep bustin' and bustin' inside o' me. It's like I died and was born again. It's really a religious experience, ma'am. I don't mean nothin' disrespectful to God. . . . I'm tellin' it straight: It's a question o' money, I'd cut out the rest and shoot my gravel on 'Stars Alive.'"

"I don't know," she demurred. "Is it plenty loud?"

"It ain't long on loud. It's got so much else you don't miss that. But I might could give him a cherry bomb first, just at the start, to warm 'im up. Then I guarantee if he's got any eyesight left in his head, that sight will carry him clear to heaven. Had a woman once so moved by it, she wrote a will and left her belongin's to the Nazarenes. Before that experience I was able to provide, Sunday was just another day to her."

"Well . . . ," she said, "he's my only kin. I reckon you can throw it in with the rest."

He turned and bent over the counter top. She stared at his back, at his sandy hair, at the paper shreds stuck to his red shirt. He was tight and slim in his shirt and jeans. He made her think of a birthday candle, all lit and ready to blow. And when he turned around with the bill, she felt like the birthday must be his.

Am I crazy, or what? She swallowed hard. "Two eighty-five?" she said to him. Godamighty, she said to herself.

"Ma'am, I got it pared to the bone. And satisfaction is guaranteed. . . . Call me Hank. You mind I know your name?" he asked.

"It's Gloria Turner," she managed to say.

"You married, Gloria Turner?" he said.

"Not me," she said. "My great-grandpa is enough for me."

She stood up then. He gave her a look that went up and down her and back again. And she wished she had on her pale blue slacks, and then she was mad for wishing it.

"He take up all your time?" he asked.

She glanced at him with a little smile, defiant and cool because he asked. "I raise hogs for a livin'," she said.

He opened his eyes on her, gold and wide. "Now, you surprised me with that," he said. "You don't look up to handlin' a hog."

Crickets were jumping out of the grass. She stuffed the bill inside her purse. "How come?" she said.

"How come?" he said. "Well, you look like a purty little girl to me. You look like you oughta be bakin' bread."

"I do that too." She waited a bit, enjoying it, feeling the crickets strike her hand. Funny the way it was with a man. You talkin' to him, he's talkin' back, and all the time it was somethin' else you was talkin' about. . . .

And then she told him where she lived.

When she climbed in the truck she looked at his card. And wouldn't you know the thing would read, BANK ON HANK FOR FIREWORKS?

I reckon I'm doin' that, she said.

When she got home, she went straight in to her grandpa's bed. She kept it in the living room. She really hated to leave him alone, but there wasn't much else that she could do, and he was good about staying put. He could get out of bed if the house caught fire. She would always shout at him when she left: "Don't you get busted up while I'm gone. Don't you go roamin' around, you hear?" And then she gave him a little hug.

He would nod and smile. He knew his roamin' days were done.

She looked down at him. He had gone to sleep. To see him now, with his legs curled up, to someone else he wouldn't be more than a bundle of sticks. But he had been handed down to her, and she said to herself, It's up to me to keep them sticks all tied up good and just as happy as they can be . . . which is what I been workin' on today.

Since she kept his bed in the living room, she tried to give it a special look. She bought colored sheets. She put her mama's best double wedding ring quilt on top and hung the bedposts with different things, like his army cap and medals he'd won, all to make him feel at home, and still it was bound to catch the eye of somebody had a mind to call and let them know, whoever they were, that in that bed was *the* most special thing around.

"What do you feed him?" sometimes they said, as if he were nothing but one of the hogs.

"What do you feed yourself?" she replied, and her blue eyes like his own flashed scorn.

Having his bed in the middle of it meant she could really keep track of him. She could sing to him when she cooked or sewed. If he went to sleep she didn't talk. If he was awake she talked a lot and rubbed his back and slicked his hair. She could tell he liked to hear her talk, and that was good, 'cause, like it or not, she had to talk. There was just so much you could say to pigs, and then she spoke with a forked tongue, like she was trying to get friendly with them and yet she meant to do them in. When she made them happy with extra corn, they fattened into an earlier grave.

While her grandpa slept she fed the pigs. They heard her coming and started to squeal, falling over themselves in greedy glee. No matter they weighed as much as a man, they seemed like motherless children to her, crying aloud for food and care, though there was a mama sow, fat as you please, lying around and munching corn, not caring about them once they were weaned, waiting around to get bred again, not giving a damn that in two months' time Gloria was planning to slaughter them.

The week before, she'd toughen herself. Real good, real good this time. She'd dump their corn and walk away. She'd circle the truck and kick the tires and say all the cusswords she recalled. And then she'd load the pigs inside and drive them squalling down the road. . . . Afterwards she'd sit on the fence of the empty pen, empty except for the three sows and Daddy Hog asleep in the mud. Most folks took their sows to be bred, but she was plumb fond of Daddy Hog and kept him on though he ate like sin. Sooner or later she'd say to them, "You musta got used to it by now," and tell them they'd better go at it again. And then she'd walk in the corn and cry. And she couldn't tell was she crying because the pigs were gone or crying because her folks were gone or because her grandpa was getting on and sooner or later he'd be gone. Or maybe it was the whole damn thing.

She reckoned that if she ever got married and had some kids, it might not hurt to sell the pigs, knowing what all was in store for them and thinking the fatback in the greens might be coming from one of them. . . . Her grandpa was the onliest thing she didn't have to fatten and sell.

His birthday got to be two days off, and Gloria tried to tell herself that the reason she couldn't settle down was that he would hit a hundred years. (It was just another day to him. He didn't remember the cake and wax or the rumpus she raised for him each year.) Then she told herself it was all the show she was putting on, the nearly three hundred bucks of it, the way she was going out of her way, and if the pigs took sick and died, then where would she be, financial-wise? But underneath, it was more than that. She felt like she'd had a litter of pigs or like she had a case of the flu. She wanted to sit, not do a thing. And then she wanted to do it all. It made her scythe the grass in front and scrub the porch and the steps and wall.

The day came. She cleaned the house as much as she could. She did the ironing, all of it. She trimmed the plants in the windowsill. Her grandpa lay in bed and looked.

"You thinkin' how come this buzzin' around?" She went to the bed and smoothed his hair. "In a little bit I'm a-fixin' you up the purtiest you ever been."

He smiled at her and showed his gums.

She held up the shirt she had ironed for him. "We got big doin's comin' up. We gonna have you a birthday cake. On top o' that a big surprise. We got to polish you up for that."

The way she talked, it was like to a sweet and innocent child, because she reckoned if you could live a hundred years, or anywhere come close to it, what all you had done was washed clean. But she never thought of his mind as gone. It was layers and layers stretching back and full of winters and summer days. She thought of him as being wise, wiser than anyone there was. He could surprise her with things he knew, the names of birds, the names of people she'd never known, and strange wars woven in and out. He was like a book with the pages mixed and once in a while a picture page so clear it made you hold your breath. Sometimes he would forget her name and call her by her mother's name. Or he might forget just who she was, but he never forgot the smile for her. Whoever she was, she was his to love. And then she would feel in the strangest way that he was taking care of her.

She was so worked up with all ahead that she had to keep on doing things. She got the cake she had baked for him the day before and stuck it full of a hundred candles. It looked like some old porcupine, come out of the woods and ready to shoot. When he saw it coming all lit up, she guessed he'd yell at her, "Down in the trench!" the way he always had before.

She fed the hens and then the cow. It was early for them and they looked surprised. She fed the pigs, but they were always ready to eat. She fed her grandpa after that and cleaned him up where things were spilled.

She found she had to talk about Hank. There was no way she could keep from it. "A man name Hank is comin' today. It's strictly business, all it is. I'm obliged to ask him to have some cake. OK with you?"

He nodded his head.

"Strictly business is all it is. You ever knowed someun' name of Hank?"

He nodded his head. "Leg blowed off."

"Well, this un' has got both legs o' his."

"Got hisse'f kilt."

"Well, this un' Hank is plenty alive."

He shook his head. "Blowed to hell."

He was getting his pages shuffled again. She brushed his hair to a silver sheen and spread it out to cover his head and got him dressed in the ironed shirt with the red stripe that made his eyes look extra blue and his cheeks pink. His face was hardly wrinkled at all. The skin of it was tight to the bone but slackened some to cradle his eyes. They were like little birds that were fast asleep in their twin nests, and when he was happy the birds woke up and hopped about. She looked for them to sing one day. "You are one good-lookin' man," she yelled.

He smiled at her and nodded his head.

She had a red mallow in bloom by the porch. She picked a flower that was open wide and pinned it to the pocket of his shirt. "You don't no more look a hundred years . . ."

Suddenly all her juice was gone. And she was thinking he might not last to 101 and what was she going to do about that? "I got to have someun' to do for. I reckon I was just made that way. If I just had me some little kids . . . All I got is them damn little pigs and ever' summer I load 'em with corn and ever' fall I haul 'em off and maybe I end up eatin' 'em."

Then she went out and walked in the corn so her grandpa wouldn't see her cry. A hawk flew by and spooked the hens. The dog growled from under the porch, enough to announce he heard the squawk. The katydids just about drowned him out. The pigs grunted and dreamed of corn. And there she was alone in the corn with katydids and spooked hens and a dog too lame to do more than growl and pigs that couldn't do more than eat. . . . She grabbed a stalk and wiped her eyes on a tassel of silk.

Then she said, "Gloria, dry up! Just 'cause a firecracker man come by . . . you and me know"—she sometimes made herself into two, just for the sake of settling things—"you and me know he's gonna shoot them crackers and move on. . . . And what kinda kid would a cracker man make? One like him with a rovin' heart . . . and then you be back where you started from."

She went in the house and washed her face and combed her hair. Her grandpa dozed, propped up in bed. She squeezed the lemons for lemonade. She parked a lemon pulp on her nose to bleach the freckles some, she hoped. Her grandpa woke and stared at her, his blue eyes still asleep in their nests. She laughed at him. "I guess I could wear a hat in the sun. You like that better?" she yelled at him.

She fetched his teeth and put them in. "You are one good-lookin' man," she yelled. Then she slid on her pale blue slacks and a shirt to match. She switched on the fan beside his bed. "You want the radio music on?" She switched it on, then switched it off. She

The Cracker Man

wanted to hear when the cracker man came. She might have to run out and flag him down if he passed the house in among the trees. She put the money in the pocket of her slacks to pay him, like he said, up front.

It was nearly five, but it wouldn't be dark for hours yet. . . . Then she heard his truck. It rattled about as much as hers. She jumped up and ran out into the yard, but it wasn't Hank. It was somebody else who'd lost his way. It was easy to do that where she lived. And then she was scared that he just wouldn't bother to come at all. Maybe a better offer came up, more money than she could afford to pay; there wasn't a phone for twenty miles. She'd been so sure she could count on him, she hadn't laid in a sparkler, even. . . . Well, I'll have to act like a fireworks show. Yell like an Indian fulla booze, wave my flashlight in his face. . . . Bank on Hank for dirt, she said.

But fireworks wasn't the only thing. It was more that a man could let you down. She had propped the card that said BANK ON HANK in front of the sugar bowl on the stove. She tore it up. She got so mad at the way a man with tall sweet talk could let her down that when he came it took her a spell to shift her gears. But then she melted like butter in the sun.

He got out and looked her up and down. "You're a purty woman" was what he said, "with a purty name to match your face." He was wearing slacks and a purple shirt with a crimson dragon on the chest. He walked around to the bed of his truck and peered inside and thumped the tailgate really good. There was something about the way he moved that said he owned the whole damn earth. She wasn't about to challenge it.

"I'm not the birthday girl," she said.

"Gloria," he said, stroking her name. "Later on, o' course, I be callin' you that. A show o' this kind it brings folks closer than they was before."

"Well, you might as well start off with it, then."

She took him inside to show him her grandpa sitting in bed like a prince on the throne, the fan faintly stirring his silver hair, the yellow-gold sheets surrounding him, the double wedding ring quilt at his feet. She had never been prouder of him than now.

Hank looked down at him with awe. It was like two chieftains face to face. She raised her voice. "Grandpa, this here is Hank," she said.

"Leg blowed off."

She laughed a bit and lowered her voice. "I reckon he knowed some Hank in a war. His memory is sharp as a tack. I couldn't tell you the wars he fought. I reckon he probably kept us free."

She saw how they eyed each other like bulls, and neither one of them looked away. Her grandpa's two little birds in the nest woke up and stood, then never stirred. She was pleased that he could hold his own and glad that Hank could see him a man and not a thing to be throwed away. "Could I offer you a glass of elderberry wine? I serve it for birthdays, nothin' else."

"Well, Gloria," he said, "I'm obliged to you, but I never drink nothin' before a show. I feel it's important my head be clear. Besides, this happens to be a show that drinkin' don't exactly fit."

"You mean like a Sunday school picnic?" she said.

"Not exactly," he said, so she still didn't know.

She poured her grandpa the least little bit and held it so that he didn't spill. He watched them over the rim of the glass. The little bluebirds raised up and flapped. "It warms him up for the rest of the year." Then she said, "I'll get him out in the yard, and we'll have us some cake and lemonade."

She was proud of her grandpa, the way he rose to his celebration, stepping out of bed like a new-hatched biddy out of the shell. She held his arm to the edge of the porch. When she and Hank lifted him down the steps, he retracted his legs like the wheels of an airplane taking off. He seemed to know he was birthday boy and took the bother to do things right. They carried him well away from the house, away from the trees and into the field, because Hank said they didn't want anything blocking the sky, and lowered him into a plastic chair.

Hank stood back, "He don't weigh as much as one o' them rockets I got in the truck, but I reckon he's got as much lift as them."

"Lift?" she said.

"How high can he make it off the ground. It's rocket talk."

"Don't ask me what I feed him," she said.

The Cracker Man

"I figgered cake and lemonade."

She laughed aloud. Her grandpa smiled and flashed his teeth, which she kept as white as white could be. Then she brought out the porcupine cake, its hundred candles all lit up, their fires bent with a current of air.

"Wow!" said Hank and took it from her. "I reckon this thing could detonate."

Her grandpa's eyes lit up and danced. She explained that he hadn't the breath to blow. "Anyway, he likes to see it burn." So they stood beside him and watched it burn. The wax ran off in a scarlet stream like lava on its way to the sea. They shouted a birthday song for him. When the cake was out and the smoke cleared, Gloria fed them cake and wax. "It makes it kinda chewy," she said. "I reckon a touch of barbecue."

Hank chewed and swallowed. "This cake has got a lotta lift."

Then she poured them lemonade. The whole thing had a family feel. The sitting around and sipping and chewing, watching the sun grow dim and sink. "It's all the dust in the air," Hank said. "Dry all over. Clouds the sun."

Gloria acted surprised to hear. Her mama had taught her when she was a kid that you had to go along with a man. As long as it was talk was all. When it come to doin', you thought again. Her grandpa flipped into a doze. "He always does that," she explained. "I think it's the wax that knocks him out. I'll wake him up when you're ready to blow."

She took the money out of her slacks and handed it over, like he had said.

He nodded and put it into his shirt. "I don't need to tell you it's guaranteed. Anything fizzles you get it back."

The dog yipped and scratched his fleas. They could hear him complaining under the porch. The hot day was cooling off. The tree frogs were tuning up. Her grandpa drifted into a snore, a gentle bass to the tenor of frogs. And everything was slow as could be, but she felt that time was running away. She wanted to hold it where it was . . . between the cake and the fireworks. Just in the quiet middle of things you chewed your wax before the end.

He looked around with his lazy eyes at the house and trees, at the pigs nearby and their farrowing house sitting homey under a sycamore tree. . . . "Gloria," he said, polite as could be and businesslike, "this place has got a lotta lift."

The sun had gone behind the trees and a lavender haze spread over the field. He said, "I'm obliged for the cake and all, but I got to set up while the light's still good."

She sat and watched in a summer daze while he set it up. His purple shirt was blended with dusk, but the dragon had a crimson glow. Some kind of paint that made it glow. And all of it, the setting up, the dragon's glow, eating her cake, the birthday song, was strictly business to him, she knew. . . . It was she who had lived a hundred years and nothing to show, nothing to show. . . .

"You reckon you should wake him up?" He had a flashlight in his hand. She saw it was dark enough for that.

"Sure," she said, coming out of her daze, and she woke her grandpa up for the fun.

"I'm aimin' away from the woods," said Hank. "Things is dry."

She pulled her chair beside her grandpa and held his hand. "Happy Birthday!" she yelled at him.

First came a volley of cherry bombs. She could feel the pleasure run through his hand. Then came a rocket that shot from the earth and burst into a shower of blooms that seemed to grow the higher they went, bigger and pinker until they met in a single flower, like a giant mallow covering them. Like a red umbrella opened up and through it you could see the sun. The sun at noon with a sunset glow. She couldn't take her eyes from it but felt the field around her burn. And then the flower sank to her, sank until she was drunk with it and almost cried when it went away. She guessed it must be "Love in Bloom," the way it peeled her years away. . . .

Her grandpa was throwing back his head. "I want to lay down," she heard him say.

At first she thought he'd had enough. Then she saw that he wanted to lie on the ground to drink his fill of all to come. "Hold it, Hank!" She ran to the house and grabbed up the double wedding ring quilt. What was it for if not for this? She got him settled laid out flat. She sat beside him on the ground.

Two cherry bombs then rocked the earth and shook her teeth. She feared that he would choke on his, so she took them out and slipped them into the pocket of his shirt beneath the mallow blooming there, while blue star showers were raining down all around like waterfalls.

A whistle came and all was night, till a tail of silver beat the sky, swish, swish, this way and that, then burst in clusters of purple and gold.... A vast explosion of red in the sky. A ball of red blown into shreds, the shreds to bits. The watermelon bust it had to be.

Her grandpa yelled it: "Down in the trench!"

A rocket swooshed to kingdom come. She thought it must have fizzled out, when shining crystals of light appeared, scattered by hands she couldn't see, diamonds of light that were flung to heaven, then fell like snow, were banked in clouds. The snowfall melted and spilled in streams, and a blue light came whizzing down to pin them both against the earth. "Godamighty," Gloria said.

Her grandpa drew his knees to his chest, like he was waiting there to be born. And she could see Hank out in front, all lit up in the blue light. A cherry bomb blew off again. "Over the top!" her grandpa yelled. Another cherry bomb blew off. "Fire, dammit!" her grandpa yelled. The dog barked from under the porch. The pigs in the pen were going wild, like a dozen possums had got inside.

Then all of a sudden out of the sky came red and purple balls of flame. They met and burst into glorious light, flickering like lightning sheets. It had to be "Passion on the Loose." Don't ask her how she knew. She knew. The cow was bellowing like a bull. The rooster thought that day had come. The pigs thought it was slaughter time and ran into the wooden fence. She heard it creak and creak again. She didn't think it could take much more. "Grandpa?" she said and leaned to him. His eyes had started to sing at last.

She lay on the ground and closed her own and dreamed she had her some little kids . . . five or six of them, maybe more.

"Grandpa! How you holdin' up?" She yelled it out and turned to him. She saw the ecstasy in his face.

"How many more?" she called to Hank.

"Two," he called. "You had enough?"

"I want my money's worth," she said. She lay back down and waited for him. She was really glad of the small delay. And then it came, his "Stars Alive." It was exactly like he said. The end of the world and the start of one, coming and coming, coming again . . . till a million stars had filled the sky. They burst into a million more. It was like her world had disappeared and nothing was left but the one up there. She heard the pigs all hit the fence. She heard it crash and she didn't care. She could only think, and know for sure, I'm glad I lived to see this day.

Suddenly Hank had her by the hand and pulled her up while the stars went on. He whooped it up into the sky: "This one really turns me on!" He grabbed her and kissed her hard on the mouth. She almost fell, but he held her up. Stars burst inside her like he said. She felt as beautiful as the stars. The crimson dragon burned her breast.

When he let her go she fell to her knees. And by the light of the final stars she leaned and saw her grandpa's face. He had a look of the purest joy. "Grandpa," she said, "did you like it some?"

But he wouldn't say.

Hank stood by. "I reckon he's stunned. I seen it happen all the time. Folks got nothin' to say for a spell. Words just ain't got lift enough."

"He sure looks happy enough," she said.

"It beats preachin' for gittin' folks high. And quicker than likker, I guarantee." She could tell that Hank was all revved up. She liked a man that could get revved up without some likker or beer inside. "Him bein' that way is why I like to finish off with 'Swing Low, Sweet Chariot.' It'll kinda bring him back to earth. That 'Stars Alive' is got such lift—I'm speakin' psychological now—it gits folks up and they can't git down. This un' here is sweet and low. Like bein' rocked in your mother's arms. Like maybe you never done nothin' wrong."

He shot it off and it did what he said, went sweet and low. It floated up and floated down. It was made of cloud with a heart of gold. It swung a little over the trees and drifted swinging toward the house, drifted, swinging its hips a bit, and settled gently on her roof. . . . "Grandpa," she said, "the shootin's done."

The look of joy didn't leave his face. She thought that maybe he'd gone to sleep. Hank swung his flashlight over him. The mallow bloom was on his chest, riding high on the teeth below where

Gloria had stationed them. A little pollen was on his cheek. And still there was his look of joy.

Hank dropped to his knees and laid his head upon the chest. He kept it there for a long spell. He stood up and brushed off his knees. "Ma'am," he said, and she was thinking, How come I'm all of a sudden 'ma'am'? "I hate to say it . . . but I think he's gone."

"Gone?" she said and fell to stroking her grandpa's face. "What do you mean? He got so happy he just ain't come back down again."

And Hank was saying, "I swear to God, it never kilt nobody before."

She sat back. "He'll come around."

"No, ma'am, I don't think so."

She struck out, "Don't call me 'ma'am.' What kinda talk is that to me? It scares me stiff you sayin' 'ma'am.' Like some kinda doctor know for sure. Call me 'Gloria.' That's my name."

She hid her face.

He dropped to his knees and took her arm. "I reckon the excitement got his heart. Him bein' a hunderd years and all, he wasn't good for a hunderd more."

"He was!" she said. "I know he was! I mean he is, 'cause he ain't gone!"

All of a sudden the roof flared up. It must have been burning while they talked. Just as quickly the house flared up, and through the windows they saw the flame. And then the flame leaned out the door and went back in and leaned again, like it couldn't make up its mind to stay. And then it leaned from a window and waved.

They sat still and watched it burn without a word, like it was just a part of the show. He locked his arm around her neck. The roof fell in, the timbers buckled. The house popped and popped and glowed. Flaring bits went sailing high and sweetly burned and sank to earth. They nestled into the bed of the truck, which Gloria had parked by the house. They gentled the cab and nuzzled the hood, till it all blew up in a red-gold flame with streaks of blue and a thunder clap that shook the earth. One of the tires went sailing up in a ring of fire. And Gloria knew her house was gone and her truck was gone, but still it seemed a part of the show.

And Hank was saying, "I swear to God it never burnt down no house before."

She was too stunned for words or thought. He shook her gently. She looked at him with eyes of stone. "My grandpa gone and my house burnt down?"

"I know it's hard to take," he said.

"My pigs is gone. I heard 'em go."

"Ma'am, I know it's hard to take."

"Don't call me 'ma'am.'"

"I won't," he said. He jerked his T-shirt free of his jeans and mopped his face. The air was hot as a barbecue. "I got to say it, he died happy. That's a real good thing. . . . I know your house and even your truck ain't nothin' put along side o' him, but it look to me like they went happy. Purtier 'n any rocket I got." He stroked her arm. "I know them pigs ain't nothin', neither, 'long side o' him, but it seem like when they busted out they busted happy."

Far back in the woods the hound dog gave a lonely howl. There drifted the smell of burning rubber, but a breeze came and took it away. And Gloria couldn't think a thing except be glad it was cooling some.

The house before them was cracking up, going black and blacker still and blending softly into night. The afterglow was caught in the sky. The rosy smoke came drifting over them like a cloud. It gently flushed the old man's face, joyous still but relaxed, at peace, the twin bluebirds asleep in the nest.

She sobbed aloud. "He don't no more look a hundred years."

"He don't," he said. "He had some lift right up to where he went out happy."

"What about livin' happy?" she said.

"He done that too. You die that happy, it takes some backup to go out happy."

The wood-burn smell was in her throat. It was very strange how going down in a sea of trouble she struck the tiniest floating raft. She climbed up on it and sat surrounded by all her life. She saw herself losing all her folks. She saw herself killing years of pigs. "What about livin' happy?" she said.

"I reckon I'm gonna go after them pigs. I got my flashlight aimed to go. . . ." But he didn't move. "It might be best when daylight

The Cracker Man

come. It's hard to corner a pig at night." Then he was talking low to himself: "I wish to God I could pack tonight inside a rocket and blow the damn thing up in the sky."

She stared at the A-frame farrowing house, which stood inside the empty pen. "I reckon I could move in there. Folks been livin' there just move out."

"Ma'am, I'm gonna git you back your pigs. I think I can lay you money on that."

"How come you callin' me 'ma'am'?" she said.

"It's just that we had us a business deal and I aim to settle that end of it."

"Well, business is over, can't you see! You think them pigs is gonna make me happy?"

"It's a start," he said. "It's a real good start.... I'll scout around." But he did not move. He looked at her, at her face staring into the farrowing house. "You got some kinfolks could take you in?"

She shook her head. "That's all my kinfolks a-layin' there."

"You got some insurance on that house?"

She shook her head.

"You got any money?"

She turned to him. "I shot it all on the Fourth of July. I was aimin' to sell my pigs for more."

He laid his flashlight on the quilt. It shot a beam across the field. "Well," he said, "the least I can do is refund what I charge for 'Stars Alive.' My policy is I don't unless it fizzles out, and this un' shore didn't fizzle out. But since it kilt all the kin you got . . ." He peeled off bills and laid them on the quilt between. He thought for a while. "I reckon it's fair you don't git charge for the last un' burnt your house to the ground. The roof it musta been extry dry." He carefully counted her out some more. "Oh, hell!" he said. "You can have it all."

She took it, wondering. "You reckon this money gonna make me happy?"

"It's a start," he said.

The tree frogs started up again like the end of the world hadn't come for her. "How'm I gonna make you understand that he was takin' care o' *me?*"

He looked around. "I reckon I could tear down my stand and set it up here somewheres about. . . . I reckon I done it a hunderd time. I'm gittin' real tired o' doin' that, tearin' it down, settin' it up. It gits to be a tedious thing. I reckon I'd do it one more time. It'll sleep one of us laid out flat."

She didn't have time for all his words, yet time was just about all was left. "How'm I gonna make you understand that he was takin' care o' *me?* He was in charge o' my life, see? A freckle-face woman is all is left, and the total thing she got in the world is her mama's double wedding ring quilt."

He checked that it wasn't under his foot. "It's a start," he said.

She tried to rise, but her legs didn't work and she sat back down. "I been so busy keepin' him happy I never had space for was I happy."

He stared at what was left of the house. "There just might be enough o' them timbers left unburnt I could stretch it out to room for two."

She couldn't tell was she hearing it straight. "You talkin' about your fireworks stand?"

He took her hand. "I ain't claimin' for it a lotta lift."

"You reckon that stand gonna make me happy?"

"It's a start," he said.

Then the whole thing hit, like a barrel of cherry bombs gone off, that the world was more than she could bear. "I just can't handle it no more. I gotta have someun' to *do* for. If I just had me some little kids . . ."

She didn't think she had said it out, but she must have done.

"Well, you gotta start someplace," he said.

"What does that mean?" she shouted at him. Maybe because she was used to yelling and it was easier to do than not. Maybe because she had to know what her life was all about.

Out in the field, a rabbit jumped over the flashlight beam, as if it was scared of a little light.

"It means I ain't takin' off," he yelled.

Raisin Faces

There were nights when she had a hummingbird sleep, as she hovered above the bloom of oblivion, dipping a moment to suck its sweetness, then hover again. But there were the nights, black holes of Calcutta, from which she emerged with a weight on her chest, her limbs in chains, and a weariness that was deep in the bone, as if she had labored the livelong night. After such nights she would sit in her chair in the breakfast nook, still a bit in chains, her mind a blank, and let the sun creep over her hands, and slowly she would begin to think, pushing her mind like a grocery cart from one thing to another thing, gradually filling it up with the children, the long afternoons they had spent in the park, the beach, the sand, and the flash of waves . . . till she had a paper sack full of things to feed upon for another day. When this was done, she removed the blue plate from the bowl of cereal Hattie had poured her the night before. She rummaged around with her finger for raisins and ate them slowly, one by one, remembering the water, the children, the sand. Till Hattie came in and found her there and exclaimed, "Miss Coralee, honey, how come you eatin' that dry old stuff?" And then she would carefully drown it in milk. Hattie came smelling of scouring powder and ever so faintly of bacon and corn. During the day it would all wear off. Or Coralee got used to it.

"Hattie, you ate up my raisins again." And the two would have them a wonderful laugh. There was nothing better than Hattie's laugh. It was gingerbread-colored like herself and full of spice, all kinds of it. And she would say, "I must of forgot to shake up that box. They sinks to the bottom, they bad about that." Then she would get down the box of raisins and shake a handful into the bowl, and she would say, "You the raisin-eatin'est woman I know." And she would add, "They good for you. They full of iron, how come they black. They put the stiffenin' in your bones."

To encourage Miss Coralee to eat, she would pour herself a handful of raisins and eat them thoughtfully, one by one. And the two of them would remember the children. Hattie had never known them, of course. She had come to work eight years ago. But she knew everything that Coralee knew, even things Coralee had plain forgot. Often she said she dreamt of the children. Sometimes in her dream she was struggling against the undertow and snatching Billy by the tail of his shirt and knocking the water out of his lungs. For it was she who had saved the child and not some stranger who happened along. "He was a chil' you got to watch out for ever' minute."

"Yes, he was," said Coralee, shaking her head, "but bright as a button, that he was."

"Bright as a shiny blue button," said Hattie.

"You remember the way he would screw up his face when somebody cornered him and kissed his cheek?"

"Sure do," said Hattie. "He was a sight."

"He got away from us once, you know. We were headed somewhere . . ." She stopped and puzzled. "You remember where we were headed, Hattie?"

"You was headed for Mississippi that time. To see your cousin lived in the Delta."

"That's right, we were. We certainly were. We had a wonderful time that year. The whole long trip was one big picnic. . . . Do you think we could have a picnic today?" As soon as she said it she knew they would. The weariness went out of her bones. She was full of glistening leaves and sky. The children were running beneath the trees. But she waited for Hattie:

"Don't see why not. Ain't fixin' to rain. What kind a san'wich you got in min'?"

"Any kind as long as you fix it with olives. But I want it to be a surprise."

"Well, it ain't that time. I got to straighten up. You be all right settin' here till I through."

Then she brought the album with all the pictures and found the ones of the Delta trip. She opened it beside the cereal bowl. "You set here and study it while I finish up."

Coralee would turn the pages, savoring each, while Hattie, moving from room to room, would sing to herself snatches of song she had learned in church. She made heaven sound like a happy land with a life as happy as life with the children pages ago. When Hattie came close, Coralee would say, "You remember Mindy's first bathing suit? She wanted to sleep in it all night long."

"Sure do. It was pink, real pink. And when it got wet it turn plum' red."

"Wasn't she funny outrunnin' the waves?"

"And all a time shriekin' fit to kill. . . . It's like I birth them chirren myself."

Coralee sighed. "Where did they go?"

"Where did who go?" And when Coralee didn't answer, she said, "Your chirren growed up, that's the trufe of it. Ain't even move off and lef' you, now, like mos' chirren takes a min' to do. I reckon they prob'ly comin' by today." She brushed up the crumbs at Coralee's feet. "My baby lef'. But not for good. One day I looks up and he be there. He stay long enough to git what he want. And then no tellin' how long it be."

"Hattie, my babies left for good."

"Now, who you think come by las' week? Got the same name. Talked like he growed up here to me."

"The ones comin' by are not the same."

Hattie shook her head. "I better he'p you on with your clothes. Case they takes a notion to see 'bout you."

"I don't want to wear that dress with the jelly."

"That jelly dress done put in the wash. I gone find me somep'n bright for you. Summer done got here all the way."

And Coralee thought, Is it summertime? Summer was children and happy time, the world of water and sun and sand. Summer had waited for Hattie to say it.

In the late afternoon Mindy came by. "Knock, knock," she said, bursting into the hall, not knocking at all. Coralee was sitting in the living room. She had gone to sleep over television plays and didn't wake up when they went off the air. Mindy switched the damn thing off. She wandered around the house for a bit, as she always did whenever she came. She skimmed the mantel with her pink-nailed fingers. Her hands were plump. "I'm checkin' on Hattie," she said when asked. "Hattie, I'm checkin' up on you," she called aloud in a jolly voice.

"Yes, ma'am, I know you checkin' on me. You have a nice trip?"

"Oh, that was over a month ago."

"Yes, ma'am, but we ain't seen you since."

Mindy was large, with lively hair. Gold with a rapturous streak of white that swept her brow and was up and away, her sole concession to middle age. Coralee watched her, half asleep, as if she were peering at a curious fish inside a tank. Mindy stayed awhile in the dining room, opening drawers and cabinet doors, slamming them shut. Coralee watched her and wished her gone. Whoever she was, she had no business rummaging around. Coralee hadn't let her own children play in the dining room. Mindy called Penny up on the phone in the hall and said she had something to talk about. "Well, pretty soon. I'm leavin' now."

"Mama, be good," she said as she left. But Coralee was dozing again.

"What did she want?" said Coralee, startled out of her sleep when the front door shut.

"Nothin' much. Jus' checkin' on us."

"I wish she'd tell me what she wants."

Then Hattie brought her an early supper. She stuffed some pillows at Coralee's back and rested the tray on the arms of the chair and stayed with her in case she spilled.

"Eat somethin', Hattie," said Coralee. "You know I do better when you eat along."

"Well, maybe I sip some coffee," said Hattie. "But I got to feed my baby at home."

"Is he here for long?"

"No tellin'," said Hattie. The skin beneath her eyes went dark. Her eyes grew older than thirty-eight.

"My children are gone," said Coralee. "But they were a pleasure for many years. I think of Penny and how she hated to have her food cut up for her. She wanted to cut it up herself. The fuss she made! You remember that?"

"She'd snatch the knife right out'n your hand. Try to grow up fast. Like to cut herself."

"Oh, my! I remember that. She was such a lively child. We have a picture of Fourth of July and barbecue all over her face."

"You want me to find it?"

"Let's have a look. I forget just who she was sittin' next to."

"She was settin' nex' to her Uncle Dave. But you can study it while you eat."

She got the album and found the place. And Coralee ate and sipped her tea, while Hattie fed her bits of the past. The children were with them and nourished her.

The next day Penny came with Mindy, and the two of them went through her things, through all her closets without asking her. They even pulled down the attic stairs, and Mindy climbed while the rungs cried out beneath her weight. Penny stood at the foot and called, "My girdle says I'm stayin' here," and Mindy replied in a voice too muffled for them to hear.

They had left the front door wide to summer and filled the house with air still chilly to Coralee. They said the house needed airing out. The ceiling creaked. The woman in the attic sounded like a squirrel got in from the roof, but bigger than that.

"What do they want?" asked Coralee.

Hattie muttered grimly, "They ain't said yet." She seemed to feel the chill herself. Her hand shook dusting a china doll.

They stared at Penny out in the hall with her high heels and her slender form in a yellow silk and her short brown hair in a stylish cut. She was like a girl high-strung with youth till she turned around. A torpor was in her olive face, which looked like something stored away. Coralee one time had said in a wondering voice, "She doesn't look familiar to me." And Hattie replied, "I reckon a doctor done made that face." But a doctor had never made her voice, which was deep and vacant, to match her face. It tended to wander away from thought.

They went away. Hattie swept the hall of the attic dust and swept their footprints off the porch. "How 'bout a picnic, Miss Coralee? It warmin' up outside real good. You rather have music on the stereo? Them songs you was singin' that time you was all campin' out at the lake."

"Why don't we have both?" said Coralee. She was past the age when you had to choose. Hattie understood and gave her choices, then gave her both.

But Mindy and Penny struck next day. They had Billy with them out of the bank. Hattie went to the kitchen and shut the door, but they sent her off to the store for food. They opened windows to let in air. Coralee couldn't think who they were or why they were always coming by. Whenever they came they made her cold. She pulled her sweater across her chest.

Mindy came right down to the point. "Mama, we've got a situation here. You're fond of Hattie. She's good to you. On the surface she is, but she's stealin' you blind behind your back."

Coralee heard the words like so many stones that were dropped on her.

"Mama, your silver is just about gone. Now, where did it go? Did you put it somewhere and then forget? I don't think you're able to carry that stuff. You don't see well, and Hattie's been stealin' it from under your nose."

Coralee was staring into their faces, trying to think what right they had to accuse her of stealing. For it seemed they were accusing her. She said at last with dignity, "Why would I want to take my own silver?"

"Not you, Mama! Hattie's been takin' it, robbin' us all."

"Robbin' you?"

"Mama, that silver goes to me and Penny after you're gone. Grandmother told us before she died."

"I never heard that."

"Well, she said so, Mama. You just forgot. She's robbin' us all. Billy says it must be reported and we go from there."

"The police," said Billy. He was short and stout, with minimal hair, but sideburns the color of weathered granite came to a point like inverted tombstones framing his face. Coralee thought they looked pasted on. There was something about him she didn't trust. "The thing is, Mama, we could get it back if she hasn't done something untraceable with it. And that may be. It well may be. We'll have to dismiss her in any event. That works a hardship on all of us. We'll take turns staying here with you until we can find somebody else."

She listened, dumbfounded. "I don't want somebody else."
They said at once, "You don't have a choice."
She was thinking in the depths of her bewildered mind that Hattie always gave her a choice.
Mindy said in a placating voice, "Wouldn't you like to have your children come stay with you for a little while?"
She looked at them, at their stranger faces. "No," she said.
Their faces tightened and then relaxed. "You don't mean that, Mama."
Her mind grew dappled with flecks of fear. "You can't take Hattie. She's all I have."
"Nonsense, Mama. She's just a maid, and we'll get another."
"I don't care what she did. If she did anything."
"But we care, Mama," Penny broke in.
"She has broken the law," Billy said with decision.
She was almost in tears. "It's not a law if it isn't stolen."
"You're not being rational," Penny said.
And Mindy said, "Where is it, then? Where has it gone?"
She closed her eyes to shut them out. "I put it away. I can't remember."
"Where?" Penny said. In her deep, vacant voice the word was like God's.
"We have searched the house. Tell us where," said Mindy.
"I can't remember." They had her at bay. She began to cry.
They circled the room. They walked to the window and bunched together like a flock of birds. Their thin legs waded knee-deep in sun. "Here she comes," they said. "Comin' up the walk. Why doesn't she ever use the back?" They turned to Coralee. "Mama, we'll give you till tomorrow to remember. And if you can't, then she'll have to go. Mama, don't tell her why we came. Don't tell her, Mama."
They went away.
Hattie laid the groceries on the kitchen table. Then she put them away. Coralee, weeping, could hear her stashing them on the shelves. She could hear milk sliding to the coldest part of the refrigerator. She could hear water running into the kettle. She was trembling all over and willing herself to have taken the silver and put it somewhere that she couldn't recall. She was willing herself to recall

where it was, to recall long enough to tell Hattie where. She was saying, Please, God, let me be the one did it. I want to be the one, please, God, please, God.

By the time Hattie came with their cups of tea, God had let her be the one.

Hattie looked at her hard. "Miss Coralee, honey, them chirren o' yours done made you cry?"

Coralee sobbed aloud.

"Honey . . . honey . . . don't you fret none about 'em. They done gone down the drive and outa your sight." She drew up a chair and stroked Coralee's arm. "Sometimes chirren can aggravate you so you got to let it out. My baby can git me so mad at him."

"These people don't seem like my children to me. The things they say. They don't like me, Hattie."

"Honey, it jus' the way chirren can be."

Coralee took the tea and drank a little. It made her feel better and even more sure she had taken the silver and put it somewhere and then forgot. She grew almost happy to think how her memory had played her a trick. "Hattie, I know you'd rather have coffee. You don't have to drink the tea for me."

"I likes 'em bofe. And it don't seem right to be drinkin' different. My husband was aroun', I took to drinkin' whatever he said. Exceptin' his likker. I didn't like that."

"You think he's ever comin' back to you, Hattie?"

"No'm, I don't. He gone for good."

Coralee sighed and sipped her tea. It seemed to her that a darkness waited. She thought it had something to do with the silver. Maybe she wouldn't be able to recall. But she wouldn't try to remember yet. "I get to thinkin' they can't be the same. They look so different."

"Your growed-up chirren? They the same, all right."

"Penny was sweet with her little curls. For the longest time she didn't know how to give you a kiss. She would just touch her little tongue to your face. . . . They can't be the same."

"They *is* the same. Ever'thing that be gonna change someday. Some way."

"Change to worse, you mean?"

"Ain't for me to say."

"Look at *me*," said Coralee. "I couldn't be worse than I am today. They say I can't manage by myself. I guess I can't."

"You a fine, upstandin' woman," said Hattie. "Your mem'ry ain't good, but it could be worse. And mostly what all you disremember ain't worth the trouble to call it to mind."

"I could get it back if I tried hard enough."

"Sure you could. But it ain't worth the trouble. It mostly trash."

Coralee's hand with the teacup shook. Hattie took the cup. "Hattie, you got to help me remember what I did with the silver. They want to know."

Hattie got up and took away the cups. Coralee could hear her rinsing them out. When the water stopped running, "Hattie," she called, "you gotta help me remember."

"Right now I gotta fix your dinner. Then I goin' home. But I fix you up for bed 'fore then."

Coralee was frightened. When she tried to think she came to a wall that stopped her mind. "Don't leave me," she said, "not knowin' what to say when they come tomorrow."

Hattie came then and stood in the doorway. Her face was dark. "You tellin' me you done took your own silver and put it somewhere and cain't recollec'?"

"Yes, yes. But I don't know where. If you could look in some of my things . . ."

"I he'p you tomorrow. Soon's I come."

"But they're comin' tomorrow. They said . . . they said . . . if I can't remember they know it's you."

Hattie put a strong, firm hand on the door. "I seed it comin'. They 'cusin' me?"

"If I can't remember . . ." She began to cry. "I got nobody but only you."

Hattie's voice was cold. "You got them chirren that 'cusin' me."

"No, I don't. The children I had are lost and gone."

"Jesus, I wisht I could be like you and see my chil' as someun' different what he was long time ago. I know he be the same one chil'. All that time he stay so sweet, this troublesome was growin' there. No way, no way to weed it out. Sweet and troublesome. Sweet and bad."

Coralee was struck with fear. "I want to go to bed," she said.

"You ain't the onliest one want that. Pull the cover up over my head and when I wake it all be gone. . . . I took it," she said, "to keep my baby outa jail. He owed a man gon' git him put in jail for good. And now they gonna git me first. Serve him right he got no mama come runnin' to, keep him outa the trouble he make. 'Cause this trouble ain't gon' be his last."

Coralee pled, "If you brought it back . . ."

"It gone already. My baby done sold it off for cash. He stole some money had to pay it back."

Coralee cried, "I'd a give you money. All you had to do was ask."

"Miss Coralee, I couldn't take your money. Them chirren o' yourn don't give you hardly enough to count. But you never looked at them silver things. I thought you'd never come lookin' for them."

"I didn't. I wouldn't. I never cared about things like that. Those people who came here said it's theirs. . . . I don't know. I can't think."

She rocked in despair, the rocker creaking, leaving the rug, slapping the floor till Hattie grimly pulled her back. "Don't git nowheres a-travelin' in that." Her face was darker than ever now. "I bes' clear out and head on home."

"Hattie . . . I'm gonna call that lawyer. He made me a will long time ago. What is his name? Started with *B*."

"Don't know nothin' 'bout no lawyer."

"He made me a will long time ago." Coralee rocked with her eyes closed, and the tears seeped from under the lids. "Get the telephone book and read . . . read the names till I say to stop. Look up lawyers and read the names. Just keep on till I say to stop. . . ."

Mr. Barnhill said he was much too busy and couldn't come. It was out of the question. Not today.

"Then come tonight. You have to come before tomorrow."

"My, my," he said, and was she sure it couldn't wait? At last he agreed to come at four. "I hope you have a good-sized piece of that gingerbread left." And he had himself a good-sized chuckle, because it had been some twenty years. Lately his memory had sprung a leak, and he was pleased to recall details.

"Fix me a cup of coffee, Hattie, and make it double, double strong." While she sipped she was trying to find her mind, where she had dropped it along the way. Beneath her breath she recited the multiplication tables—the twos, the threes. She found she couldn't finish the fours. The fives had wholly disappeared. She tried to name the capital cities, but they had gone with the tables she'd lost. She wept for them. I used to think straight. What happened? she asked. She recited the Twenty-third Psalm aloud. She whispered the rhymes the children had loved.

"Bring the children, Hattie," she said.

And Hattie, looming like doom in the doorway, laid the album in her lap. "What good they gon' do us now? You rummage aroun' and pickin' 'em outa the book like raisins. Raisin faces is all they is."

"I remember things when I'm with them. I touch their faces and think of things."

"Things done happen long time ago ain't gonna he'p us none today."

Coralee drank the bitter brew. "I let my mind get away from me."

When Barnhill came—he was running late—she didn't know him, he had changed so much. He seemed too old, no match for the people she had to fight. And had to beat. She peered from her chair with anxious doubt at his bushy white brows, at his pink cheeks as pink as a brick, his creamy moustache like a piece of pulled taffy scissored off. He hadn't had any of this before. Even his voice had a sandiness that sounded old. She was afraid he was as old as she, and if he was, then he wouldn't win.

He patted her shoulder in a knowing way and, sitting before her, fixed her with an indulgent eye. "Now, what can I do for you?" he said.

She was conscious of Hattie harbored in the kitchen, sounding each word for a prison ring. "Did you make me a will?" she asked in a voice as firm as she could make it sound, just to be sure he was the same.

"Miss Coralee, I made you an excellent will. I reckon it was twenty years ago."

"Did I sign it?" she asked, for something to say.
"Of course you did. And got it witnessed. All of that."
She gazed into space. "I want it changed."
He pulled his watch chain, slid his thumb and finger down it, dropped his eyes. "I wouldn't think there'd be a need."
"People change their wills. I want it changed." Then as he made her no reply, "The telephone book is full of people who can change a will. All it takes is run my finger down the page and stop when I come to the best in town. I want it changed and changed today."
He smiled at her. "Well, now." he said. "I see it's a matter of some concern. . . . You tell me how you want it changed."
She pulled her sweater over her chest. "I have this maid who looks after me."
He inclined his head. "I believe you have children in town," he said. "Perhaps they should . . ."
"I don't have anyone but her."
"Surely . . . ," he said.
But she hurried on. "She took some silver to sell for me. I didn't have any use for it. I never have company in to eat. Most of my friends have moved away. Some have died. . . ."
He listened to her with his bushy eyebrows slightly raised and his fingers touching across his vest.
"Certain people . . . have got the notion she sold the silver without askin' me."
"I see," he said with a knowing nod, and he seemed to be looking at rows of cases, similar ones.
"They want to make trouble. . . ."
"Prosecute?" he said. "On your behalf?"
She grew confused. "Make trouble," she said. Her hands were shaking. "I thought if you would change my will and let it say I leave it to her . . ."
He interrupted. "That wouldn't do." He seemed to consider. "If she broke the law . . . if she took the silver when she shouldn't have, and that would be easy to prove, you know, then willing it now wouldn't make it right with the law, you see. . . . A lot of silver? What value?" he asked.
Her mouth was dry. "I don't recall."
"You don't recall what you told her to sell?"

She shook her head. Her mind was beginning to slip away. Into the threes and then the fours.... She began to tremble. "I just don't want any trouble," she said. "Please, no trouble. I just don't want her taken away." Her voice choked. "I can get the money to pay your bill." And then she was thinking how little she had, and how did she know what it would take.

"Well, well," he said. It was plain to see he had counseled a thousand old ladies before and knew at what point they began to cry and knew at what point he would say, "Well, well." He drew out his watch and studied it. "This watch belonged to my father," he said. "Haven't had it worked on in twenty years. Wonderful the way they made them then." He put it back and fingered the chain. "Miss Coralee, I see you've got strong feelings here. There *is* a little something we could do. It might be a little ... but in this case ... You could sign a deed of gift dated back to a time before she took the silver. It would mean you had already given it to her. So who is to say what she does with it?"

She couldn't help crying with joy and relief. "Can I sign it now?" she said through tears.

"Hold on," he laughed. "I have to draw it up, you know."

"I'll have to have it before tomorrow."

"Well, what if I send my girl from the office around real early? You can sign it then. She can witness it."

He stood up then and patted her shoulder. "You dry your eyes. It's gonna be fine." At the door he added, "I hope she's grateful to you for this." And then he let himself out the door.

"Hattie," she called with joy in her voice, "did you hear what he said? He's goin' to make it all right for us." When Hattie came toward her across the room, it was as if she had lost and found her all at once. She hadn't ever seen her before, not really seen how fine she was, tall enough for the highest shelf, her skin the color of fresh-brewed tea and her gingerbread laugh that was full of spice.

"Miss Coralee, honey, you done so good. You spoke right up to that lawyer man."

"I did, didn't I, Hattie?" she said.

But it wasn't going to be right at all. The girl from the office never came. Coralee sat before her cereal. The raisins in it were hateful to her. When Hattie arrived, she was full of tears. "Did you call that office place?" asked Hattie.

Coralee had never once thought of that. "Hattie, you dial." He had seemed too old to remember things. She tried to recall the things that were said the day before. She only recalled it would be all right.

But the line was busy and busy again. When Mr. Barnhill was finally there, he said, "Good morning, Miss Coralee. Well, well. I've given it thought. It won't be possible to proceed as we said. I'll have to get back to you later on." She heard the never in his voice.

She could scarcely report his words to Hattie. Betrayal was all she could recall. Hattie was grim. "Them chirren o' yourn has got to him. I heerd in his voice he got a mind could be changed for him. It don't matter none how they done it. Lord, Lord, what I gonna do?"

"Maybe another lawyer would do it. That one seemed too old to me."

"Ain't no time, no time for that. Your chirren be here any time."

Coralee began to cry.

Hattie said in a high, tight voice, "How'm I gon' think with you carryin' on?" Coralee choked down her sob. "You got some kinfolks lives outa town?"

Coralee closed her eyes to think. She remembered the capital city of Maine. She whispered a line of the Twenty-third Psalm. . . . "There's a cousin a mine . . . in Jacksonville. I never did like her all that much."

"Never min' that. You tell 'em how you done recollec' you sent that silver along to her. You tell 'em you give her a piece at a time. I wrop it and took it down to mail. And you done sent her that gifty deed. It hold 'em off for a little spell. Till I can git myse'f outa here." She picked up her purse.

"I won't say it right. You know I won't."

Hattie laid her purse down with a joyless cry. "You tellin' the trufe. I got to fill in what you forgits." She sat in a rocker facing the door. "I mostly skeerd o' that banker man. Anything money they cain't turn loose. . . . I gits to dreamin' it was me done fished him outa the water that time. Shoulda lef' him to drown hisse'f."

"That was my Billy. It's not the same."

And suddenly they were on the porch and letting themselves in with a key they had. Billy and Mindy were in the room. They seemed to fill it with Judgment Day. They stared at Hattie as if they thought she had her nerve.

"Well, Mama," said Mindy, "did you remember?" It was plain she had not remembered her girdle. The streak in her hair fell across her cheek.

Coralee sobbed a single breath. "Remember what? If you're talkin' about the silver, I did." She told it all, her fingers clutching the arms of her rocker. When she had finished she shut her eyes and asked God please to forgive her lie.

"A gifty deed?" said Mindy to Billy.

"I think she means a deed of gift."

"Well, what about it?"

"I don't know how she got the thing, if she got it at all. But she knows the term. I don't think Barnhill would draw it up."

They spoke as if she were not around or couldn't hear or had no sense.

"The whole damn thing is just insane. I don't think I believe a word. I'll have to check with Cousin Mabel. I haven't heard from her in years. I have her address somewhere at home. Or Penny has it. We'll try to call. What if Mabel does have the silver?"

He ruffled a sideburn and smoothed it flat. "We'll talk about that when we know the facts."

Without even saying good-bye they left. Hattie raised the curtain and peered outside. "Sweet Jesus, they got the po'lees! They talkin' to him. And now they bofe of 'em drivin' off." She turned to the room. "But they be back, direc'ly they speak to that cousin o' yourn. Merciful Jesus, they be comin' back!" She sat abruptly, unable to stand. "They comin' to git me pretty soon. I got to git outa town real fast. I got to leave. I got to go."

"Where? Where?" said Coralee.

"Jus' git me a bus ticket somewhere fur. Fur as I got the money to pay."

"Take me with you," said Coralee. The words came out as if they had been in the roof of her mouth for a hundred years. And she was back to a little girl saying them to her black mammy that time whenever it was she left. Nobody told me why she left. She had to go was all they said. Coralee climbed the gate and screamed. Screamed to go and was left behind. Nobody ever took care of me and rocked me to sleep the way she did.

"You crazy?" said Hattie. "You talkin' crazy. I got no time for studyin' you."

"Take me with you," said Coralee. "I got nobody but only you."

"You got them chirren is causin' this trouble."

Coralee cried, "My children are lost and gone for good. How many times do I have to say? You're the only one remembers them and knows what page to find 'em on."

Hattie stood and grabbed her purse. She looked around the room they were in, at fine chairs backed with linen squares and the table with china dancing dolls and curtains of lace and picture frames of shining gilt. "You got in your min' to leave all this? You mighty crazy to swap all this. What you think you swappin' it for? Ride on a bus no tellin' where."

"What good is it? What good to me?" She began to rock. "It's like . . . it's like I get to losing who I am and when you come I know again. . . . I'd rather lose this than who I am. In the night it's like I lose my name. It's like I'm born all over again and all they say is stuff me back inside again. At night you're gone off home but here. I need someone gone home but here and comin' closer all night long."

"Ain't no way it can be that way. Things done changed the most can be. You be nothin' but trouble to me. White and black don't mix no way. I got no money comin' in. The work I gits, it might be long time comin' my way. You ain't do nothin' but slow me down, so likely they cotch us and bring us back and claim I done stole you 'long with the silver."

Coralee was shivering, winter cold. Too cold to climb the gate and scream. She held her handkerchief pressed to her eyes, pressed so hard that her eyeballs ached. She heard no sound, nothing at all, till Hattie was whirling about the bedroom, opening drawers and slamming them shut. Then she was back, saying, "Take that handkerchief down from your face. I brung the money, what little you got."

Hattie was standing there holding a suitcase, holding her purse and Coralee's. "We got to hurry. I brung them raisins for you to eat."

But in the doorway Coralee turned. "We have to take the children," she said.

Hattie gave her a look of bleak despair. "We got no room for that heavy thing. I got your grip here packed to the brim."

"We can't go off and leave them here."

Hattie stood still and shut her eyes. "Jesus, give me strength," she said. She put down the bag and opened the album. She ripped the pages out of the binding and stuffed them into her own handbag. . . .

The Wake of a Cry

Sometimes it would begin to seem as if he were back in Tennessee. The warm, marshy nights were haunted with frogs and the sounds of birds falling asleep in the bush. The early mornings glistened with trees, and insects screamed aloud in the grass. Yet deep in the pit of himself he must know, he must always know, how much he was here. The glistening trees were alive with snipers. If they crossed a stretch of open ground, it was always the line of trees he feared. But on a morning in early August they were set upon in the head-high grass. He heard a sound like the cry of a bird. The cry itself seemed to strike his thigh. He fell over backward with a deep surprise. And then he was not surprised at all. The body springing to block his sky belonged in his dream, so familiar it was. So familiar it was, that to fire into the plunging form was something he seemed to have done before. He had killed a thousand times in his dreams. He fired and blew it back and away, not even hearing his weapon's sound. If not the doing, the ease with which it was done amazed him.

The sky grew black with the clap of his thunder. He thought for a moment he had shot himself, till the pain in his thigh screamed through the thunder and cleared his head. The hours of his life raced into his wound, and he had no tomorrow, no yesterday, only this now that was his forever.

Then he seemed to be striking the earth once more, breaking against it like a shallow wave, and spreading like water across the sand.

The world around him grew final and still. He thought of crying aloud for help. There were eight in his squad. If any were left, they must have retreated into the jungle. If he called, the snipers would pick him out. Best to lie still, let them think he was dead. But his heart was beating into his thigh. He knew that he could not last as he was. So with infinite care, lest he stir the grass, he unbuckled the belt from around his waist and strapped his thigh tight above the pulse. The pain grew intense and stopped his mind. . . .

When he came to, the sun was a flame directly above him. The ground was spongy beneath his head, and the heat of the sun had sharpened a smell of decaying weed. It sharpened as well the scent of a body not far away. He had blown the body back and away, but it had not dissolved for him into air. He could not determine how near it was, yet its presence was unmistakable. And now it was shrilling that he was alone, more alone than he'd ever been. In the heat of the noon the insects were still. Not even the call of a bird was his. His leg was on fire. He could smell his blood burning under the sun.

And then he was lost in the drift of his mind. . . . He was dying at the age of five with his mother, watching the cold come into her eyes. He was dying as his wife walked out of his life and into the car and drove away. In a dream he was running behind the car and falling when it disappeared in the trees. You had to be careful about the trees. They were full of snipers, he thought as he fell. He was struck and falling into the grass. He was aiming and blowing the shadow away. And something was throbbing now in his past. Her car as it disappeared in the trees. . . .

His mind stopped whipping the past with the present. He must concentrate on being missed and the men in his squad returning for him before the others came back for their dead and found the American still alive. He made the scene come close and clear: Did Gannon go down? We can't leave Gannon back there in the field. He tried to think they would make the words and care enough to come back for him. He had been with them little more than a month, and all they shared was a rotten war. They shared a danger and a lust for home. They shared a passionate lust to live, and this had seemed to make them one. All for one and one for all. . . . Maybe seeming was all it was.

Cautiously he moved his head. The soil beneath was marshy, rank. The crushed green ribboned about his face. He became aware that his helmet was gone. Had it fallen off as he struck the earth? His fingers stumbled about in the grass. He felt that a part of him was lost, that finding it would help him live. When he shifted his body his blood broke loose. After that he lay still and willed it to stop, his blood to stop. By an act of his will he must keep it from flowing into the sun. His mind was tensing and sealing the flow. As if it were blood, his fear broke loose.

All at once from the ground through the roots of the grass came a tremor of sound, the faintest movement. He tried to believe that it was an insect fanning the air or a small bird drumming the grass with its beak. Painfully he pressed his ear to the earth and lay in an agony of listening. It came once more: the humming or moaning of a human voice. He was gripped with the terror of being at the mercy of the shadow body he had blown away. His heart pumped blood with a surge into his thigh and awareness left him. . . .

Slowly he was rocked back into the sun and the smell of vegetation. He was on the swinging bridge he had crossed the day before. Was it yesterday? Don't look down, they said. Look at the other side and know you're going to make it. You had the crazy feeling you were blowing in the wind. Rocking, swaying in a wind that wasn't there. . . .

But the bridge was yesterday. He heard the call of a bird. His desire flew after it into the jungle and wandered about in the quiet shade. The trees over here were like caves of green. You could walk for a mile and forget the sky. The trees had a kind of rain of their own—bits of bark, and seeds with wings, and feathers that drifted into your hand. The feathers were falling from birds that were different from ones he knew. Some of them flashed and flamed in the dusk, like flowers glowing along the boughs. He had saved a green feather. It shone in his mind. And part of the shining . . . part of the shining was a presence in the grass, a presence like his own that was trapped and stunned.

He tried to think why it wasn't dead, and what it would mean that it wasn't dead. He had nothing at all to fear from the presence. He chanted it dumbly to clear his mind. They were fallen enemies who had done their worst and now were powerless to strike again. In a single moment their war had ended. His own had ended. And all of the dying had ended with this. Watching his mother die, watching his wife drive away through the trees, watching his father building his wall, brick by brick, till it walled him in and away from his son. Trying to wave as he boarded the plane, but his father

The Wake of a Cry

already had turned away, turned perhaps to his own war, which he had always kept from his son. It's nothing to talk about, he said. He had stuffed his war in a duffel bag and whipped his son for opening it. . . . All of it came to this in the sun. You were always hurt, one way or another. One way or another, you were always alone.

The pain in his thigh stole up his body and into his chest and became his aloneness and he wanted to pray. He moved his lips. But the sun was burning the words in his mouth.

Then abruptly there sprang from the grass nearby a cry that began as a wail in the throat and mounted the air and circled the land and fell with a low-pitched scream to the earth. It seemed to Gannon to shatter the sky and rock the ground, as if their encounter had gathered force and echoed now in some larger place. It pinned him against and into the earth with a shrill astounding of all his senses. Before it died, he lifted his cry—silent, sustained, a chiming of pain. It came from his depths through no will of his own. It made no sound, but he knew the tensing of all his limbs, the surge of his chest, the way the walls of his throat grew wide.

In the wake of this cry they lay as one. Gannon was dazed. His wound had opened and the world poured in. And it seemed to him nothing could be locked out. He wondered if this could be death at last, when nothing forever could be locked out.

The sky was pressing against his eyes. He kept them closed to erase the sky. He seemed to be swaying upon the bridge, holding on, climbing up and down but holding on. Don't look down, they said. He heard them above the skreak of the rope. Or was it vine? Holding on. This time you didn't think of the snipers. You made it, they said. Until they told you, you didn't know. Because the rolling wouldn't let you go. . . . He could not have said how long he rocked in the sky, rocking, swaying in a wind that wasn't there. No target for snipers in a wind that wasn't there. He wouldn't die, they wouldn't get you till you reached the other side. . . . And then he was still, but his heartbeat was tolling the tossing bridge. And a pulse in his thigh was the child his mother caught in the swing to thrust him down and away again.

After a time, recalling his helmet, he moved his hand with extravagant care, exploring the porous, rancid soil. First, one hand was shuttling through grass, out at his side, above his head, stretching as far as he could reach. Then the other hand began its shuttle, till he touched a shape that was not a helmet. Profoundly shocked, he withdrew his hand. After a moment he twisted his head to see in the shadows striped with sun the edge of a sandal broken and worn. The scent of its rubber, alive in the heat, had been there all along for him. The smell of it was the smell of fear. And again he was in the wake of their cry, as if it had sounded a moment ago. His hand and the foot and the cry were one. Once more his blood had flooded his mind. And then it was gone. The blood was gone and his mind was clear.

Above in the air and just to his right, there began to arise an image of water. At first it was scarcely more than a shimmer, like the feather retrieved and placed in his wallet. Then he named it water by the way he could see in it moving clouds, tassels of green, the insects pricking its surface like rain.

He opened his eyes and still he could see it. The sun had shifted away from his face, but just where its shaft struck the tips of grass, he could see the water. Now white with cloud, now glassed with sky, it glanced and quivered before his eyes. . . .

Profoundly he knew that the image was shared. A dream of water had struck the air, as if a hand had smote a bell, and then its echo had echoed against the sounding bell. That was the singular part of it. Not the image itself but that it was shared. Such a thing had never happened before, not even in the first good days with his wife before he learned he was still alone. They had been lost in their separate worlds, groping for words that would make them one. Across a solitary place their lips would meet and taste the dust.

Now wholly, deeply he was not alone. While his mind lay stunned it had been possessed. He drifted in wonder because it was so, and then in pain, and again in wonder. Slowly the perilous thirst invaded. His fingers crept to the canteen still attached to his belt but fell away. For the thirst sprang from that other throat that had forged the cry that became his cry. Like a flame it licked the roots of the grass and crept through the soil and became his own. The thirst of the other became his own. He began to know how it stabbed the throat and the tongue was a stone. He harbored and held the image of water and would not release it or let it fade.

His mouth drank for an endless time, drank of the image he harbored and held. Something below him smelled of green. Beneath his mouth the water shuddered and lengthened to a stream with floating leaves. He was stumbling in water, flowing with it through arching boughs, swimming and wading, his feet bruised with rushes. Bodies strange to him were swimming toward him. And yet he seemed to have known them before. He could see how morning kindled the flesh. In the stream the sky was woven with leaves. A woman caught and hurled a branch between the wings of her floating hair, and in her mouth a jungle flower. Shawled, she was, in her swirling hair. Her breasts bloomed from the water and fell. Along the bank the naked children flickered with sun like candles winking among the trees. He was full of welcome and full of light, remembering a scene he had never known. Never in all his life had known, so how could it be there waiting for him? Was it a haunting of his mind with another's dream of going home? Richer because the dream was shared.

The memory-longing pooled with their blood and disappeared into the ground, where it seemed to have roots in his mother's arms. He had been so young, so fresh to the world, that he scarcely knew she was not himself. When he cried and she held him close to her, he could feel his own tears flood her throat . . . and the pain of weeping that turned to joy, for they wept as one. It seemed to him now that long ago they had wept as one for this very hour. They had wept for him here and wept for the dreamer whose dreaming he shared.

His mind stole in and out of the grass in search of something remotely his own. Something lost that would help them both to live. He could not seem to recall what it was. His fingers drifted, remembering the helmet. And then he found it above his head. It was lying dome up. His fingers slipped over it, slipped again, but he inched it downward and onto his breast, where he clutched it tightly with both his hands. The effort consumed him.

Something was throbbing again in the past. The sound of her car as she drove away. But the sound grew close. Was she coming back? He listened, his fingers gripping the helmet, till the pulsing seemed to come out of it and all his body throbbed to its beat. . . . The sound of her car became the chopper. He heard it over the line of trees, the chopper, rescue, angel of mercy . . . always so for the man gone down. He heard with joy its hovering wings. One hand released the helmet and threshed the grass to a beckoning. Oblivious of his surging blood, he whipped the grass as the chopper whipped the sky above. A little more and the grass would fall, he would lie exposed. He heard the motor closer now, weaving a circle above the trees, stitching him into his pattern of days, the warm nights that were haunted with frogs, the birds that fell asleep in the bush. . . .

"Over here . . . ," he wanted to cry. But he made no sound, for something began to clutch his throat, the fear in the man who lay with him. His eagerness was lost to fear. And then his fear fell into relief, as the chopper beat itself away. He heard its faint, staccato roar retreating into a silent sky. The gray smoke of his own despair dissolved into the other's joy.

His mind no longer belonged to him. He lay with the certainty of it now. When the body is breached, the mind is breached. He had never been told of this before. Strangely, he felt a kind of peace that he had been told of it at last.

He slipped away again into the past when his mother had died and he was five. She was lying inside the finest box he had ever seen. Its handles were carved, the color of gold. He had watched it lowered out of his sight, and then his father took his hand and made him leave the box behind. But jerking free of his father's hand, he ran back over grass and stone. They were shoveling dirt upon the box. He understood it was something he was forbidden to see. He was too astounded to feel any grief. He could not think why his father would allow such a thing to be.

One day—it must have been after that—he caught a green frog in the hollow of a tree and placed it in the hollow of his sandpile bucket . . . the very pail he held now on his breast. . . . While the frog waited for his hand to release it, he was filling the pail to the rim with sand. He smoothed it level and traced with his finger in the sand a frog.

He left the frog in the sand all day. In the night he kept waking up to the dark. Whenever he did it was hard to breath. At daybreak he ran to empty the pail, and out of the mound of sand the frog leapt free. It seemed to leap straight from the middle of the earth and into the sky. The boy was overjoyed. He leapt with the frog. He leapt with it into the weeds and the hedge. For a long time he lived in the mind of the frog. He knew when it wanted to flick its tongue at the insects, and when it wanted to lie still in the shade and drink the dew, and when it grew restless and wanted to jump, how it felt to be green, to coil into a spring and to leave the earth. One day, without thinking, he left the frog and became a bird and knew how it was to look down from the tree and to sail like a kite and make a shadow on the ground. . . . Now the face of the bird was shimmering like water and becoming the face of the shadow in the grass. He could not begin to think what it meant. Unless it meant that his life had been growing to this, seeking forever this union in the grass. . . . It sang to him, the whole of his life, unfolding and flowing into this release.

The sand pail surfaced out of his childhood and became his helmet. He shifted it slowly close to his face and saw that it belonged to the other. But now this did not matter to him, for his joy sprang from the helmet he held, like the frog from sand.

The man beside him withdrew into sleep, losing their sky, releasing their pain. They slept for a while and woke to one another and slept again. He wove for them both a dream of his mother, how she put him in the wagon that was shining red and knelt beside him, laughing, and kissed his hair. At once he was gathering the hair of his wife and holding it safe while she knelt and drank from a pool that glimmered like the feather he had saved. He had saved it for her.

Dream or memory or desire . . . the man beside him held it greening for them both.

Once, in waking, his lips touched his mother's dying eyes and his father's eyes . . . and the eyes of his wife. Like mourning. Or prayer. Beside him in the grass, lips were moving with his.

And then they were rocking the bridge together, breaking its roll, leaning into a wind that was never there, moving together to the other side. Before they reached it they couldn't die. There was something that said you wouldn't die till then.

Before they reached it, endlessly rocking, the roll of the bridge was stirring the grass. The voices began to say he had made it, and then went strange. A shadow fell. The helmet was lifted away from his chest. He tensed for the blow. And the shadow left. . . . I am already dead or the blow would come.

And dying was losing a helmet they shared.

He was fallen into darkness when they took him away.

After he could get around, they gave him a job shuffling papers in the rear. The war was on forever. It was six months before he found a man from his squad, and then it was someone who was on his way home. When Pearson bent to sign, he looked up and saw it was the Pearson he knew, and that he had given up the slick of shoe polish on the place going bald.

After the greeting he got around to asking, "You know who brought me in?"

"You lookin' straight at him. I reckon you owe me." He kissed his papers noisily and creased them down the middle. "Man, I drug you to the chopper with a hole in my hand, and then I got inside with you and bled over you. All the way to the hospital. You don't remember that?"

Gannon shook his head. "I reckon I owe you." And then he had to say it: "Was one of them there?"

"Back where I drug you from?" Pearson shook his head. "You was all alone."

"I blew him off me. . . ."

"Nobody, only you." Pearson put the papers in his shirt and sighed. "You lose some blood, enough of it, you off your head."

"They came and got him, then. But he was there."

Weaving together their dreams and blood. . . . Time had sealed it from all denials. Like the pain of his wound, it would never wholly leave him for the rest of his life.

Bread upon the Waters

On Visitors' Day at Larabee Hall, Elvie played a piece by Chopin. It was a difficult piece, but Elvie's fingers flew over the keys in careless rapture. The visitors, mostly ladies, watched her with benign, bright eyes.

Larabee Hall is an orphanage. But since the word is filled with unsavory associations, of pathos, of iron discipline, of scant, repulsive meals—in a word, of Oliver Twist—this orphanage, being sponsored by a church denomination and founded so to speak on love, of course was called a Hall.

Elvie had been a Hall child since she could remember. Now that she was ten she saw that it was not the best life might have offered, but it was all that was available. She resigned herself—if resignation is bestowed upon a child so young. More accurately, perhaps, she waited, and on the whole behaved agreeably. She had a small, round pixie face with lips that pouted, not from petulance but from a slight protrusion of the teeth, and blackish hair chopped off below her jaw. It was rather a lot of hair, and when she played the piano it fell into her eyes so thoroughly one marveled she could see the keys. Her eyes, when one could glimpse them, were alert and amber brown, and in them one could see that even now at ten she knew herself for what she was.

One of the ladies on that leaf-bright autumn day was Lena Winters. She was thirty-nine and handsome, and her husband's earning powers made possible a generosity that became her tall, distinguished figure. Indeed, at the end of the entertainment, seated at the superintendent's desk, she penned a check to the Hall with an angular grace that was pleasant to behold.

"What was the little pianist's name?" she smiled as she handed it to the Head. Miss Travis styled herself Head Worker instead of superintendent. Her dignity was safe. With her burnished dome of hair and her long official teeth and her eyes that could nail a commitment to the floor, she looked for all the world like a superintendent and not like a laborer in the vineyard at all.

She took the check and carefully withheld from it her gaze. It was her official custom to bridle the inclination when she harvested a check, as if she trusted the amount as she trusted her God. She fixing her trusting eyes on Mrs. Winters' own. "Her name is Elvie Miller. We encourage her all we can, but of course our resources are so very limited. Miss Leech, who teaches sewing, gives her lessons in music. On her own time, I may add." She gave a small involuntary sigh. "We have a hardworking staff, Mrs. Winters, we do." Then she permitted herself a tiny glance at the check. "It's friends like you, Mrs. Winters, who make it possible to go on."

"I'll just make a note of the name," said Lena Winters in a gracious tone. Straightway she wrote it down in the margin of her checkbook.

"I'm sure it will encourage her to hear about your interest."

Miss Travis slipped the check beneath a paperweight of heavy glass that sheltered in its depths and magnified a photograph of Mr. Larabee, and only in a cyclone could the check have blown away. It was as if that benefactor, a man of weight in life as now in death, had taken the check into his keeping for transmittal from the grave.... Often Miss Travis felt that he ran things from the grave, as he had in life. Often she wondered if his heavenly reward had been divine permission to interfere in the affairs of his earthly benefaction. He had left a will quite literally infested with provisions, timed-released like a pill.

Surely no more than ten days later Mr. Winters appeared at Larabee Hall. Unfallen still were the yellowing leaves that had traced their shadows on the hoods of the visitors' limousines. He was shown at once to the office of Miss Travis and given the one upholstered chair reserved for benefactors, and there he awaited her return from some remoter portion of the Hall. Mr. Winters had a noble, weary face, much older than the face of his wife, and above it a clean, hereditary, utter baldness.

While he sat, he pushed about the paperweight containing Mr.

Larabee, as if he were engaged in a nervous game of chess. The check from Mrs. Winters had long since been converted into necessary things.

Presently Miss Travis swam into the room. He released the paperweight. Expressionless, he rose as from the depths of the sea.

"Do forgive me," said Miss Travis. "One of our workers has taken to her bed. Flu," she confided. "It makes a shortage, but we carry on." She looked herself a little feverish. She sat with a sigh. "Do sit down," she implored. She revealed to him her teeth in a tight official smile.

"My wife explained on the phone, I am told, that I would call for the . . . the child."

"For Elvie Miller. Yes, indeed. Mrs. Winters is so kind. So more than kind. And little Elvie is of course on pins and needles with excitement . . . and has been packed for two days, I might even add."

Mr. Winters shrank from the charities that seemed to require his presence and his voice. He gave to these as little of each as he could. He was obliged to sit again. "Did my wife make it clear that this is limited in nature? In scope, that is?" An infinitude of blessings would not be heaped upon the platter. "She simply wants the . . . child to have . . . such as . . ."—his eyes were fixed on Mr. Larabee—"such as musical training?" He had lapsed into a question, as if for him the whole affair was coming unglued.

Miss Travis was ready with official glue. She moved in with reassurance. "Oh, perfectly understood. So more than kind."

"But no adoption . . ."

"Oh, perfectly."

"And was it made clear to the . . . child?"

"To Elvie? Oh, perfectly." Miss Travis gave a little smile. "Elvie is quite at home with the thought that no one will adopt her. People rarely want a girl of her age. They want the little ones. Before they're formed, you know. And now and then an older boy but not a girl. And Elvie, when she came to us—but of course I have explained all this to Mrs. Winters—was not available for adoption. Her father had departed—who knows where?" She raised her superintendent's eyes. "And the mother simply could not support them all. The child was sent to us. But the mother has since passed away, and of course little Elvie is now available. But then," Miss Travis sighed, "her best years are behind her."

"Yes," said Mr. Winters. An affirmation seemed required.

"Of course we dream . . . ," Miss Travis said in an almost singing voice, but sensing the other's alarm she hurried on. "I do admire Mrs. Winters. Such a vital, enthusiastic person. So many, many interests. So generous with herself and with her time, you know. You must be proud of her."

"Yes," said Mr. Winters belatedly and stood. "Now may I take . . . the child?"

"Indeed you may." She rose and went to the door. It seemed to remind her. She turned back at once with an arch, official smile. "There's just one thing. In my note to Mrs. Winters I believe I mentioned it. The matter of the braces . . ."

Mr. Winters thought of suspenders. He looked at sea.

"She may not have thought to mention it." Miss Travis sighed. "Elvie's teeth are badly out of line and growing worse. The nurse considers them most desirable. The braces, that is. But the expense, Mr. Winters! They are quite beyond us. And I thought . . . well, it would indeed be lovely, while Elvie is with you . . ."

"Of course," said Mr. Winters. "We'll take care of it."

"She has been prepared for them," Miss Travis said. "Emotionally." Then she went again to the door and caroled, "Elvie . . ."

Elvie appeared at once. Mr. Winters, disconcerted, supposed the child had been there all the time. She was carrying a battered little suitcase. And from what he could see of her face through the hair, she did not look at all on pins and needles.

Elvie was driven through the Hall gates in a large gray car with softer seats than she had ever seen before. It was such a quiet car that she wouldn't have known that she was going anywhere but for the scenery changing. The driver wore a gray cap and was large and silent like the car. Mr. Winters sat beside him, not so large but just as silent. Elvie sat in back. She was silent too until she saw the lions made of stone beside the entrance. Then she pressed her nose against the window and said, "Wow!"

The house where Lena lived was in the finest part of town, so fine that it was scarcely like a part of town at all. It was a wild and wooded spot, primeval in its tone. In the midst of the wilderness was a Garden of Eden, and in the midst of the Eden was Lena's home. Lena herself had planned the garden and the house. They were always changing like the shadows in the forest that had made a place for them. The garden changed its flowers and its gardener once a year. The house would change its furnishings, its servants, and its guests. The mass of men and women have it in them to survive a single invitation, no more. Lena Winters had a talent for pruning and replacement.

As for Mr. Winters, he was of course beyond replacement. Lena could not recall when first she had gazed with deep depression on his noble, weary face. His bald head had become for her a tiresome abstraction for the nature of their union. But extremity of barrenness will pass into abundance with the passage of time. A generous cornucopia of nothing at all. Lena could surround her marriage with a shifting plenitude. But alas, Mr. Winters was a cipher in its midst.

It was a long ride from the lions to the front door of the house. Elvie slumped into the cushiony back seat of the car and fixed her rigid gaze on Mr. Winters' barren head. She stared it into grand prize in an Easter egg hunt. She saw it filled with chocolate with marshmallow at the core.

When they stopped before the big house and the driver let them out, Elvie said to Mr. Winters in the slenderest voice, "Back yonder . . . was them lions?"

He skimmed her with his eyes. "I think we ordered lions."

"They look real mean," she said.

"I think we ordered that."

Elvie was captivated but kept it to herself. She had ordered 3-D glasses from a catalog once. Susan kept the catalog under her bed.

The house inside was rather dark. Mr. Winters, as if by magic, disappeared into the dusk. Elvie was conducted up a curving flight of stairs and then up another by a girl in a black dress, who had caramel-colored skin, a black ponytail, and a little white apron hardly bigger than her hand. She carried Elvie's suitcase and dropped it with a thud inside a pretty room at the top of the steps.

The room had white curtains printed all around with trailing blue ivy and a bedspread whose ruffles had the same design. The rug beside the bed was the blue of the ivy. And opening off the room was a little bathroom whose tiles matched the rug. Elvie did not guess that the bathroom was her own. It made her quite uncomfortable to think that anytime no telling who might come into her room on the way to the bathroom, for it clearly had no other door. Left alone, she did not like to risk changing her dress or to put away her clothes, as the girl had told her to. So she simply did nothing in the middle of the floor. She heard her stomach growl like the lions at the gate.

The girl with the apron was prowling in the hall. Soon she stuck her head inside and bounced her ponytail. "Well, do it now. And don't put nothing on the bedspread if you want to get along."

So Elvie put the contents of her suitcase inside a bureau drawer, with most of it to spare. Then she kicked her empty suitcase under the bed and sat in a fluffy little chair to wait. At last she thought to herself, If there's anything I hate it's when you got to sit around and got no guarantee what is coming next, so you got to brace yourself for ever'thing there is, and the longer you got to brace the stiffer you get. She wished she had the nerve to say a damn but she didn't. Alma Wiggins said it and would probably go to hell. She said it when her chemistry set leaked on her pink panties in her bureau drawer, which had happened more than once. It happened all the time. Alma said there were chemicals that when they got together were mean as hell. Like some people she could name but she wouldn't, she said. Elvie's stomach growled some more.

After a while Lena Winters knocked and entered. Thinking she was on her way to the bathroom, Elvie politely averted her eyes.

"My dear child, welcome. Are you quite, quite at home?"

"Yes, ma'am," Elvie said, and she got up as she had been taught to do when Miss Travis addressed her. She stood in front of Lena Winters with her head bowed a little and the dark, straight hair swinging forward till it nearly hid her face.

Lena looked her up and down with speculation. Then she sat down gracefully on the bed. She did it so lightly that she never disarranged the bedspread in the slightest. And the blue ivy on the ruffle twined about her slender ankles as if it loved to have her there. "Did Miss Travis tell you how much I admired your playing?" she inquired, smiling.

Elvie looked uncertain. "She said it was the reason you took me out."

Lena laughed. "Took you out! It makes you sound like a library book, now, doesn't it?" And she laughed again all by herself, for Elvie did not see that it was funny. In fact, she had never been to a library. Miss Travis had a room with books, but you never took them out; you sat and read them on the spot. And if you tore a page Miss Travis knew who did it.

"I took you out because I wanted to know you better," Lena said. She had a gracious, charming voice. It was one of the nicest things about her. And now her face was so lively and really pretty that Elvie stole a glance at it through the dark wings of her hair.

"I've been thinking about you quite a lot," Lena went on. "I've been thinking it would be so nice to have a little sister." There was a warm note in her voice that made it almost husky. "We must see a lot of one another. And then you can decide." She put her elbow on the bedpost and rested her pointed chin in her hand. "I want to make you like me as much as I like you."

Elvie looked away in some confusion. She did not understand how Mrs. Winters could possibly like her so much when she had hardly ever seen her. There were only two or three people that Elvie herself really liked, and these she seemed to have known forever. One of these was Mr. Tom, who drove the bus for them whenever the children from the Hall were going out together. He also went for groceries and supplies of various sorts, and anything in the whole world that needed fixing he could fix. The others were Susan and, except on rare occasions, Mary Jane.

Lena was saying, "And while we're waiting for you to like me as much as I like you, we're going to give you music lessons. You will play, play, play.... There's a wonderful big piano in the music room downstairs, and you must feel free to use it whenever you like. Any time of day you can pop in and play. You must forget about the Hall and just be happy here and play your heart out for a while. And then we'll have to see about other sorts of lessons. But I imagine the music is all you really care about ... now, isn't it?" she smiled.

"No, ma'am," Elvie said. "I like geography and learning about insects."

Lena brushed it away. "But music is the best."

"No, ma'am," Elvie said. "I like geography best."

Lena did not say a single thing for a moment. Then she laughed and stood up and held out the fingers of one hand to Elvie. "Come over to the mirror," she invited her. "I want to see something."

She pressed Elvie down upon the bench before the dresser. She ran the pretty ivory comb through Elvie's hair. Then she parted it down the back and began to braid it carefully, one side at a time, with a mysterious little smile caressing her lips. She looked at Elvie's brown, startled eyes in the mirror. "Wait, wait . . . ," she entreated. "Just wait and see."

When she had finished she felt around in the dresser and found two rubber bands—it was almost as if they were there for the occasion—and secured the braids, which she lifted high and gently to make a coronet. "Charming!" she exclaimed. "Just look at yourself." Then she found convenient hairpins and fastened the braids in place. She drew away her hands. Still they circled the head, sweetly forming a halo, only to fall again and with butterfly fingers caress the coronet. "It needs to be a little longer, but it will be soon. . . . Don't look so grim," she laughed at Elvie in the mirror. "You'll like it so much better. Don't you feel as light as a bird with it up so high?"

Elvie dropped her eyes to the dresser scarf. Her head felt naked, even chilly. But Lena put her face down close and tilted Elvie's head and made her look at herself again. "Such a charming age!" she said. "Almost a woman and still a little girl. Could anything be more fun? Charming," she said again into the mirror. "Just the way a little pianist should look."

And then she said quite solemnly to Elvie in the mirror: "You must leave it like this. It will please me."

Elvie stared at herself and dropped her eyes again.

Lena took away her hands but continued to gaze at the Elvie in the mirror in a gentle, friendly way. "Look," she whispered. "Aren't we almost like sisters?" She smiled quite beautifully. "If we're going to be sisters I must call you something else. I could never have a little sister called Elvie." She shook her head playfully. "Elvie doesn't sound like my sister at all. . . ." She narrowed her handsome black eyes, tilted her head, and then laughed. "Margaret!" she said. "'Margaret' just suits you with your hair like that. It sounds like a little princess who plays the piano." After a moment she added, "I'm going to call you Margaret.

"And now," she said, turning away, "there's time enough for you to have a nice long bath and put on your very nicest dress for supper."

She walked to the door and, with her hand on the knob, gave a final, gracious smile to the Elvie in the mirror. "Be very, very careful not to muss the hair."

After she was gone Elvie stared at herself for a good long time. She wondered if Mary Jane and Susan were turning cartwheels and standing on their heads in the grass behind the Hall. When the weather was nice, all the girls at the Hall of a certain age, which is in between being too big and too small, did tricks on the grass before the bell for supper. It was just about the happiest part of the day. They always played "Statue," a game of slinging one another, and each one has to stay the way she falls, not move a muscle even, and the prettiest statue wins. Alma always cheated—she moved—and so they never let her win.

Elvie put her hand up and pressed the hard ridge of braid across the top of her head. She guessed it would really hurt if she stood on her head. . . . She was getting up her nerve to say a damn, but she didn't.

Mr. Winters left in the gray car and didn't stay for supper. Mrs. Winters had a lady full of lace come to eat. Lena took one look at Elvie and how her braid had not survived the bath and told her she could eat in the pretty breakfast room. She said it was the prettiest room in all the house and that she wished with all her heart she could have her supper there with her own little sister. But she couldn't of course. So Elvie sat surrounded by morning glories in the wallpaper and chewed her food. She didn't chew too well, since her teeth were out of line. It was not like food she had ever had before. Not all that good, she thought. Not worth the trouble to chew. Not what she would expect, considering all the rest—the lions at the gate and this paper on the wall, which looked expensive to Elvie.

In the night she awoke to hear a woman screaming. At first she was sure that it was Mary Ellen in the middle of a nightmare. Then she knew it wasn't; it was real-life murder going on with Mrs. Winters on the floor below and maybe it was Mr. Winters back from where he went and killing his wife. If it wasn't so high up she would have jumped out the window if it hadn't been dark. But then she remembered that Mavis Sisley's mother had two boarders who tried to make a baby almost every night. Mavis' mother told her not to listen when the lady screamed, but Mavis did. She said it sounded worse than when your teeth are drilled. . . . It occurred to Elvie that if it worked on Mrs. Winters she wouldn't need an orphan and would send her back. Elvie covered up her head and hoped it would.

She woke up hungry, her stomach in a growl, and with no earthly idea what to do with the day. She saw herself in the mirror, and the braids were still there but after a rocky night had begun to bristle. Elvie was famous for electrical hair. . . . If the folks in this house got a porcupine in mind, well, they gonna be happy, she told herself. She grinned and made a terrible face in the mirror, and then made another more terrible still. At the Hall she was famous for that as well. She could make all the younger kids turn and run.

No sooner had she dressed than the girl in the apron came in without a knock. "You're supposed to be at breakfast while I make your bed." She flung off the bedspread and draped it on a chair. "Don't sleep with this on you if you want to get along." She shook her ponytail. "Fold it up nice before you crawl in bed."

Elvie stood and watched her work. She inquired if Elvie had heard the peacocks in the night. "They is one bird there ought to be a law against, the way they carry on. . . . I thought they was pretty when I took this place. Now I wisht I had the nerve to shoot 'em all dead."

She popped the pillow with her fist and snapped her ponytail as if it were the last girl in a line of Crack the Whip. "We had to change the curtains and the spread for you. Different rug, different chair. Different strokes for different folks. She had an aviator in here before you come."

"What happened to him?" Elvie asked.

"She dumped him, that's what."

Elvie pondered that one. "Was he nice?"

"Too nice . . ."—and she rolled her eyes at Elvie—"to the wrong one."

Elvie pondered further. "Where do you live?" she said at last.

"One floor up." She pointed with a finger and waggled it a bit, along with her ponytail and tight little rear. "At the tippety top. The lower down the higher up. Remember that." She popped the other pillow. "She's got you in between, so watch your step."

"Why?" said Elvie.

"There ain't a why. It's just a dicey place to be." At the door she turned. "And don't lay on the bedspread or she'll dump you too."

Elvie stood and listened to her stomach growl. Then she found some paper she had brought along for letters she had promised to write. She sat on her feet in the fluffy chair and wrote to Mavis Sisley: "There is a woman here can make a bed but she don't make a dab a sense I swear to God. And they give me a bedspread I reckon come from Jesus Christ. They got peacocks here and I aint seen them yet but I can tell you what they sound like when I see you. Which I hope to do."

The girl slipped her arm inside the door and gave her fingers a snap. "You better get on down if you want to get along."

It was at breakfast that Mr. Winters mentioned the braces. They were sitting in the morning glory room overlooking the tangle of the trees beyond the polished lawn. "Miss Travis spoke about some braces." He stared into his egg cup.

Elvie stole a glance at him. His face had a look of playing Statue at the Hall and somebody threw it and he couldn't let it move. His eyes made her think of the buttonholes that Susan made in sewing class, all sewed together. If she got the button through she had to pull it with her teeth. . . . Elvie's toast was the loudest she had ever chewed. She had to swallow it to stop the racket. Then she stole another glance at Mr. Winters. The skin beneath his eyes made her think of a mess Alma made with her chemistry set whenever she got mad. Elvie chewed some egg and guessed that he was working on a pipeline. Susan's father had been ruptured by a pipeline. Elvie herself would rather starve than work around one.

Lena was looking past him with the brightest impatience. "Braces!" she exclaimed. "Well, what an idea!"

Mr. Winters just skimmed her with his eyes, which had somehow made it through the buttonholes. "She wrote you, I believe."

Lena gave a girlish smile. "Miss Travis may want braces. Margaret doesn't."

Mr. Winters consulted Elvie with the stare of a statue. The sun chased the shadow of a leaf across his gleaming skull. Then his face contracted and seemed to feed upon itself in a look that Lena seldom saw but knew for an obstinacy as utter as his baldness. "We are committed to the braces."

"Nonsense!" Lena broke out, scattering her bacon with the fork. "No little girl wants braces." She smiled at Elvie. "Do you want braces, Margaret?"

Elvie explored her teeth in secret with her tongue. She did not look at Lena Winters. "Yes, ma'am."

Lena studied the morning glories on the wall before she spoke. "No one ever wants braces." She said it slowly, "How could you possibly want them?"

Elvie swallowed her piece of toast. With her hair in the new way, her ears were feeling cold and large as buns. She saw that Mr. Winters was expecting her to speak. "Miss Travis said I got to think of the future."

"Whose future? Her future?" Lena asked almost rudely. "The future of Miss Travis I'm afraid is drawn in charcoal. Margaret's is every bit in lovely color."

"Go on," Mr. Winters was saying to Elvie. He sounded kind.

Elvie looked into her plate. "If I have braces . . ." She felt at once a little sick. "If I have braces now . . . later on, somebody . . ." She could not go on.

"Somebody what, dear?" Lena asked.

Elvie did not answer.

"Will adopt you?" Lena prompted.

"Marry me," Elvie said.

There was a long silence. Mr. Winters stared into the yolk of his egg. A different woman with an apron had come into the room and now was pouring coffee with one hand and milk with the other at the very same time into Mr. Winters' cup without spilling a drop.

Lena laughed with irritation. "Miss Travis speaks from her disappointments."

Mr. Winters' face contracted once again. "She is to have the braces, whatever it involves."

"But the future is the future!" Lena cried at once in a lively tone. "And now is now." She did not look at Mr. Winters. She looked at the morning glories clutching the wall. "How can I bear Margaret wearing braces? She won't be a little princess with her mouth all full of wires. And I'm sure she couldn't play the piano at all."

Mr. Winters rose. "I expect the conference to last through dinner." Elvie thought he stood as if he had been thrown against the flowers on the wall and told not to move or else he couldn't play.

"You'll call . . . ," Lena said.

But Mr. Winters cheated. He had moved and was gone. Lena shrugged. Then she rose and followed. In the midst of crunching her cinnamon toast Elvie heard their voices beyond the door abruptly lowered. They said at the Hall she could hear a fly walk.

"How long is this trip?" she heard him inquire.

"Your questions have a way of confusing me, Henry."

Elvie stopped crunching her toast to listen.

"The Dutch aviator lasted three weeks. And the boy with the shriveled leg lasted two. And the Little Theater, the retreat for artists, and the shop for Kitty. And the little antique dealer, what was her name?"

"They failed me," she said. "So what is your question?"

"I wondered, that's all, how long is this trip."

"Well, don't let it spoil your lunch," she said.

And then she was back with a lovely smile. "Now we have the whole wonderful morning to ourselves. Mr. Lovett is coming to give you a piano lesson at ten. You must play your very, very best for him and make me proud." She dipped her fingers in her water glass and tamed Elvie's bristles with a few icy strokes. Then she brought some hairpins from her very own room and restored the coronet, which had begun to slide.

With Mr. Winters, Elvie wondered about the trip and whether she was required to go along.

Mr. Lovett came. Elvie thought he looked something like Mr. Larabee inside the paperweight. Perhaps it was because he had the same wavy hair. If he had not charged the moon and more for his lessons, he would have insulted Lena by very firmly closing the music room door. But included in the cost was his smile of regret at cutting himself off from the rapture of life that was Lena Winters. In truth, women made him as nervous as a cat, and he absolutely could not have them breathing down his neck. If he charged enough and smiled enough, he did not have to put up with it at all.

When the lesson was over, he sent Elvie out to play in the sun. Then he tiptoed to the door of the study, where Lena sat leafing a magazine.

"Did we disturb you too badly?" he asked.

"I could hardly hear. Mr. Winters went to so much trouble, you know, to make the music room as soundproof as possible." She added graciously, "I should really like to have heard you at work."

Mr. Lovett included another smile in the price. Then he entered and sat down in the shadow of a floor lamp twined in a loving way with wrought-iron grapes. What followed he would bill as consultation of course.

Lena's eagerness was subdued and flattering. "Mr. Lovett, tell me exactly what you think."

Mr. Lovett studied his slender hands. "She can play one piece," he said finally.

Lena smiled. "You mean she plays one really well."

"She plays only one at all. This . . . this thing of Chopin."

Lena stared at him.

"She doesn't read notes, which of course . . ." He raised his eyes. The grapes on the lamp after all were mistletoe. He shuddered a bit. Decadent taste, he thought.

"I heard her once," Lena cried. "She played beautifully."

"Was it this . . . Chopin?"

"I . . . I'm not sure."

"Da-da-da . . . da-da . . . da-da-da . . . da-da," Mr. Lovett sang helpfully.

"It may have been."

"She learned it from a sewing teacher. She attacks it quite as if she were darning Chopin's socks. She never saw the notes."

Lena flushed. "But that . . . that in itself is remarkable . . . is it not?"

Mr. Lovett shrugged. "'Chopsticks,'" he observed, "is in the repertoire of every plumber, every pharmacist in town. I have heard it flawlessly rendered by a child of three."

Lena was silent. "But she had . . . that is, has she . . . feeling?"

"Feeling? Musical feeling at ten?" Mr. Lovett swept the mistletoe with his smile. "At the moment she has the gusto of a 'Chopsticks' devotee." He played a scale with one hand on the arm of the chair. "We must begin at the beginning. Just as if she had never played this . . . this unfortunate piece. I shall bend every effort to erase it from her mind. She must unlearn it, if you understand. Her fingering is barbaric."

There was a lengthy pause. "There is something to consider," Mr. Lovett said. "She memorized this Chopin for some occasion because she was promised two helpings of dessert for a week." He rose. "She prefers geography," he said, "and, we must face it, bugs."

"I do thank you," Lena said with her most enchanting smile. "I shall be in touch."

After he had retreated, she wandered to the window. Out of the tangle of the trees came Elvie with her two hands cupped together. Her braids had come undone and swung about her ears like bangles. Midway across the lawn she stopped and opened her hands the merest bit, and carefully, rapturously, she peeked inside.

Lena explained it wonderfully to Miss Travis on the phone. Onerous duties had intruded. Miss Travis understood, of course. She knew what duties were. Then, blowing a little kiss, Lena bid Elvie good-bye before she left to cut a ribbon for the opening of a garden for the blind. Or was it a listening gallery? She must check it on the way.

Late that afternoon Mr. Tom came along with the bus to fetch Elvie. She had been packed and waiting for an hour in the porte cochere. Now and then she'd made a dash to chase the falling leaves. When she saw him round the curve, she ran out into the driveway and flagged him on, just as one of the orphans always got to do at a crossing for a train. They took their turns hopping out and flagging, and it was just too bad there weren't more crossings around.

"Whoa," she called out. "Whoa, there, Mr. Tom." Then she jumped up happily beside him and they drove away, just the two of them, with all those orphanless seats behind them bumping along and raising dust. She was glad to see he looked the same as before. Friendly hair and nice little chicken-pox holes in his face.

When they passed the lions, Elvie rolled her window down and roared at them until they disappeared from view. "Them two lions," she said, "is just about the best thing they got. I wouldn't give you two cents for all the rest."

Mr. Tom stole a glance at her. "You all right?" he said at last.

"You bet I am. Fine and dandy."

"Food OK?"

Elvie nodded. "But guess what. She changed my name to Margaret, and she fixed my hair like this."

He glanced at her with sympathy.

"They had to go on a trip and they couldn't figure out how long it would be. I was scared I'd have to go along."

Suddenly Elvie pulled down the braids and tickled her nose with the feathered ends. Then she jerked off a rubber band and stretched it around her front teeth. "Look, braces," she said and grinned at Mr. Tom, and the two of them laughed fit to kill.

Meanwhile back at the Hall, Miss Travis, it must be sung, had nailed the braces. She knew her benefactors well and why and when they benefacted. Now and then she cast an orphan like bread upon the waters and always with a cunning hand.

She bared her own official teeth and tapped them lightly with a finger. In the act of confiding to Mr. Larabee beneath the glass a note about the promised check, she happened to look out the window by her desk and witness Elvie driving up with Tom. And such are the remarkable coincidences in the world of the mind, she found the very image that had occurred to Lena Winters. "It's like she was returning a library book"—for Miss Travis put on comfortable grammar in her thoughts as she put on slippers in her bedroom—"right after she took it out."

She pondered it, she tapped her teeth, and then allowed herself an unofficial "Damn."

Valley of Summer

They had been lost for almost an hour, weaving the car through the leaf-bright hills. Ellen was driving. He'd never tell it by gesture or word, but her driving made Judd nervous as hell. His hands shook, his face was gray, and his eyes were full of the miles they'd gone. It reassured her a little to know that behind the wheel he would have been more nervous still.

She'd gotten him out of the bed for this. "Take Judd along," her boss had said. "I hear he's back from his holiday." Judd's holidays were ten days alone with a bottle. The newsroom would have it so. "The fresh air will do him good."

What he meant was that it would do her good. She was surfacing from a bad divorce. He knew it and knew she needed the work, knew she needed to get away. But he didn't say it. Instead he said, "He's the best damn cameraman, drunk or sober.... Tell him I said."

"Tell him that?"

"Tell him I said to go along."

So she called him up. "McRaney's got us a thing to do. There's an Indian burial ground in the hills. He wants a Sunday feature, with shots."

She could hear in his voice how sick he was, how sick he was of being sick, how close to the grave he felt himself. "I'm not sure."

"It's not till tomorrow. You'll be OK." He didn't agree but he didn't protest. "You will, Judd." She mentally supported him. She liked to have him go along. He never drank when they were alone. He was only a big, sad, used-up man, graying, older than he should be, with something steel underneath it all, with love for her underneath it all. She would catch him with the sigh in his eyes. He found her beautiful, she knew. Beneath his gaze, she felt herself grow into it. Even after he had looked away, she was growing beautiful for him, this sad man who would be afraid to take her youth, even if she should offer it—which she never would, it was understood. She was twenty-four; he must have been all of fifty-five. . . .

He rarely talked, but when he did she saw how much he had read and knew. She saw that their roles should be reversed, that he should be doing the Sunday features and she should be doing the camera work, except that her shots were out of focus, and when he wrote (she had read some things), what he tried to say was out of focus, a little bit the way he was. Maybe good for a literary piece, but not what the paper wanted at all: Whittle the thing to a fine point. Sentiment was all to the good. She could work it up to a fine lather, then razor it off to just a trace. Let it show you had bled a bit but staunched the flow. Well, that was the way McRaney liked it. She had never written for anyone else. That was the way she buttered her bread.

She glanced at Judd. He had bled a bit from his morning shave because of his hands, which always shook and were shaking now. It was hard to believe that his pictures showed no trace of it. "You want us to stop for coffee somewhere?" And then she laughed. They were in the wilds.

He managed a rather watery smile. She saw that he wanted it over and done. Did he need a drink? She didn't know. She would try to make it easy for him. She wanted whatever was best for him. At times she felt that he was her child.

"We're losing the light," he reminded her, like a child who might be afraid of the dark. He meant he needed the light to shoot.

"I think we might be lost," she said.

And then the truck was approaching them. A gray Chevy pickup hogging what little road there was. It slowed but came relentlessly on. Ellen pulled so close to the edge that leaves of the trees that rimmed the ravine flew in through the open window like birds, a flock of them, and brushed her face.

The pickup stopped. A man got out and came up to them. She could not see his face for the leaves. "You mind backing up a hundred feet? It's wide enough down there for two."

She took in his voice. It was civil, and it sounded safe.

"Better do it," said Judd. "I would."

She went into reverse while Judd turned in his seat to watch. "Pull over now, and lock your door."

The man was approaching them again. His face and voice were friendly enough, a stocky man of medium height, his graying head beginning to bald, his kindly face beginning to line. He came close and bent to them. "I wonder if you have lost your way." He was dressed in dirty brown work pants and a rumpled shirt. The hand that rested on the window ledge was sun-browned, the creases soiled. "The mountain roads are confusing."

His speech was reassuring. They took him into their confidence.

"The graves?" he said. "Oh, they're not here. I could turn around, though, and guide you there."

They protested that it was out of his way.

He laughed. "One way is as good as another." He tossed it into their hesitation: "I'd just as soon go yours as mine."

It was hard to believe him serious. Was he laughing at them or at himself? He scanned the sky and turned his head to face the sun. "It's late in the day for much of a look." He was leaning over to see them in the dusk of the car. His eyes were blue. They noted Judd's camera in the back.

Ellen trusted him at once. In an instant she would trust or not. She could be wrong, as she'd been with Hank, the man she'd married. Or she could be right, as she was with Judd, the man she hadn't. It took her longer to deal with women. "Wouldn't it be better just to go back and try tomorrow?"

He protested, "When you've come this far? From the city?" he asked, and Ellen nodded. "I'll tell you what. My house is half a mile from here, and I have a map of the hills there. I could save you a lot of time, you know. You could follow me."

She could not take it in at once. Judd was silent, as if he had given up on the day. She looked ahead at the winding road, an asphalt ribbon in need of repair. The air, she noted, was growing cold. It was late October after all. She looked at her watch. Judd was losing the light.

His voice was gently coaxing. "The road gets narrower, I'm afraid, and a little rough. But it's really not your best approach."

Well . . . ," she said, "that's nice of you." While he turned around she buttoned her jacket against the cold. She drew in behind and followed him. "OK with you?" She glanced at Judd.

He nodded at her. "OK with me. But what will you say when he wants to feed us a cozy supper?"

She laughed at him. "We're total strangers. He won't do that."

"He was looking at you as if he would."

She was trying to keep the truck in sight. "You're crazy, Judd."

"I saw the look in his eye. He will."

"Too bad you didn't get it on film." She smiled at the road. "You're always looking into a lens. Even when you aren't, you are. You imagine one in front of your eye. I can tell when you look at me like that."

"Such vanity is beyond belief!" But she knew that he sneaked quick shots of her when he thought she wasn't noticing.

They were spiraling down a narrow road. The truck was below them through the trees. Ellen had to brake from time to time. "I'll bet this is murder when it rains." Judd's hand was gripping the seat, his knuckles white. She tried to make it light for him. "You reckon this is a trap," she said, "a den of thieves and murderers?"

He offered at last through clenched teeth: "My blood is on your reckless hands."

"McRaney will get the bill for it."

Their eyes were on the swift descent and failed to notice the change at once. They drove through trees that had scarcely turned and then through trees that were summer green. The air grew ever so faintly warm.

And then they were abruptly there. The forest was gone; the road was gone. They pulled to a stop in open space, with grass and trees of another kind. The truck was out of sight somewhere. They looked around them curiously and then with a vague uneasiness. They braced themselves against delay. "I think we made a mistake," said Judd. In the distance they saw their man emerge from trees through which they could dimly discern a house.

"I'll give him twenty minutes," she said. "But God, Judd, would you look at this!"

"I'm not believing it," he said.

They got out and stood by the car to watch their host approaching them across the grass through fallen leaves that were drifting slowly out of the hills. There were lemon trees in a tiny grove, oleanders along a walk, and bougainvilleas against a wall. They were not in bloom, but they looked at home.

Coming close, he welcomed them. "My name is Jonathan Quinn," he said. With a smile of pleasure he listened to theirs. They saw that his shoes were caked with soil.

"How do you manage this?" said Judd.

"Manage the summer, you mean?" said Quinn. He seemed delighted at their surprise. He thumped the mud from his heavy shoes and flicked it from his trouser leg.

Ellen was shrugging her jacket off and tossing it into the rear of the car. "Isn't it warmer here?" she asked.

"Feel the ground." He insisted, "Feel it."

She smiled at him uncertainly. Obedient, then, she knelt in the grass and placed both hands upon the earth. "But yes," she said. "It's so. It's warm. You must feel it, Judd."

He was faintly amused. "I take your word." He held out his hand to help her rise.

She did not rise. She gazed at the autumn they had left. She saw herself slipped through a ring of fire fashioned of hickory, oak, and birch. She saw herself narrowed down into earth that was faintly warmed by the flames above. Like a Muslim at prayer, she dipped her forehead into the grass. "Not really warm but something close. It's like a nest the birds have just left."

Quinn nodded approval. "That's very well put. That's exactly it."

"And you have grass on your nose," said Judd.

She rose and wiped it with her sleeve. "How on earth did you find this place?"

"My wife says that it found us. . . . The Indians found it long ago. They called it, I'm told, the valley of summer or, as some would have it, valley of the fledgling. They buried their dead high up in the hills."

"The graves?" Ellen said.

"The burial ground I'll direct you to. They seemed reluctant to bury them here or anywhere close. It's strange, you know. Perhaps they feared the spirits of the dead would alter things." He had the storyteller's voice that beguiled one to attend his tale, a gentle, richly cadenced voice, with confidential undertones suggesting they were the first to hear.

To reinforce the summer for them, he led them into the lemon grove. The leaves had a lively citrus smell, a wayward tang of bitterness. He went on in his grave tone: "This is one of those spots of the earth that defy the seasons, don't you know. You see how the hills protect us, but more than that, there are underground streams that run warm. Even in winter the earth is warm. When late November comes to the hills and the cold air plummets down from them, you can see the mist rise out of the ground, shrouding us in the promise of spring.... You would get a glimpse of it later on, when the air above us cools for the night."

"The Garden of Eden," Ellen said, half in earnest, half in jest.

"Hardly the Garden of Eden," he laughed. "We have a seasonal change of sorts. There are other places like this, you know, but they're rare, I think, so very rare." He was slowly leading them toward the house.

Ellen said, "Judd, we must have some shots. It belongs with the story we've come to do."

"Please, no photographs," said Quinn. He grew alarmed. "No photographs. My wife would be distressed, you know."

"Just as you say. No photographs." She smiled at him. "The Muslims say it steals the soul. Perhaps the soul of a place as well."

He did not smile. "I trust you to honor our request."

And she replied, "We shall honor your valley in memory."

His humor was instantly restored. They were passing through oleander shrubs as tall as trees; and just beyond, they were flanked by roses deep in bloom. Quinn had walked ahead of them. The low stone house was almost hidden among live oaks and flowering quince. Bees hummed at the open door.

Inside, the hall was dimly lit. They followed him into the dusk of a room. Ellen tried to capture a word for it, perhaps for the feature on the graves. This curious place, this very room, began to seem its prelude. Here was the valley of summer distilled, intimacy somehow distilled and disconcerting in its force. The walls painted with life-size figures and giant fruit in earthen hues, the books on tables, stacked in corners, the grand piano massively there, the bowl of rushes. It seemed to her a room in flux. Things would be added or taken away. Its pattern would shift from day to day. Even the painted fruit would change, the figures drift along the wall. Its season of ripeness would remain. She stood in search of the key to it.

They could see beyond through an open door an arbor of vines, below it a network of sun and shade. Quinn left the room to enter it. "Elsa," he called, caressing the name as he stood dappled with shadow and light. Beyond the arbor were brakes of fern and in the air a glancing shimmer, as if there might be water near by.

"Elsa," he said, "I have brought you pilgrims in search of the graves." He turned back to them. "They were broken into from time to time, the graves, you know. But I dare say they're worth your while."

A woman appeared, her back to the light. They could see only her slenderness against the ferns in shimmering air. Then she entered the arbor and stood in its shelter, motionless, observing them without a word. A small wind that stirred the vines swept the shadows across her face and wove the sunlight in her hair.

"This is Elsa, my wife," said Quinn. "And these are . . . anyway, Ellen and Judd. They lost their way. We'll give them supper and a bed for the night. Or beds? Which is it?"

Ellen said, "You're very kind, but we'll be on our way when we've seen the map."

His gentle voice grew insistent, the coaxing, storyteller's voice. "It will be dark so soon, you know. The dark falls in the hills like a hawk. It catches you quite unaware. And what can you see of the graves in the dark? Not even a moon will be out till late. And as for pictures . . . not a chance." He waved his hand.

"Of course," said the woman, "you must stay." Her voice was rich but hesitant, cool. They had fallen upon her like the hawk.

Judd broke in: "Stay for the night? We couldn't do that." He sounded alarmed and almost rude.

The woman advanced into the room. She gazed at Ellen without a word, her chin lifted, a trace of a smile.

Judd dropped back. "My God!" he whispered, and Ellen heard. She could not speak. The woman before her resembled her. More than a likeness, she imaged her. No matter the woman was shorter than she, the dark hair longer and caught behind. The eyes, the lips ... the face was the same. Ellen could but stare.

Judd roused at last to cover for her. "If we leave soon we can make it," he said. He sounded dazed and a little sick.

And Ellen, grasping the thought of Judd, was thinking he shouldn't go on today and that if she had to take him home, tomorrow she'd never get him back. Then she panicked that Judd would win and they would be committed to leave. She stared into the open air, dimly feeling its shudder of light, as if the shudder were in herself.

"I'd like to stay." The merest silence followed her words, so abrupt they were. Ellen herself was amazed at them. At once she knew that what she had said had nothing at all to do with Judd. It had to do with the woman's face and its power to haunt if she did not stay.

"Of course!" said Quinn. "That settles it. . . . Now what can I offer you to drink?"

"Thank you, nothing at all for me." She would have been glad, too glad, for a drink. But she stood in silence supporting Judd, willing his no. I need you, Judd.

"Thank you, no," he echoed her.

"Well, supper it is," Quinn cheerily said. "You'll find it very simple, you know. We live a simple, quiet life." He led them out to the patio. He turned to them with a comfortable smile. "Indian voices surround us here. This is the hour for them, you know." His wife had quietly slipped away.

The valley, defined by a narrow stream, glistened and curved like a new moon at the foot of hills far into fall. They stood in silence before the scene. The hills rose sheer, curved slightly like two archers' bows, each drawn in battle against the other. Quinn was saying, "You see how the stream has cut through rock to make its bed. At bottom and top are softer rock. It was harder going in between. . . . Our valley gets deeper by the year. The hills grow taller. And those of us who live here smaller . . . until, I suppose, we disappear." They watched the brilliant rain of leaves, eddying downward in the sun. "Another month," Quinn promised them, "and the forests will have shrugged them off, and the stream will be under a blanket of them, till the spring rains come to move them on. . . . My wife has done a painting of it, with a glint of water among the leaves. . . ." He called their attention to the pool. "Each morning I rake them from my lake."

They were standing before a little pool ringed with water hyacinths. A water lily was gleaming white, improbable, its stamens gold. The green pads were brushed with gold. "It's beginning to close for the night," Quinn said. "But tomorrow morning you must see." He added, "The water is always warm."

"The springs?" she said.

"Perhaps not springs but currents, you know. Warm currents that move below. In the winter rain it's a striking thing. Each drop creates a drop of mist, almost white, like a tiny pearl, as if a hand had thrown them down. They make the sound of whispers." He paused for a bit and smiled at Ellen, as a storyteller will pause and smile. "It's a haunted pool."

But it was his wife that haunted her. It seemed to her that if she entered the room again, she would find the woman a painted figure smiling at her from the wall. And yet the woman was in her throat . . . and in her breath. . . . A face in the pool stared back at her. With a small shock she turned from it.

Quinn went on in his cadenced voice: "The Indians had a curious lore. They thought that here was the center of things, or so it's said. The sun sank here and was trapped below and slowly, very slowly escaped, up through the water, up through the earth. At the end of each day it was trapped again. . . . I'm told that is why their burial ground was higher up. Here the spirits of the dead could be trapped in sun and sink with it and try to escape and be trapped again . . . and never get to the Hunting Ground."

Ellen was thinking while he spoke, Why are we speaking of Indians when in this house is a woman, his wife, who has my face, or I have hers, and nothing has yet been said of it? The hills had sobered with coming night. The light they held had drifted down, as if it sank from heaviness, and shimmered on the hyacinths. She felt herself drawn into sun, to sink with the spirits of the dead.

She turned to be sure that Judd was there. It seemed to her he shunned her eyes.

"Perhaps we shall eat out here," said Quinn. "We often do. We eat early and wait for dark, and when it comes we let it ripen, then go to bed. The power lines don't come to us. We have a generator of sorts, which gives us the light that we require. Quite early, though, the lamps grow dim, and then we have primeval dark. We're very quiet here, of course. My wife is an early riser, you see. She likes to sculpt and paint, you know. She's fond of the very early light."

"And what do you do?" Ellen suddenly asked. Her work with the paper had made her bold to probe for what she had to know.

"I keep her safe," was all he said.

To be the woman a man kept safe! Hank would leave for days or weeks, with never a word when he finally showed. Ask me how I've been, she'd say. I see you made it, was all he'd say. . . . Sure, I made it. I made it, Hank. I brushed my teeth and fed my face. . . .

Quinn was saying, "You must excuse me while I change."

It was all as if they were planned-for guests, with invitations a week ago. When he was gone, Ellen turned to Judd. "You saw it," she said. "I'm not insane."

A yellow leaf came out of the sky and fell on the surface of the pool. "Yes, I saw."

"Then why doesn't he say it out? Why doesn't she?"

He shook his head.

"Talk to me, Judd."

He straightened his shoulders wearily. He never seemed at home with them, the weight of them too much to bear, until he strapped a camera on. "A twin is born and what does he say when he sees the other come after him? Go back inside, we don't need two? If it were someone who looked like me, we'd say, well, look, we don't need two. . . . But a beautiful woman? There's never enough to go around. A double helping the world needs."

"How can you make a joke of it?" She walked away from him at that. "Don't leave me alone with her," she said.

"You were the one who said to stay."

She turned to him. "I know I did. At first I wanted to see it through."

"And now you don't. . . . Do you want me to tell them we have to go?"

She shook her head. "They're fixing food. When food is involved, you have no choice but to see it through. And then it will be too dark to go. If we can get lost in broad daylight . . ."

"We'll stay," he said.

"We'll stay, all right, but I won't sleep."

"Yes, you will. You're worn out."

He was always right when it came to her, always somehow tuned in to her. Perhaps he was tuned in to everyone and had to drink to shut them out.

The air was opalescent now. The sun was sinking behind the hills. A giant shadow darkened the stream. Like a rising flood it mounted the hills. . . . At last their host in fresh attire was gazing into the valley with them. "When the shadows rise . . . soon they will swallow all of it. . . . I'm glad of a lodging for the night."

She did not know how to answer him. He spoke as if it were all a story, the rising shadow, the coming night. His wife . . . herself were a part of it, no more than a story for him to tell. He began to disperse things around a table. She tried to look involved with the pool. A pool was serviceable for that. Whenever there was nothing to say, you could stare at water, pretend that it gave you long thoughts, pretend its spell had silenced you, make it through till time to go.

At last there came his kindly voice. "It's here," he said, "what there is of it."

She turned and there he smilingly stood, holding a chair for her to sit. For a long moment she thought with relief that his wife had chosen not to appear, but no, the table was set for four. And she was there. In the naked light the resemblance was more striking still. She seemed to have changed her dress for them. She wore a slender denim skirt and over it a white peasant's blouse, the neck embroidered with a trace of red, the full sleeves pushed to bare the arms. Waving Judd's help aside, she seated herself across from Quinn. Her smile was an echo of his own, but sweet, remote, impenetrable.

Ellen could only stare at her, but Elsa seemed unaware of it. She was anxious as to their ease at table. There was a hearty soup with beans and generous slices of coarse bread. "We make the bread ourselves," said Quinn. Then purple grapes, which he said were snatched from above their heads. And afterward a strange tea they sweetened with honey and laced with milk. "We have our own bees here, you know."

He called their attention to the mist, which faintly now invaded them. A milkiness in the amber dusk, for all the world like the tea they drank, the air sweetened with fragrant bloom. "I'm glad you remained to see it," he said. "It's the cool air falling out of the hills and onto the warm earth where we are. The Indians had a name for it, but I can never remember it." He turned to his wife. "Can you, my dear?"

She shook her head, gazing into the mist. "It's a beautiful name, but I've lost it too."

Quinn poured each a glass of wine, which he said was made of the honey and grapes. It was very soft. "It allows the dark to ripen," he said, "and then it will give you pleasant dreams." He spoke at length to Judd of bees. The wine smelled of the grapes above. Birds were nesting among the leaves and cheeped in whispers and stifled cries.

The women were left with the thing they shared no one had named. It was like an uninvited guest whose presence provoked a curious dread and robbed them of the power to speak.... At length the men fell silent too. They let the darkness ripen for them. The moon abruptly cleared the hills and spilled itself upon the mist and turned it into a kind of smoke. The trees and shrubs were smoldering. It gathered the arbor into cloud. Now drifts of smoke invaded them, making them islands in the night. The woman's face had disappeared, yet Ellen felt it touched her own.

Quinn released her when he stood. "We shall retire now," he said. "I'll show you where you are to sleep. It's prudent to ready yourself for bed before the lamps abandon us. We'll save the map for morning, I think. That way it will be fresh for you."

He led his guests into the darkened house, switching on lights for them as he went, and out upon a narrow bridge that linked the house with a small lodge. He explained to them in his quiet way: "This was built for my mother, you know, but she couldn't bear our quiet life, and after a while she gave it up." He reached inside and switched on a light.

They were in a bedroom simply furnished. "I'll just open a window or two. No one is ever here, you see.... Oh, yes, the bathroom is next to this, and another room with a bed beyond." His hand had never released the door. "I'm glad you chose to spend the night. Very much the sensible thing. Oh, yes," he recalled, "the windows. I'll leave them to you if I may. And do remember the lights will go."

When he had gone, they stood in a daze. The night had become a story he had told them in his tranquil voice, and now that they had been put to bed it seemed to have no reality. Judd roused and found the other room. "I'll take this one in here," he called.

"You have the bathroom first," she said. There was a mirror above a chest. She turned from it and dropped to the bed. She looked at her watch. It was only nine. My God, they live like the Indians. The weariness was in her bones. The room had a faded-flower smell. If I should raise a window now, the damn mist will come inside. She lay back, and soon it was lying awake for Hank— she could not break the habit of it—wondering where he lay that night, even now that she didn't care. Worn with wonder . . . many a night . . . trying to see a woman's face and if it was anything like her own.

She heard Judd in the bathroom. Then the silence grew intense, as if the mist had muffled sound. She closed her eyes and let the mist enclose the lodge. After a while she roused herself. In the bathroom, she shut her eyes against the mirror and washed for bed. Then she took off her skirt and blouse and lay across the bed again. She saw Judd lying upon his bed, used up and needing a drink. She felt the trembling in his hands. She found that she was trembling too, her whole body tuned to him, the way he was always tuned to her. At last the trembling sprang from fear. . . . Not fear, she thought, uneasiness, not knowing what the hell went on.

She stood and quickly dressed again. She found a door that opened upon a tight little hall, and then she was knocking on Judd's door.

She waited so long for him to come that she was beginning to be alarmed. At last he opened the door for her. She saw that he had been undressed and had just thrown on his clothes for her. Through the opened shirt she saw the silver hairs of his chest. His eyes were bagged with weariness. She entered his room without asking. "I want to know what is going on."

He buttoned his shirt with a trembling hand. "Could you be more specific, please?"

"It's like they were lying in wait for us." She gave a nervous laugh. "For me." She waited for him to surface for her, to leave off fumbling with his shirt.

He rubbed his face. "It's just a damn coincidence. . . . I think you're making too much of it. I got the impression they didn't notice a damn thing. Nothing. Zilch. It's all a matter of angles . . . light. I can shoot a face from a different angle, different light, and you wouldn't see it the same face. Angle, light, it's the same as a viewer's point of view. It gets on film what's in the mind. Not just the subject's, the viewer's mind."

"You're not making any sense to me."

"Look," he said, "I can make anyone, with limits of course, look like someone entirely different. I shoot a family picture, see, and what they want is a family resemblance. A family look. They never know it but they do. It's why they have the damn thing made. They won't like it if it isn't there. So I get the lights and the angles right for each of them, and then they do. They want to see the way they feel. Or maybe the way they want to feel."

She looked at him impatiently. He talked the way he wrote, she thought. Everything slightly out of focus. "Why are you telling me this? You saw."

He turned away from her. "Well, I did. All I'm saying, I think they didn't."

"You're wrong, Judd. She saw it, she did." She began to pace his narrow room. The bed was narrow, too small for him, with a low rail as if for a child. I'll make him take my room, she thought. "It was like . . . well, she saw it, that's all."

He stood away from her, looking at her. "They're cool, all right."

She turned to him. "Let's leave," she said. "Write them a note and just leave. Before the lights go out on us."

He began to laugh. "I've never seen you like this before."

"There's never been a like this before. . . . Talk," she said. "You're supposed to know everything there is."

He looked around the room. "You want to sit down someplace?" he asked. There was a chair beside the bed.

"I want to take it standing up."

He shrugged and laughed. "What's to take? They say everyone has a double out in the world somewhere."

"Tell me something new," she said. She came to him. "You know everything, so what does it mean?"

He turned a little away from her. "The German Romantic poets," he said, "were always yapping about the double, the *doppelgänger*, the double-goer. Then the fiction writers took it up, English, French, Russians, the works." He turned to meet her troubled face. "Well, body and soul . . . the body wandering, seeking its soul, something like that. It's murky stuff."

"That's all?" she asked.

"In Norway they had the *Vardøgr*. . . . "

"Go on," she said.

"The Talmud says . . . None of this has anything to do with you. . . . Before the prophets prophesied, they saw themselves, the Talmud says."

"I know you," she said. "There's more to it." She came close to stare him down. "When it happens it means you're going to die. Right? Unless of course you're a bloody prophet."

He caught her to him. "No!" he said.

She sobbed once and stifled it. She felt his trembling hand on her back. "You're . . . too beautiful to die!" His trembling lips were in her hair. She knew how much he wanted her . . . and wanted a drink but needed her.

She broke away. "I don't have time to die," she said. "I've got an assignment to do the graves. . . . God," she laughed, "that sounds weird!" She covered her face. "You're right. I'm making too much of it. It fell upon me like the hawk." She tried to smile. "I'm really tired. Good night, Judd."

At the door she turned. "It's like she hollowed me out inside." She waited there. "I think it's the damn divorce," she said. She'd never spoken of it before. "It's just . . . I lost it who I am."

His voice was thick. "He's a goddam fool."

"Maybe. Maybe not," she said. "I think your lights are going out."

In her room she took off her shoes and skirt and lay on the bed to wait for dark. It was like waiting for death to come. Nothing you did would hold it back. As a child she had been afraid of the dark. . . . It wasn't just you were at the mercy of terrible things you couldn't see. It had to do with being small and the dark could easily wipe you out. It was like you were on the schoolroom board and the black eraser wiped you out. You weren't dead, but how could you know if you couldn't see? Sometimes you even began to cry, just to hear that you were there. . . . Divorcing Hank was all of that—the dark eraser that wiped you out. And so was a woman who had your face before you ever came to be. She could say to you—her silence had: This is mine, so you aren't here.

It gave her a comfort she couldn't explain that Judd's light was failing too. Separately they would lie in the dark. Together they would lie in it. His room in town she had never seen, but even there she would meet herself, for lining his wall would be shots of her, large and small and nothing framed, just loving film. . . . She could not rid herself of his arms holding her and trembling, the big, loving, used-up man, like her father and like her child and always dreaming of something more. Dreaming to stifle the thirty years that he had lived before she did . . . and maybe here was the place he could, where time didn't seem to matter much, nothing changing the way it should, the night warm when it shouldn't be. And she was trembling because he was. God, I hate you, Hank! she said. For leaving me washed out to sea. For leaving me in need of a man who's needing me and it shouldn't be.

She could see the lamp in the mirror. It was slowly giving up its light.

The knock on the door was very faint. She caught her breath. But this was the door to the narrow bridge. He must have an outside door as well. He must have walked in the mist to come. She lay waiting for him to leave, but the faint knocking came again. At last she rose to let him in. It seemed to her she had no choice. For she was afraid of the dark tonight, and so was he. So was he.

She unlatched the door. "Judd," she said. But it wasn't Judd; it was Quinn who stood wrapped in mist on the narrow bridge. She could not speak for her surprise.

"Forgive me," he said in a troubled voice. "I meant to give you a flashlight." He held it out. It was damp with mist. But he did not leave. "Please . . . there's something I need to say."

She simply stood.

"But if I may . . . May I just come in?" He pressed beside her into the room. "Please sit. I must say some things." He seemed distraught, oblivious that she was half undressed.

She did not sit and neither did he. He paced the room distractedly. "I swear to you I didn't see it. . . . I swear to you I didn't see it. She doesn't believe me but it's so. I have wounded her, and that I would not do for the world, for all the world, my beautiful wife."

She sank to the bed and watched him pace in the fading light.

He paused before her. "Forgive me but I did not see. I cannot imagine why I didn't. You were there in the road and you were lost, and all I wanted to do was help . . . and perhaps I thought it would make a pleasant evening for her. We're so alone here, don't you see, though it's the way she's wanted it. But then perhaps I did see and didn't know. Maybe it's why I wanted to help, was drawn to you because of her. To do for you was to do for her. Maybe it's why I made you stay. But if that's so, then why, why?" He seemed to be pleading for her reply. "Not to hurt her, never that!"

She shook her head.

He stared at her in the light that now was all but gone. "I see it now. Why didn't I then? I think my eyes are filled with her, and I am blind. . . ."

She could not tell what he wanted of her. It was all as if he were telling a tale, an Indian legend about the dead, and yet he seemed to cry to her out of a real and present pain. "Your wife," she said, "she couldn't think . . ."

"That I wanted you? Oh, never that! She knows my love. She trusts my love. My whole life encircles her."

The mist had come through the open door. He shut it out. "That mist . . . that mist she loves. But I have grown to fear it," he said. "It blurs us. It muffles even the things we say."

She was so weary she could not think.

He began to pace. "You must forgive me for breaking in. I had to talk to you, you see. I had to assure you I didn't see . . . didn't have some little trick in mind."

"I believe whatever you tell me to." Though she did not know what that could be.

He stood before her once again, smaller than Judd but just as old and needing her to understand. "My beautiful wife has looked at time and will not let it plunder her. She chooses to live where the earth itself has canceled time. Timeless legends were waiting for us, and we have become a part of them. Timeless too, do you understand? She will not speak of her age or mine. She will not acknowledge the passing years. Children remind her of passing years—they grow, they change so fast, you know—and so she has chosen to live without. And not to marry. . . . No, she has never married me. Marriage would lock her into time. . . . In spite of it, she is my wife. My wife, my wife she will always be."

Suddenly he began to weep. He blindly reached for a chair and sat. She did not know what to do for him.

He struggled with it. "Forgive me," he said. He wiped his eyes. "My wife is under a kind of spell. She dreams her life. At times I think she is dreaming mine. I have no existence outside her dream. We move like sleepwalkers through the days. . . . And I would gladly go on with it . . . but look at me!" In a broken voice he commanded her. "The years have taken their toll of me. I haven't her gift. I haven't her will for stopping them. Already she slips away from me. Into her immortality. Out of my reach, do you understand? When I hold her at night and stroke her hair, between us is lying this younger woman that she has dreamed. I think she dreams her for both of us. But I don't want this girl of the past . . . this young girl who is like yourself. Forgive me, please, for saying it."

He could not go on. The room was fading into dusk.

At last through her weariness she asked, "And what has this got to do with me?"

"Oh, but you see I brought you here. You are alike." He stared at her. "So much it is like a blow to her. She thinks I struck her deliberately, to show her what the years have done, what she has chosen not to see. That you are young and she is not. That winter comes in spite of all. My wife is a strange and beautiful creature. She doesn't want the world we are given. I have tried to give her the world she wants. And now I have taken it away." His voice broke.

She lay back. She felt a mounting desire to laugh, but in her weariness she slept. She woke to hear him speaking of her, the wife he betrayed, the wife he loved. Yet not his wife.... Between her waking and her sleep, she knew the wonder of growing old with such a man to love one so. She knew the woman to be a fool.... Yet Ellen was still afraid of her, because you were supposed to die. If you met yourself, which one would die? She was lost in the mist of a waking sleep dissolving into the valley mist, and she feared as a child alone in the dark, and questioned so.

They were in total darkness now. He seemed to be unaware of it, for his voice went on in its gentle way. She was even glad he was there with her to keep her fear of the dark at bay....

And now he was into another tale, another legend, incredibly. She caught a beginning or an end.... Wed to a mortal, the goddess of dawn was granted eternal life for him. But she had forgotten to ask the gods for his eternal youth as well.... "I call my wife Aurora," he said, "the goddess who forgot to ask...."

By then she was asleep again: The goddess was painted upon the wall of the room where she had met herself.

When she awoke there was morning light and Quinn was gone. For a while she thought she had dreamt his coming. Surely some of it was dream. She washed and dressed and knocked for Judd. She found him walking around outside and rejoiced to see that he looked refreshed. Much of the gray had left his face. It was as if he had come in the night instead of Quinn and together they had outslept the dark. Its remnant mist was smoking in the brakes of fern.

"You had a visitor," he said. He stroked the stubble on his chin.

"I fell asleep on him, I guess."

"Someone I should be jealous of?"

She laughed at him. "Let's get out of here."

"Without the map?"

"Without anything."

"Without coffee?"

"We'll get it somewhere."

But Quinn was there and beckoning. "I have your breakfast. I've drawn a map."

They joined him on the patio now blanketed with brilliant leaves. The hills shouted their red and gold. Plump little clouds were on the wing, casting shadows that dipped like hawks into the valley and rose to skim the fiery slopes. The stream flashed in the early light. The water lily stretched its throat, devoured sun. He had spread a modest repast for them. He poured them water from an earthen jug. "We dug it up in the garden," he said. "It's not as if we'd robbed the graves. Curious markings, don't you think?" He held it up for them to see. "My wife is just a little unwell and begs to be excused," he said.

So this is the way it ends, Ellen thought, not with a bang but a whimper. She suddenly would not have it so. She was still lost, weaving her car through the leaf-bright hills, searching for something that she had lost or never found, searching for something besides the graves. Nothing that happened came by chance. She grew afraid she would never know why she was here. "But I must see her before I go."

He looked alarmed. His eyes that were rimmed with weariness pled. She saw that he longed for them to leave, and yet he dreaded it as well. "I'll tell her what you wish to say."

She remembered how he had said before that he kept her safe. And who will keep you safe? she thought. She wanted safe all faithful men. Rarer were they than Indian graves. People should visit them instead and grant their loyal hearts' desire. "Just for a moment. I won't stay."

He put down the vessel and came to her. "She's very fragile. . . . I beg of you."

"We're all fragile, I promise you. The grave robbers have broken in."

He nodded as if he understood. Behind him, Judd looked up, resigned. He never questioned her change of mind. Quinn pointed to the end of the house. "Around the corner at the end." She felt his anxious, weary eyes upon her as she walked away.

At the end was a covered porch. Ellen stood on the flagstone walk among the leaves that struck her face as if the autumn that raged above would turn the valley into fall, and all who came there into fall. But after all, no one was there. She lacked the courage to mount the steps. She noted the easel, the canvases stacked against the wall, and a half-created form of clay that rested on a wooden stand.

Elsa came from within the house. She saw Ellen and stopped at once. The glance between them was sharp and full, as if in the clearing two does had met, and startled, threatened, prepared to seek the cover of trees.

Ellen spoke at last. "I cannot be your enemy."

Elsa turned away. She held in her hand a ball of clay. She coaxed it into another shape and pressed it into the half-created form on the stand, as if to go on with the task at hand was the only refuge left to her.

Now in the sharpness of early light, the resemblance still had power to shock. Yet there was something the years had done. A slackening of the mouth and chin. Ever, ever so slight it was . . . the eyes withdrawn into the bone . . . ever so slight the shadows below. Ellen was caught in the promise of it. This is how I will look one day.

Still the woman, half turned from her, went on with the work of molding, stroking, indenting the clay, as if her hands would shape a decision her mind could not. Quinn had said, I haven't her will. . . . That will was fallen into these hands. The silence deepened in her face.

Ellen waited, unable to leave. Whatever I came to this valley for . . . whatever I came for isn't done. It seemed to her that the woman's hands were intent on shaping both their lives. And Ellen relinquished that right to them. The hands and face had preceded hers. She felt the pressure of probing hands, the searching fingers imprinting her. The dark that had erased the child. The hands that could erase her now. When the leaf struck, she almost fell.

Slowly Elsa turned to her. "Come to me." There was scarcely a welcome in the voice.

Uncertain, Ellen climbed the steps. She was looking into her own eyes and saw that they were filled with tears. "Please allow me," Elsa said. "I want to remember how it was." She took Ellen's face in both her hands. They smelled of clay, and Ellen thought of the graves above. Her face was cradled as a child's. The fingers gently caressed the cheeks, the mouth, the chin; they fluttered softly about the eyes; they brushed the throat. . . . For the first time Ellen knew her beauty, not as the face that Judd could love, the flesh that fastened bone and vein—but deep in the bone a given thing. Beneath the hands she grew into beauty deeper than hands could give or take.... In a spiritless voice, Elsa said at last: "I am saying good-bye." And Ellen knew she meant the face that had been her own. "You have changed me ... you have changed my life...."

"Say good-bye to *me*. I am more than face."

Elsa dropped her hands.

"Do you forgive me?" Ellen asked.

In silence, Elsa met her gaze. With the back of her hand she brushed her eyes.

But Ellen said, "I want more. I want your blessing so I can go...."

Elsa pressed her fingers into the clay.

Ellen went on: "So *I* can change. I need to be more than I was before, and who is to make it happen but you? Bless me and make me twice as much ... so I can know when I lost my way was the best thing I ever did."

"Yes. Yes." And weeping, Elsa turned away.